THE PREDATOR

VAMPIRE NAVY SEAL

S.B. ALEXANDER

This is a work of fiction. Names, characters, places and incidents either are the product of the author's imagination or are used fictitiously, and any resemblance to locales, events, business establishments, or actual persons-living or dead is entirely coincidental.

Copyright © 2022 by S.B. Alexander.
All rights reserved

No part of this publication may be reproduced, transmitted, decompiled, or stored in or introduced into any information storage and retrieval system, in any form or by any means, whether electronic or mechanical, including photocopying, without the express written permission of the author.

Please do not participate in or encourage piracy of copyrighted materials in violation of the author's rights. Thank you for respecting the hard work of the author.

Cover designed by Hang Le
Cover copyright © 2022 by S.B. Alexander

The Predator
Book two: Vampire Navy SEAL – Sam and Layla Series

First Edition: April 2022

E-book ISBN — 13: 978-1-954888-19-7
Paperback Print ISBN — 13: 978-1-954888-20-3
Large Print ISBN — 13: 978-1-954888-21-0

Audiobook ISBN — 13: 978-1-954888-22-7

1

SAM

The odor of wet dog burned my nostrils as I stalked into the infirmary with one purpose in mind—tear out Dane Gray's canines with my bare hands. My eyes flashed from green to silver and my fangs lowered slow and deadly.

Dane was responsible for what had happened to Ben. I couldn't exactly prove it, but Ben's wound was definitely from a large animal. Bears were a possibility, but they were rare in and around the city.

For the last eleven days since the ambulance brought Ben in, he'd been in and out of consciousness, and as the days passed, his condition wasn't improving.

It felt like a dagger stabbing my heart over and over again anytime I looked at my best friend. He'd been through hell and back since I'd become a vampire. He'd been the product of an experiment gone wrong, and as a result, he was half human and half vampire. The vampire in him should have been healing him, which led us to believe he'd been bitten by a shifter. According to Doc, their venom could be poisonous to vampires. Not so much for humans. I was curious about whether Ben's half-human side would become a shifter.

Tripp had said no unless an alpha had bitten him. Despite that, I was thankful a clerk at a gas station not far outside the state forest had found Ben behind his establishment and reacted quickly. Luckily, one of the paramedics on the scene knew Ben was a Navy SEAL stationed on the naval base. He'd gotten ahold of us, and we'd rerouted them here.

Tripp marched toward me, his bronze eyes pinpricks. "Back away. We don't know that Dane's pack is responsible for Ben."

I glowered at the alpha in the distance as he and a bald dude gave Dr. Vieira their rapt attention.

I gritted my teeth. "He is. I feel it in my bones."

Tripp slapped a hand on my shoulder just as Dane sat in a chair and held out his arm. He was there to give Doc a blood sample for his research. We'd agreed to help the Gray Pack uncover why one of their own had died from a shot of a drug used by Layla Aberdeen and her sisters that night at the club.

Tripp guided me into an empty patient room. "We invited them in. We are not getting into a fight. Not here. Not now. Are we clear?"

Growling, my fangs clicked into place as rage boiled inside me. I was one second away from ramming my fists into the glass supply cabinet. "Who's the bald dude?"

Tripp swiped a hand over his sandy-blond hair tied into a ponytail at the nape of his neck. "Dane's beta, Ross. Look, after Doc pulls their blood, I have a plan."

I retracted my fangs. "Care to share?"

"Just follow my lead." He sounded as frustrated as I probably looked.

I tucked my fury away for the time being, stretched my neck one way then the other, and trailed behind Tripp. If he had a plan, I was sure it was a good one. Unlike me, Tripp had an uncanny way of extracting the truth without beating someone over the head.

Blood flowed from Dane's arm into a vial before Doc switched the filled tube with an empty one. Ross was engrossed in something on his phone as he waited his turn near the stainless steel counter along the sidewall opposite Doc.

Dane lasered his dark eyes on me as though he was ready to leap over the black countertop and tear out my throat.

That rage I held so tightly was about to burst as I approached.

Tripp pressed his hands into the edge of the counter. *Easy, Sam,* he said telepathically.

I sidled up to him. *I'm cool,* I lied.

Dane swung his gaze to Tripp. "Did you work out your issues with the hunters?"

"Let's stay focused on why you're here," Tripp said.

Ross's bald head shot up from his phone, his hazel eyes glinting beneath the stark bright lights overhead. "The Aberdeen women need to atone for what they did to one of our own."

I tucked my fisted hands into the pockets of my cargo pants, staring him down. "Touch any of them," I barked, "and you'll deal with me." If he so much as said Layla's name, I might tear him to shreds.

Ross whistled. "Sounds to me like you have it bad for one of them."

It was hard not to. Layla Aberdeen was beautiful, wild, tough, sassy, feisty, and bold as fuck, and she was all mine.

Sam, take it down a notch. Tripp's caustic tone blared in my head.

Easier said than done. Layla was embedded in my psyche, my skin, my veins, my brain, my dreams, and every part of me. I hadn't been able to stop thinking about her since she left. The way she made me feel like a god among gods, like she was my other half—which sounded fucked up on so many levels. A relationship between a human and vampire wasn't unheard of. After all, my mom had been human. But my mom hadn't been a hunter and had no desire to burn my father at the stake.

Regardless, eleven days had passed since Layla had left. Eleven days of hell, not being close to her. Eleven days of sleepless nights, thinking of her and every other screwed-up thing happening in my life. I'd been tempted to get my ass on a plane and pay her a visit. Maybe that would calm me down. Hell, I knew it would. But the auburn-haired goddess wanted some space to clear her head, and I wanted to be there for Ben.

However, if she kept ghosting me and not responding to my texts, then, vampire hunters be damned, I would storm their Montana ranch.

"Okay, Dane," Dr. Vieira said. "Ross, it's your turn."

The two traded places.

"Sam, I would like you to meet my beta, Ross Gray," Dane said.

Ross and I exchanged a glare.

"I see you and my brother will get along great." Sarcasm dripped from Dane's voice as he smirked.

I envisioned my hands around their throats, snapping their necks.

As if Doc knew what I wanted to do, he piped in, zapping the tension strung between Dane and me. "I would like to run an autopsy on your dead shifter." He inserted the needle into Ross's arm. "Is it possible to bring the body to me?"

"It isn't," Ross said, "but we did extract some of her blood before the burial."

Dane slid a box across the lab bench to Dr. Vieira. "We kept it refrigerated."

"Mm," Doc said as he finished pulling Ross's blood. "Not as good as doing an autopsy, but I might be able to work with this."

"How long before you have any results?" Ross asked.

Doc tore off his nitrile gloves and deposited them into a trash bin near the sink. "I'm not sure. The blood samples will go to our lab for a full toxicology workup. We have a small number of the darts that were recovered from the club. I'm having the drug analyzed as well."

Wyman, who had hired Layla and her sisters to capture me, was still in our custody. He'd given the drug to Layla to knock me out so he could turn me over to his former employer—the CIA. Regardless, he'd learned about the drug from none other than Layla's father. As far as Wyman knew, it was a highly concentrated human sedative that the Aberdeens had been testing when Layla's father was killed. I was one hundred percent certain Layla didn't know that tidbit. In fact, she'd given us the impression she had no clue what the drug could do.

But I wasn't about to divulge that part to the

shifters who were salivating to seek revenge on the Aberdeens. I couldn't blame them. If the tables had been turned, I would have wanted the same. Still, we couldn't allow shifters to take out humans.

I zeroed in on the conversation.

"You don't think there's wolfsbane in the drug?" Dane asked Doc. "That's the only thing I can think of that would kill us. Can it do the same to your kind?"

"It hasn't been known to," Dr. Vieira responded. "But as a doctor, I won't say it's impossible. However, not one vampire died at the club that night. Your shifter was the only death." Doc wiped his hands with a paper towel. "I might need more blood from you and your pack. Will that be a problem?"

"No," Dane said. "Just let me know what you need."

"Good. Now, if you'll excuse me, I would like to pack up these samples for the lab," Doc said.

Dane scrubbed a hand along his angular jaw. "I have one last question. Why didn't Roman Brown react the same way as the other vampires in the club? From what he told us, the drug paralyzed him, but he was still awake."

"It's highly possible Roman has access to an antidote to counteract sedative-type drugs," Doc replied. "We have one handy for that very reason, and the SEAL team is given a dose when entering into combat or potential situations with our enemies."

The Council of Elders had interrogated Roman until they were blue in the face. According to my old man, who was an elder, Roman wasn't talking. My father had taken the next step to read Roman's mind, but the fucker was smart. He knew how to clear his head, so my father couldn't get a damn thing from him—either that or Roman had a mind-blocking potion like ours. After all, he'd worked for a pharmaceutical company, so it wouldn't have been a shocker for him to have access to drugs.

Doc glanced up at the six-foot-five alpha. "I'll let Lieutenant Tripp know when I have concrete results on your blood samples." He collected the tray of samples along with the box Dane had given him and headed in the direction of his office.

Silence descended before Tripp cleared his throat. "Dane, if you have a minute, I'd like to show you something. Follow me." Tripp didn't wait for the shifters to answer. He pivoted on his heel and stalked toward the patient rooms that banked one wall in the infirmary.

Dane and Ross exchanged a suspicious look but followed Tripp into Ben's room.

Once the four of us surrounded Ben's bed, Dane's eyebrows pinched together. "You want to show us a patient?" It sounded as if he had never seen Ben before. Maybe I was wrong about him.

The heart monitor beeped as Ben's chest rose and fell.

Tripp pulled back the blanket, exposing the bandage on Ben's waist.

Dane's Adam's apple bobbed as nervous energy floated in the air.

A muscle jumped along Ross's jaw.

Tripp lifted the taped gauze to expose Ben's massive wound.

I fisted my hands at my side.

Dane pointed at Ben's mangled waist. "What's this? Are you trying to say we did this?" His tone bordered on a growl.

I glowered at the shifters. "Did you?"

Dane's eyes flashed red as his canines clicked into place.

Tripp jutted out his chin, calm and reserved.

"We're only asking. Obviously, this is a shifter bite."

"That could very well be from another animal, like a bear," Ross said smugly.

Tension, thick and angry, dangled over Ben.

It was Tripp's turn to show his fangs. "Do you think we're idiots, beta? If it were a bear, I'm sure Ben wouldn't be here. That's a wolf bite. I should know. I've seen plenty of them. Wolf blood runs in my family."

If they were surprised by that, they didn't show it.

I didn't detect any guilt or that they were hiding anything. Then again, they weren't exactly human, which meant they knew how to hide their true emotions.

Dane flared his nostrils. "So, you're accusing me or my pack of doing this to your man?"

"One of your pack members, Vera, had been Roman's sidekick," I said. "She wanted revenge for her sister's death."

Tripp's eyes morphed from bronze to liquid black. "Let's not forget, Dane, that you were taking orders from Roman that night. You were desperate to do his bidding because you owed him a favor."

Dane's claws, sharp and deadly, grew from his fingernails as his red eyes bore a hole into Tripp. "I ought to rip out your throat."

"For what? Asking a question?" Fury fueled my elemental powers, causing Doc's rolling metal table to fly across the room. "Seems to me, you're guilty."

Ross, who had been standing at the foot of the bed, stalked up to me. "I don't like you." His eyes morphed from hazel to shimmering blue.

I was beginning to learn that the alpha had red eyes. His beta's were deep cerulean-blue, but Vera, if I remembered correctly, had amber eyes in wolf form. Interesting hierarchy of physical transformations. Then again, my family had different eye colors that aligned with how powerful we were.

Ross and I were nose to nose, chest to chest, and both of us were breathing fire. "Feeling's mutual, beta." I itched to do something other than stare at the jerk. "Who in your pack attacked Ben?"

A deep grumble shook the walls. In a flash, Ross was pushed aside, and Dane dug his claws into my neck. "Back the fuck down, vampire."

I grinned as I gripped his balls. "I could crush

your jewels in a flat second, so take your fucking paws off me."

"Sam," Tripp warned, "this isn't the place."

Pain etched Dane's face as his canines dripped with venom.

I snarled, pushing Dane so hard he stumbled into the medical supply cabinet, almost breaking the glass doors.

He lunged at me, swiping his sharp claws down my face.

Motherfucker.

Ross and Tripp intervened.

Dane shrugged Ross off as his red eyes bored a hole in my forehead. "Touch me again, and I will rip out your throat." Then he brushed his hands down his jean-clad legs, retracting his canines as well as his claws. "Keep your man in line, Lieutenant, or I'll have to do it for you."

It was Tripp's turn to show a side of him not many saw as he spit fire at Dane, standing toe to toe and eye to eye with the alpha. "Let's get something straight. I don't take orders from you, and if you want our help with the drug, I suggest you answer our question. Did you or did you not tear out Ben's flesh?"

Ross ran a hand over his bald head. "Just tell

them, Dane. Then we can get the fuck out of here. These vampires are making me itch."

It was useless even to acknowledge the brazen barb. "Karma's a bitch, man. But you're right. The faster you dogs leave, the better we'll all be."

Dane backed away from Tripp, sighing. "We have a new pup in our pack who couldn't control himself. When your man escaped from Roman, we had one of ours chase him. Things escalated. The two got into a fight. Our man went down, and yours disappeared."

Kraft had mentioned that he and Olivia had found a trail of blood in the snow that night.

I rubbed my throat. "He dies, I'm coming for you." I pointed at Dane. Fuck his beta. I wanted to take down the big bad alpha.

Dane arched a thick dark brow, which was in stark contrast to his white hair. "You can try, vampire. But you'll fail."

Tripp pinned me with daggers, no doubt daring me to engage.

I bit my tongue for the time being and stalked out. I needed to release some fury, and short of getting laid, I had something else in mind.

2

LAYLA

Rianne, Jordyn, and I sat in the wide-open kitchen of Uncle Jack's rustic log home, surrounded by exposed beams on the ceilings, weathered wood, antique metals, vintage glass, and earth tones that complimented the design, not only in the kitchen, but throughout the eight-bedroom home.

Jordyn popped up from her seat at the wood-topped island that held six guests comfortably. "Let me make sure no one is listening before we chat." She sped out like wildfire.

My sisters and I hadn't had a chance to talk about our next move. It was the first time since I'd gotten sick that I'd been upright—I felt ten times better. I was a little behind on what was going on around the ranch and what my sisters had been up to. Jordyn wanted to head back to Massachusetts to chum up to the vampire military. At least, she'd dropped that bomb the other morning while I'd been in the bathroom puking. I wasn't sure about Rianne. She and I hadn't talked about what she wanted.

"Are you sure you're feeling better?" Rianne studied me, her brown eyes appraising as she fiddled with a paper napkin across from me. "You still look pale."

A few days before, I'd gone to a walk-in clinic, and the doctor had diagnosed me with the flu. I'd figured as much. I hadn't been eating right. My stress level had been through the roof and taking vitamins had never been on my list. Truth be told, I'd been relieved to hear him say the flu. I'd been worried that Sam's blood had done something permanent to my system.

I cradled the coffee cup in my hands. "It'll probably take me several more days to get my strength back, but I do feel human again." Metaphorically speaking, anyway. When I was with Sam, I seriously thought I'd been changing into a bloodsucker, which was impossible. I set my cup down and rubbed under my eyes. "The dark circles are showing, aren't they?"

She nodded. "And your blue eyes are grayish."

"I'm sure once I get food in me and inhale some crisp mountain air, I'll look better." The sun shone through the large window over the sink directly ahead of me. "Maybe horseback riding will do me some good, or a long walk."

Smiling, Rianne gathered her long brown hair, draped it over her shoulder, and combed her fingers through it. "I'm sure Poncho misses you." She picked a stray hair off her red sweater. "Mom loved that horse."

After she died four years ago, Dad had brought Poncho to my uncle's ranch. Dad had been too distraught to look at the horse. My sisters and I had felt the same way. "Have you done any riding?"

She shook her head. "No. I haven't been anywhere near the horse barn." Sadness bled through her words.

I was sure returning to Montana brought out emotions my sisters and I had buried—or tried to, anyway. "So where is everyone?" I suspected my younger cousins were in school, since it was ten in the morning, according to the clock on the microwave. "And I can't find my phone. Have you seen it?" I'd thought I'd left it on the nightstand by the bed, but it wasn't there or anywhere in the bedroom. I was curious whether Sam had tried to call or text me like he had been prior to me coming down with the flu. Not that I was returning to Massachusetts.

She rubbed her pink glossy lips together. Rianne rarely wore makeup, but a rosy blush colored her cheeks, blending well with her lip gloss. "The uncles made a trip into Bozeman to scope out horses. Most of the cousins are in school, and Aunt Tab went out to the workshop to get a box of mason jars. She's making her famous elderberry jam."

My uncle had a humongous two-story workshop that functioned as a weapons room with loads of instruments to combat vampires—or anyone, for that matter.

"Mom loved elderberries," I mumbled. "You know, we should visit her grave and Dad's, too, while we're here."

She set the napkin she'd been toying with into her empty cup and straightened on the barstool. "Look, Jordyn filled me in on possibly going back to Massachusetts. That's a bad idea." Her tone bordered on disgust.

I sipped my black coffee. "I agree." One, we had no reason or purpose to show up on Sam's doorstep. Two, after all the problems we'd caused, I doubted the military vamps, except maybe Sam, would welcome us with open arms. But I wasn't eager to run back into his arms. I felt human again, and Sam would only make me feel like the crazed animal I'd been while in his presence.

She flinched. "You do? I thought you were into Sam."

I snorted through a laugh, almost spitting out my coffee. "What? Did you think we would date?" I glanced around to be sure no one was listening, suddenly curious about what had happened to Jordyn.

"Sam isn't going to leave you alone, Layla," Rianne said with a hard look on her face. "Don't get me wrong. I appreciate him saving my life. I didn't want to come back here either. But I've had plenty of time to think about how my life isn't hanging out with vampires. Frankly, I want nothing to do with them, and neither should you."

"What does that mean, then? You want to live here?" My stomach began to swirl with nerves and despair. I wanted my sisters to be happy, but Rianne didn't like my uncle any more than I did. Unless someone had brainwashed her.

"Actually, I would rather live here than with vamps. Come on, Layla. That's not who we are. And let's not forget that you were fucked-up when you were with Sam. It was like you changed overnight."

I pursed my lips. "That was because of his blood."

She scratched her neck. "I still don't understand why you even tasted his blood."

So many things had happened in that short time span that I was beginning to wonder if I'd dreamed all of it. But she was right. And I had explained to her and Jordyn why I'd bitten Sam—he'd been on the verge of sinking his fangs into me. My quick response had been to bite him, although I had no reason to chomp on him during the throes of sex. But I wasn't about to divulge that.

"It's in the past," I said. "There's no sense in hashing it out again."

She sighed. "For a second, I swore you were turning into the creature we hated and hunted."

"Believe me, I thought I was too. But our parents would've told us if we carried the gene."

She laughed. "You sound like you still believe you could turn into a vampire. We don't have the gene. Even if we did, you would need Dad's blood to make the change, and if he were alive, he would have to be a vampire."

I swallowed a big gulp of coffee as I shivered. "I know. Let's talk about something else." I wanted to put the past behind me.

Jordyn breezed in with a huge smile, rosy cheeks, and a glint in her light-brown eyes that told us she was up to no good. I swear, our younger sister had been giddy for some reason. Then again, I'd been bedridden, so I'd probably missed something.

She slipped her phone into the back pocket of her black jeans. "Coast is clear. Cousin Noah is cleaning out his truck. The other cousins are in school. But we should talk before Aunt Tab comes in from the barn."

Rianne hunched her shoulders. "There's nothing to talk about."

Something was off with her, but I couldn't pinpoint what.

Jordyn fixed herself a cup of coffee before sitting beside Rianne. "What do you mean? We need to figure out our next move."

Rianne stuck out her chin. "I know what mine is. I've been waiting for Layla to get over the flu to tell you both. I'm heading into Bozeman today to talk to an Air Force recruiter." She'd had that dream of the military and flying jets for as long as I could remember, yet she didn't sound as excited as I thought she would.

Jordyn lost the gleam in her eyes. "What? You can't leave us."

"Jordyn," I said in a quiet tone, "we're not going back to Massachusetts. It's suicide. I'm also taking a break from hunting." I couldn't say I would completely give up our family heritage, but I needed to do something different for a while. "I've been thinking of the police academy."

Both of my sisters reared back.

Rianne perked up, no doubt relieved that I wasn't about to date a vampire. "That's great. You would make a kick-ass cop."

Jordyn gnawed on her bottom lip, suddenly despondent. I couldn't help remembering that look when she lost her best friend in the seventh grade. Marybeth Wilson and Jordyn had been inseparable since first grade, but Marybeth moved out of state when her parents divorced.

I tucked my auburn hair behind my ear. "Jordyn, you realize that if we go back to Sam and company, Uncle Jack would cut off our heads."

She mashed her lips into a thin line. "Since when do you care what he thinks?"

Rianne turned in her seat slightly to face Jordyn. "Why are you so hung up on the military vampires? Have you forgotten that Roman kidnapped you and a wolf shifter wanted to kill you?"

Jordyn pushed up the sleeves of her soft, pink V-neck sweater as if getting ready to throw down with Rianne. "I want to do some good in this world. Why not help them protect humanity?" She regarded me. "You told us that Sam's father, Steven Mason, approached Dad to work for him. Did Steven ever tell you why?"

I dipped back into my memory and the conversation Steven and I had had in the viewing room on the naval base. I couldn't remember if I'd asked him that very thing or not. "I don't recall. What does that matter, anyway?"

"Well, I called him," Jordyn said. "I asked him why he wanted Dad to work for him."

Rianne and I looked at Jordyn like she'd lost her mind.

"Are you kidding me?" Rianne's voice rose in pitch.

I pinched my eyebrows together. "What did he say?" I *was* curious.

Jordyn tugged on the sleeves of her sweater so that they covered half of her hands. "Steven knows how good our family is at hunting them. He wanted Dad to join his team to help his government police their kind. Maybe be a scout or representative for them. Steven feels that a human might be better to talk to those within our government who are privy to vampires."

"Obviously, Dad didn't take him up on his offer," Rianne said. "Why?"

"According to Steven," Jordyn said, "Dad felt his brothers would disown him and that would put us"—she circled her finger among us—"in a bad predicament. But Steven did say Dad had really considered it because the money was great."

"It is suicide," Rianne said. "I'm not exactly a fan of Uncle Jack, but he and the others—cousins, uncles, aunts—they're still our kin."

"It was also suicide to team up with a former CIA agent to turn Sam Mason over to the CIA," I said. "Think about the ramifications if a human government got ahold of Sam. They would try everything in their power to build super soldiers or highly engineered vampires who could be stronger than Sam. Dad would've been adding more of them to the population. That goes against the family ethos."

"He wanted the money, and that plan was better than betraying family," Rianne said.

The lesser of two evils, I supposed.

Jordyn sipped her coffee. "If we work for Steven, we can protect humanity and help to ensure no one like the CIA can build armies of vampires. I think we should meet with Steven. He had to cut me off for another meeting, so I didn't have a chance to broach the subject of us working for him."

Rianne shook her head as the color drained from her cheeks. "No." She climbed off the stool. "I don't want anything to do with vampires." She checked her phone. "I need to go. Noah is driving me to Bozeman."

Speaking of the obnoxious cousin, Noah waltzed in. "I heard my name."

Fuck. I pinned a horrified look at Jordyn then at Rianne.

Rianne didn't seem fazed, but Jordyn appeared to be sweating bullets.

Horror gelled my blood. "Eavesdropping?"

He smirked, dragging his fingers through the

unkempt blackish-brown hair curling around his ears. He resembled his mom, Aunt Tab, with his dark hair and eyes, although he had a light dusting of freckles on his face like his father. "Now, why would I listen to a bunch of women?" He strutted over to the pantry, his cowboy boots clicking along the weathered wooden floor.

True. He didn't listen well—not to anyone, in fact.

He ducked into the pantry.

"I'll take care of him," Rianne whispered.

Noah came out with a protein bar. "So, Layla, I see you're over your vampire sickness." His tone held too much derision.

I was tempted to flip him off but decided not to expend too much energy on him. "I see you're still an asshole."

His lips tightened as his biceps bulged. At twenty-two, he was in great shape, tall like his father, with a broad chest and slim waist, and I had no doubt he didn't have any trouble snagging a lady. What turned me off about my cousin was his crass and obnoxious attitude. He had three younger brothers, a younger sister, and one older brother. Of the clan, he was the biggest jerk aside from his father.

Rianne grabbed her canvas messenger bag from the desk near the arched doorway. "Let's go, Noah. I don't want to be late."

Noah walked over to me, leaned down, and whispered in my ear, "So did you fuck one of the bloodsuckers? I bet you did. That was the reason you were sick. You're going to hell, cousin."

"If you don't get your disgusting breath off me, I might kick you in the nuts." Digging my nails into my jean-clad legs, I jerked my head at Rianne. Surely, she hadn't told Noah.

Without looking at me, Rianne rushed over and grabbed Noah's arm. "Stop it, Noah, or *I* will ruin your chances of ever getting laid. I'm sure the ladies won't appreciate you not being able to please them."

He muttered a swear word. "I'll be in the truck, Rianne." Then he marched out.

"Find out if he heard anything before he came in," Jordyn said.

Rianne hiked her bag over her shoulder. "Don't worry. How about we meet at the Deer and Elk around five for dinner? I'll check in when I'm done with the recruiter."

"Whatever you do, don't invite Noah," I replied.

"He's not that bad," she returned.

She had a soft spot for him. They were the same age and had gone to school together. He'd always had her back, so she stuck up for him. What I wasn't sure about was whether she had given Noah any indication that I'd slept with Sam. I was sure she wouldn't have, but she was acting a little off.

I jumped up and hugged her. "Good luck. Fingers crossed that it goes well."

"Wait," Jordyn said. "Are you enlisting today?"

Rianne shrugged. "Not sure. I want to hear what the recruiter has to say first."

I snagged my cup. "Convince Noah to join with you," I teased, but deep down, I was serious. I wasn't an expert on how to knock some sense into him, but he could certainly benefit from a well-disciplined structure. Not that my uncle Jack wasn't a hard-ass, but from what I'd seen over the years, he'd gone easy on his sons. In his eyes, they walked on water.

After Rianne left, I poured another cup of coffee. "You don't think Rianne would tell Noah I slept with Sam?"

"I don't think so," Jordyn responded. "Is that what he whispered in your ear?"

I could really use some whiskey in my coffee to settle my nerves. "He asked me if I fucked one of the vampires." I glanced out the window. The mountain range rose in the distance beyond the horse barn and workshop. "It looks like a great sunny day to explore. Let's go horseback riding."

"Sounds great." Jordyn sounded despondent.

I spun on my heel, and when I did, the hot mug slipped out of my hand and crashed to the floor. I jumped a mile as memories careened back of that cold, dark morning when the house we'd been renting exploded. I swore I *would* have PTSD. Not only from the house blowing up but from my ordeal with Sam, Roman, Vera, and everyone and everything that had happened to my sisters and me.

Jordyn waved a hand in front of me. "Layla." Her soft tone drew me out of my haze.

I squatted to clean up my mess while Jordyn snagged the roll of paper towels.

As I went to grab the mug, a jagged piece of the ceramic where the handle had been dug into my hand, breaking skin. "Shit."

Jordyn wiped the floor. "Did you cut yourself?"

I popped up. "I'm fine." But as I turned on the faucet to clean the small amount of blood that pooled around the wound, my throat became scratchy and dry. I stared at my hand, licking my lips. Suddenly, the need to taste my own blood hit me like a freight train.

No freaking way.

Images of me sucking on Sam's wrist like a starving animal danced before me. I grabbed my trembling right wrist and examined the blood like it was the most amazing thing I'd ever seen.

Jordyn shut the faucet off. "Layla, what's wrong?"

I licked my lips again then brought my hand to my mouth and was ready to suck the blood from my palm when Jordyn shook me.

"You are not about to do what I think you're going to do."

I blinked. "What? It's my blood. Haven't you had a cut on your finger and sucked the blood off?"

Her chest heaved. "Sure, but after what you've been through, I don't think that's a good idea."

"What's not a good idea?" Aunt Tab asked as she entered the kitchen with a box of mason jars, looking a bit out of sorts. Her salt-and-pepper hair was mussed. Hay clung to her ribbed black top, and her jeans were dirty at the knees.

We needed to stop talking in this house. Before long, the family would string us up and beat the crap out of us for even mentioning vampires.

I washed my hands quickly. "Staying inside all day."

Jordyn tossed me a dish towel. "We're going to take Poncho and Yankee out, if that's okay?"

Aunt Tab flicked strands of her hair away from her face. "Don't be long. I'm making lunch. It should be ready around one."

We had a few hours. My body would probably protest if I rode a horse any longer than that.

"Glad to see you up and about, Layla," Aunt Tab said.

I gave her a warm smile. "I feel better."

Jordyn yanked on my arm. "See you later, Aunt Tab."

"Is something wrong, Aunt Tab?" I asked, knowing she probably wouldn't tell me.

Aside from her unkempt physical appearance, which probably stemmed from her rooting around in the workshop or barn for mason jars, I detected a hint of despair in her dark eyes.

I wondered if she and my uncle had a spat.

"I'm fine." She didn't sound convincing. "Go. Enjoy the sunshine."

As I left, I got the feeling her sour mood had something to do with me.

3

LAYLA

An hour later, Jordyn and I were riding down the dirt path along the edge of the property. The wind was cold but light. The weather in February averaged high thirties to low forties during the day and below freezing at night. Despite the cool temps, the fresh Montana air felt amazing. Inhaling, I turned my face toward the late-morning sun as Poncho trotted alongside Yankee.

Jordyn cleared her throat. "I love the energy here. It's the only thing I miss about living in Montana."

I righted my head and blinked. "That and our parents." I was tempted to suggest we ride to the cemetery, but it was too far on horseback.

Jordyn adjusted her knitted brown scarf so it covered some of her chin. "Layla, are we going our separate ways?"

A shiver ran through me. I hated to think that we were. Rianne, Jordyn, and I had been inseparable since Mom had gotten breast cancer, even more so when our father died. But we needed to do something with our lives. "It's time, sis, to move on."

Silence followed us as we took a detour off the beaten path. Snow capped the mountains along our right side. There were open fields to our left, and a defunct ranch that had once been occupied by our great-great-grandparents lay ahead.

"I hate this place," Jordyn said as we approached.

An eerie feeling gripped my soul. Images of vampires burning, screaming, and fighting for their lives flashed before me as I caught a glimpse of the firepit in front of the boarded-up house and barn.

It was the very place where my uncles drank beer and laughed as they tortured vampires. I couldn't say I hadn't enjoyed watching them burn or seeing how satisfied my father had been to watch them die. But after spending time with

Sam, the hatred I'd harbored for them was slowly waning. Another sick feeling dropped into the pit of my stomach when I pictured Sam hanging from the makeshift structure over the firepit, his body going up in flames.

I choked as acid settled in my throat. I couldn't discern whether what I was imagining was real or not.

Jordyn came to a halt with Yankee, a mare who had a beautiful brown coat with white spots on her muzzle. "You look like you've seen a ghost. We should go back."

I yanked my scarf away from my neck, suddenly hot and panicked as I pulled on Poncho's reins. "I'm fine."

"Did you have a vision?" she asked as though she was talking about the weather.

Fuck, I hope not. The thought of Sam's flesh burning to a crisp sent my heart galloping, and not only because I might have seen Sam's demise. My chest hurt at the notion he could die. *Oh, crap. I can't have feelings for him.* Sex was one thing. Feelings for him... no way. Not an option.

"Answer me, Layla." Panic laced her tone.

"I don't know. But if I did, then Sam is going to die."

She sucked in a sharp jagged breath and pointed to the pit. "You mean burn at the hands of our family?"

I shrugged. "It's nothing. Sam can't die. He's too powerful."

She stared at me like I had five heads. "Holy shit. You have feelings for him."

"No, I don't."

"You are so lying through your perfect white teeth," she said, suddenly giddy.

"You're right. We should go back." I hadn't had anything to eat, and my stomach didn't feel so well.

"It's okay, sis. I'm rooting for you and Sam."

I let out a laugh that felt like the weight of the universe had lifted off my shoulders. "Only you would."

"Look, it's weird. I know. But you can't help who you love."

"I'm not in love with Sam," I was quick to add.

She bobbed her head in patronizing fashion. "We were brought up to hate vampires. They have no souls—Dad taught us that. But after meeting Sam and the other military vamps... they're not evil like the ones you and I have come to know. Which is why we should consider talking to Steven Mason. We can help to rid the planet of the evil ones."

"You're not going to let this go, are you?"

The light breeze ruffled her long brown hair. "I get that Rianne wants to join the military. I'm all for her doing what she wants, and I want you to be happy as well. But I saw how you looked at Sam after everything went down with Roman. You were also happy when you talked to Rianne and me about what had happened between him and you. Frankly, I've never seen you glow over a guy."

I snorted. "Glow, huh? The sex was amazing. I won't lie. But that's all it would ever be with Sam and me. I'm not going back, Jordyn. I can't and won't lose myself like I did."

"So you wouldn't mind if I go, then?" Jordyn asked in a hesitant tone.

I studied my sister, who resembled our mom with a button nose and heart-shaped lips. "If I recall, you mentioned something about wanting to bed a vampire. Is that the real reason?"

A hawk flew over the firepit, landing on the wooden T that my uncles had built to string up vampires.

She swiped a hand over Yankee's mane. "I'm

not going to lie and say that I don't want to experience what it's like to have sex with one of them, but it's not about that. It's about protecting humans, which is what our family stands for. If I'm not mistaken, that's your moral code as well. I mean, if you want to be a cop, that means you want to protect. So let's put our skills to use."

I heard what she was saying. I wholeheartedly agreed about protecting humanity. "I don't know. I'm afraid, actually."

"Layla Aberdeen, afraid? Nonsense. You're the toughest woman I know. You would die for Rianne and me. What has you spooked?"

"What if I revert to the crazed animal I turned into when I was around Sam? I don't want to get like that. I felt like I didn't have any control."

She laughed and snorted at the same time. "Says the woman who called out Sam's name in her sleep the other night."

"What?" My jaw practically hit Poncho.

"Sounded like you were having a pretty intimate dream too." She waggled her eyebrows.

I shouldn't have been embarrassed, but heat pinched my cheeks hard. Then something else whacked me upside the head. If I dreamed about him, did he have the same dream, as he had when I'd been sleeping in the women's barracks?

She squinted and twisted her lips, holding back a grin.

I dug my heels into Poncho. "Let's go." Talking about Sam, vampires, and watching the hawk study the pit below him was making me want to hurl.

We headed back toward the ranch in silence, lost in our own thoughts. And I couldn't shake the thought that maybe Sam had had the same dream as me.

About half a mile in, I asked, "Have you seen my phone?"

"So you can call Sam," she teased in a playful tone.

I rolled my eyes. "I'm worried. What if Uncle Jack has my phone? If Sam's been texting..." I didn't want to think of the consequences, especially if Sam did experience my dream with me or was dropping comments about our steamy night together. Then my vision blurred for a split second. "Jordyn, did you dispose of the pregnancy test?" I was sure she had.

"Whoa. Where did that come from? Of

course. But what does it matter? The result was negative."

The notion that one of us could be pregnant might not sit well with our family. Then again, they shouldn't care. We were old enough to start families. "True, but I just don't want to answer more questions," I said.

"Surely, they know we couldn't get pregnant by a vampire, if that's what you're worried about."

I sniffled and wiped my nose with the back of my gloved hand. The cold air always made my nose run. "You're right, we can't, but I still don't want to hear their opinions and all that." Noah would have a field day, for sure.

Another round of silence followed us until I said, "I miss Mom. I would give anything to have her here right now." She'd been wise beyond her forty years. She knew how to calm me and make me feel like I could conquer the world.

Jordyn frowned. "I do too."

The rest of the way, we reminisced about our parents, talking about how Mom loved baking and Dad enjoyed woodworking. He'd built his own workshop on the five acres of land we'd lived on.

Before long, the one-story home with high peaks, timber siding, and a stone facade on the front came into view. Three of the horses were grazing in the pasture behind the property. A beat-up gray truck, a Suburban, a golf cart, and a three-wheeler sat outside the six-car garage—or rather, workshop. No one parked their cars inside.

My uncle Jack made his money on horses and cattle. Over the years, he'd done well financially, but since Uncle Ray had gambled away most of the money from the family business, Uncle Jack had been trying to replenish what they'd lost, which was probably what he and Ray were doing in Bozeman.

After the horses were back in their stalls, Jordyn and I headed into the house. As we shucked our boots in the mudroom, Aunt Tab's voice filtered in.

"Sam, you need to stop calling and texting her," Aunt Tab said. "My husband will burn you alive. Do you understand?"

Jordyn's wide-eyed look met mine before I bolted through the mudroom then the laundry room, skidding to a halt in the kitchen.

4

LAYLA

The color drained from Aunt Tab's face as I ripped the phone—*my phone*—from her and ended the call. I wasn't talking to Sam. Not then. Maybe not ever.

"*You* had my phone?"

Jordyn rushed in on my heels and sucked in air.

I narrowed my eyes so hard it hurt. "Why?"

Aunt Tab rubbed her lips together, seemingly deciding how to answer. I suddenly understood why she'd looked like something had been bothering her when we left to go horseback riding.

"I was in your room this morning when you were in the shower," Aunt Tab said. "Your phone was vibrating. I saw the text and got curious. Then your uncle Jack poked his head in to tell me he was leaving, and..." She lowered her gaze to the knife beside the cutting board on the island where she had tomatoes, an onion, and celery ready to be chopped.

I gripped my phone as I created some distance between us, settling at the end of the island. "Please tell me Uncle Jack did not read the text." I held my breath. I had no idea what the text was about, but considering Sam's previous ones were rather steamy, I would bet my uncle went through the roof.

Jordyn slid onto a stool across from Aunt Tab. "How did you get into her phone? You need her passcode."

Aunt Tab lifted her dark gaze. "The text was on the screen."

I was kicking myself for not turning off the show-preview feature. Then again, I'd never needed to hide my messages. But stupid me should've thought about that before entering their house.

I set my phone down on the island. "The bigger question is why you kept it."

She picked up the knife and began slicing a

tomato. "Your uncle took it and tried to unlock your screen, which he couldn't. I planned on returning it, but I got sidetracked. I'm sorry, Layla. I was being nosy. Your uncle told me that you girls were too friendly with the vampires. He saw how Rianne threw herself at Sam Mason. I was curious to know more. And I'd been meaning to ask, but you got sick, and with everyone in the house, I could never get Rianne and Jordyn alone." Regret threaded through her words.

Anger bubbled to the surface, making me shake. "Are you sure you want to know, or are you spying for your husband?"

Aunt Tab was a nice person who treated me with kindness and had been a great friend to my mom. But she was loyal to Jack. Therefore, I couldn't trust her.

She focused on chopping vegetables. "I'm trying to help."

"Help?" I parroted. "Snooping in my business is not the definition of helping." She'd never come to my rescue when my uncle berated me.

"I adore you girls," Aunt Tab said. "I want what's best for you, and vampires aren't."

Anger morphed into fury. "With all due respect, Aunt Tab, you don't know what's best for me or Jordyn or Rianne. You haven't done any-thing for us since our mom or dad died."

She set the knife down, wiped her hands on her apron, and sighed. "You're right. I should've been more attentive and involved, especially when your mom passed away. I can't change the past, but I want to be there for you now. All three of you seem lost." She gave me a warm smile. "I love you girls. Let me help."

Jordyn and I exchanged a suspicious look.

I couldn't shake the feeling that she was fishing for Jack. "I can't trust you." In no way was I about to share what had happened between Sam and me. Besides, that was old news and in the past, to use her term, which was where I wanted Sam and me to stay.

She moved the tomatoes to the back of the cutting board, and then chopped celery.

I rubbed my temples as a headache loomed. "What do you think, Jordyn? Should we clue Aunt Tab in?"

Jordyn shrugged, pursing her lips. "Depends. Aunt Tab, how do you feel about us working for vampires?"

My aunt's head shot up, and, at the same time,

the blade missed the celery and snagged her fore-finger. "Ow."

The sight of blood scrambled my brain as I froze.

Jordyn hopped off the stool and skirted the island to help Aunt Tab.

"Layla, get the first aid kit," Aunt Tab said calmly. "It's in the pantry on the top shelf, off to the left."

I couldn't move as Jordyn examined the cut.

"Layla." Jordyn's tone was screeching and harsh. "Snap out of it. First aid kit."

I shook my head and bolted into the pantry and grabbed the kit. When I returned, Aunt Tab was at the sink, running water over her cut.

Jordyn took the first aid kit from me. "Aunt Tab, sit on the stool."

Aunt Tab tore a paper towel from its holder near the sink then sat on the stool. "It doesn't look like I need stitches."

Jordyn proceeded to unpack the necessary supplies as though she'd been a skilled nurse for many years.

I had normally been the one to respond quickly in tense situations, but the blood seeping into the paper towel was messing with my head.

"What's wrong, Layla?" Aunt Tab asked. "You look pale."

Fear obviously washed over Jordyn.

I picked up the knife, staring at the blood on the blade, and images of me sucking on Sam's wrist came soaring back. My pulse quickened as my tongue darted out. Before my brain could catch up with my actions, I was licking the blood off the knife as if it was a spatula that had choco-late-cake batter on it. I moaned as the sweet, tangy blood danced on my tongue.

Aunt Tab screeched, "What are you doing, Layla?"

Jordyn whipped her head at me, horrified.

Aunt Tab tore the knife from me and threw it in the sink. "What did those vampires do to you?"

The clanging sound made me flinch, and I briefly closed my eyes, scolding myself.

Aunt Tab wrapped her finger in the paper towel since Jordyn hadn't yet bandaged her wound. "Your uncle was right. Something hap-pened to you girls."

I dug my nails into the palms of my hands. Jor-dyn's suggestion to leave and work for Steven sud-denly sounded good. If anything, I didn't want to be there when my uncle came home. I swallowed, hoping to clear the tanginess from my tongue. "You want to know what happened to us?"

Jordyn shook her head, and strands of her brown hair fell forward. "Don't, Layla. Aunt Tab isn't ready to hear that."

Aunt Tab closed her wounded hand into a fist. "Jack will be home soon. Given the events of the day so far, I think it's best if you two leave for a few hours so you can think about where you go from here. Plus, I might be able to calm your uncle down."

I doubted that. Uncle Jack listened to no one.

"Why? Are you going to tell him what I just did?" Her answer would tell me if I could at least begin to trust her.

She regarded me with equal parts sadness and concern. "No. It's bad enough he blew his top when he read the text from Sam."

Jordyn packed up the first aid kit, leaving out a bandage. "You should put a Band-Aid on your finger."

Aunt Tab moved a wispy strand of her salt-and-pepper hair off the side of her face. "I'll be fine. But I have one question for Jordyn. Were you serious about working with them?"

Jordyn shrugged. "Does it matter?"

Aunt Tab opened the Band-Aid. "Word of advice. You're welcome to stay as long as you like, but while you're living under our roof, you have to watch yourselves. You can't be saying things like 'working for vampires' or"—she eyed me—"licking blood off knives."

I agreed with her. But I had no explanation for my actions except maybe having vampire DNA.

5

SAM

Roughly two hours later, sweat poured off my body in buckets as I rammed my fists into a punching bag, picturing Dane's head then Ross's face. I was trying like a motherfucker not to think. So much had transpired since Layla had rocked my world. Not only that, but rather than text Layla for the umpteenth time, I'd called her before I started beating the shit out of the bag.

"Shocked" didn't even begin to describe how I'd felt when Tabitha Aberdeen answered Layla's phone. But that shock had quickly transformed into outrage. Layla was ghosting me for some reason, and my ego was turning black-and-blue because she didn't want anything to do with me—either that or Jack was forcing her not to talk to me.

My fist connected with the bag, punch after punch, left, right, left, right. I blew out a breath and hit the bag again.

The door to the gym squeaked open, sounding like nails on a chalkboard and only further inciting my rage. The punching bag came off its chain and flew against the padded wall, practically ripping it open.

"I'm surprised you haven't torn that thing to shreds by now." Jo's sweet voice did nothing to ease my fury. She glided deeper into the room with her black hair tied up in a high ponytail, wearing yoga pants and a tightly fitting tank. "Need a sparring partner?"

I growled. What I needed was to get my ass to Montana. Maybe then I wouldn't feel like I couldn't breathe. "No. I might end up hurting you."

She snorted. "Doubtful, brother. You know I'm stronger than you."

I wiped the sweat off my brow with a towel. "Not anymore."

She picked a sword from one of many on a table along the far wall. "Want to test that theory?"

I dropped down on the slatted wooden bench. "Tell you what. Let's go down to the water's edge, and I'll show you how strong I am." Using my elemental powers wasn't the smartest thing to do, especially in the middle of the day. Too many chances of some human seeing us.

She wielded the sword one way then another. The blade glistened beneath the gym lights. "It's been a long time since I practiced my powers, but now isn't the time. Get up and spar with me."

I shoved my hands through my hair. "Sorry, sis. Not today." Her powers might rival mine, but not when I was angry.

She frowned as she returned the sword to the table then joined me. "I'm worried about Ben, too, but he's in good hands with Dr. Vieira. And you'll be happy to know that I spoke to Doc before I came down. Apparently, there's a wolf in Dane's pack with blood that has healing properties. He's not sure if it will work on someone who's only partially human, but it's worth a try."

I guessed I would've learned that if I hadn't stormed out of the infirmary.

She placed a hand on my knee. "Ease up, Sam. You're wound tight."

That was an understatement. "Let's hope it works."

She shuddered as sadness wafted off her. "Ben has been through so much, and I can't bear to see him like that. I also don't want to have to call his dad."

Christ. Mr. Jackson would have a coronary. He blamed us for everything bad that had happened to Ben since Jo and I became vampires, although Mr. Jackson wasn't aware of our vampire status—or Ben's, for that matter. We wanted to keep it that way. For years, Mr. Jackson threatened my father, saying he would go to the police and anyone who would listen to him about how my father was an evil man.

I twisted the towel into a knot, tempering the need to damage something other than a punching bag.

A beat of silence passed before Jo spoke. "Any word from Layla?"

I tossed the towel into a wicker basket close by. "Funny you should ask. I thought she'd been ignoring me, but I called her phone when I came down here. Her aunt answered. I think her uncle might be holding Layla hostage." I was going with that theory because I couldn't bear the thought of Layla not wanting anything to do with me.

"I doubt that," Jo said. "Layla and her sisters don't strike me as the types to allow anyone to boss them around."

I popped to my feet. "Something's not right. I'm going to Montana." I collected my gym bag.

Jo had her hands around my arm before I took one step. "Are you nuts? The Aberdeens will skin you alive."

I pushed out a long-suffering sigh. "I know, but I have to see her."

She batted her silver eyes. "I've never seen you this smitten with a woman."

I snorted. "Smitten? Somehow that word and my asshole nature don't match, sis."

She laughed. "Very true, but you like her a lot, Sam. You're falling for her, aren't you?"

I pulled on my sweaty hair. "No. Yes. I don't know." Hell if I knew what love felt like, and if the pain in my chest or the empty feeling in my stomach were any indication, then fuck love. I didn't want any part of it. "Look, it's more than my feelings. I think Layla is in trouble."

"Then see if you can have our scout in Montana check on her," Jo said. "Webb or Tripp should have his info."

My father did, as well, but he was tied up with making sure Roman Brown was shipped off to our vampire prison in Puerto Rico.

I kissed her on the forehead. "Thank you. I don't know why I didn't think of that."

She giggled before she dropped down on the mat and kicked out her legs. "Maybe because you have your head up your ass, consumed with thoughts about Layla. Love will do that to a person."

I collected my bag and hiked it over my shoulder. "I need a shower before I talk to Tripp." A renewed sense of purpose overshadowed the brooding feeling that had been making me an ornery jerkwad since Layla left.

She bent her upper torso over her thighs and touched her toes with her fingers. "He was on the phone with Webb when I passed him in the hall outside the control room."

"Everything okay?" Webb wanted to be part of the team to escort Roman to prison. He wanted to make damn sure he saw Roman behind bars.

"As far as I know," Jo said. "You don't have any gut feelings, do you?"

Ben's situation, the shifters, and thinking about Layla meant I hadn't thought much about Roman. "Not at all. But now that we're talking about him, I wouldn't be surprised if Roman did try and break free. He reminds me so much of Edmund Rain."

She shuddered as she curled her legs underneath her. "Please don't say his name." Jo had nightmares about him even though the vampire was dead by her hand.

"I'm sorry, sis."

Her silver eyes morphed to violet as her emotions changed. "It's been five years since I killed him, but I always get chills when I hear his name. We do need to find out how Roman knows about Abbey."

"For sure, but he isn't talking. And he blocked Pops from reading his mind."

She raised her gaze to mine. "I bet I could get in, but Webb and Dad said no."

I didn't agree with them. If anyone could break through a memory bank, it was my sister. But I wasn't in charge. Besides, with Roman locked away to rot in prison, I was sure whoever he'd gotten his intel on Abbey from wouldn't stay in the shadows too long.

I held on to the straps of my bag. "By the way, how is my niece?"

Abbey was my niece by proxy. Her mother had been murdered by Abbey's father, Edmund Rain, not long before Jo killed him. There was no other family that we knew of on her mother's side to take Abbey in. Edmund had a brother and a sister, but he'd never spoken to them, at least since my father had known him. I wasn't sure how long that was, except that Edmund and my father had been friends for many years before they became enemies.

Nevertheless, after Jo and Webb married, they'd taken custody of Abbey. She needed a parent. As a vampire, Jo couldn't have kids, so she jumped at the chance to be a mom. More importantly, Abbey was a special little girl who, if the prophecy was correct, didn't need her father's blood to turn into a vampire. According to our late grandfather, Abbey would slowly lose her humanity as she aged, and at sixteen would be a full-fledged vampire.

We were watching her change right before us. At ten years old, her powers were getting stronger.

Her ability to read the future was becoming sharper. She could open a door with a wave of her hand. Jo had been looking into Abbey's mother's family history to see if Rachel had any relatives who were powerful witches.

"She's good. She's in the library. Alia is tutoring her."

I grinned, remembering the days when Alia Costner tutored Jo and me. "Is she still having nightmares?"

"Yeah. But she still won't talk about them."

The door to the gym burst open, and Abbey ran in. Her big blue eyes were filled with fear.

Jo was on her feet in a nanosecond. "What is it?"

Alia hurried in, trying to catch her breath, her blond hair swept on top of her head with wild strands around her face. Like Abbey, alarm swam in Alia's blue eyes. "I'm so sorry." She rubbed her hands together as anxiety swirled around her.

Tears cascaded down Abbey's rosy cheeks as she trembled.

Jo dropped to her knees and clutched Abbey's arms. "Talk to me."

Alia sighed, blowing out the air through her

nose. "She had a vision while we were in the middle of a history lesson."

Abbey's bottom lip wobbled. "Grandpa and Dad are in trouble," she cried. "You have to call Dad."

I dove into my bag for my phone when Tripp rushed in. His skin was stark white, his bronze eyes glued to Jo, powerful terror jumping off him and clinging to me.

I staggered where I stood. "It's Roman, isn't it?"

"A bomb went off in the basement of the building, inside the tunnel leading into the prison cells," Tripp said on a heavy breath. "The helicopter will be ready in fifteen minutes."

Abbey threw her arms around Jo and cried.

Alia touched her hand to her mouth.

Jo rubbed Abbey's back. "Shh. I'm sure Dad and Grandpa are okay."

Somehow, I didn't think so. If Abbey had a vision, then she knew their fate, and by the looks of Abbey bawling her eyes out, it wasn't good.

My heart hammered against my ribs. *Motherfucker. Can my life get any fucking worse?*

Abbey pulled away from Jo, who was white as

a ghost. "Mom." She shook her head. "Grandpa isn't going to make it."

My heart fell to the floor.

Jo fixated on me, tears filling her silver eyes as they shifted to violet.

"Pops can't die," I muttered. My father was one of the strongest vampires I knew. He'd been around for well over a century. Yet even as I said it, a voice in my head screamed, *You're wrong. Vampires die eventually.*

Abbey shuddered. "He needs your blood." Then her teary blue gaze landed on me. "Uncle Sam, he needs your blood too. It's the only way he'll live. But he doesn't have long."

Fuck.

"How long?" Jo asked.

Abbey blinked away a tear as she swallowed, hunching her small shoulders. "I don't know."

Hell if my old man would die on my watch— but even as that thought ran through my brain, I couldn't help thinking about what Alia had taught Jo and me about the power of three. Ben was fighting for his life, and now my old man. Who was next?

Jo and Abbey ran out with Alia.

Tripp and I kicked our legs into gear, and as

we left, I asked, "Can you give me the number to that scout we have in Montana?"

He jerked his head at me as he closed the door to the gym. "Something wrong?"

"I don't know." But that eerie feeling I'd had earlier about Layla had multiplied tenfold.

6

SAM

The whirr of the helicopter blades was muted beneath my headphones. "How much longer?" I asked the pilot into my mic.

Boston's skyline stood out against the deep-blue sky, the glare of the setting sun gleaming off the John Hancock Tower.

"We're five minutes out," the pilot replied.

Tripp tossed a look over his shoulder from the seat beside the pilot. "Webb just radioed."

Jo clutched her chest and pushed out a squeaky sigh. "Thank God."

I grabbed her other hand and squeezed. "Dad will be okay too." I infused as much confidence into my tone as I could.

"Jonah, Webb, and a team of guardians are trying to move rubble to get to your father," Tripp said.

Jonah, my father's personal guardian, wouldn't let my old man die. Jonah and my father had become friends when they were both in prison. My father had been accused of murdering the secretary of the navy, and Jonah had been our enemy, working under Edmund Rain until Jonah learned Edmund had killed his soulmate.

"Any word on Roman?" I asked.

Jonah had called Tripp when we boarded the chopper to give him an update. Apparently, the explosion had taken out the tunnel that connected the prison cells to the transport loading dock. "Nothing yet," Tripp said.

Hopefully, the fucker croaked. I leaned back in my seat and gazed out, praying my old man would make it and that Abbey's vision wouldn't come true.

A 747 approached the runway at Logan Airport to our right, and to our left, the skyscrapers stood tall and ominous. The traffic below was at a standstill for rush hour. I was grateful we had the chopper. Otherwise, we would have had no chance of saving my father.

The pilot banked left, skirting past Logan Airport and over the Charles River. Our headquarters weren't far from Fenway Park.

Jo bounced her knee, ready to tear out as soon as the helicopter touched down.

I squeezed her hand again and gave her a reassuring grin.

She feigned a smile as her anxiety seeped from her pores. "Did you get ahold of the scout in Montana?"

"Yeah." I'd called Conrad, a scout on our payroll, just before boarding the helo. "Conrad says he hasn't seen anything out of the ordinary. But he's investigating."

About two minutes later, the pilot landed on the eight-story building that was home to the Council of Elders and all of the vampire administration services for North America. The stone structure spanned a city block and was enclosed with a high security fence and guards who patrolled the grounds. Humans thought the building was home to a data center owned by one of the bigger cable companies in the country.

Webb stood by the open door of the building, waiting for the pilot to power down the engine. Jo, on the other hand, didn't. She took off her seat belt and jumped out with the rotor blades still spinning. She threw herself at Webb. He caught her in an emotional embrace, as though they'd been separated for years.

Sighing at the knowledge that at least one person I loved wasn't dead, I climbed out, threading my fingers through my hair. I stalked up to my brother-in-law while Tripp talked to the pilot.

Webb gave Jo a hard and fast kiss before the two separated. Then Webb and I exchanged a quick hug.

"I'm glad you're okay, man," I said. "And my father?"

Webb frowned as he regarded his wife. "We're still clearing the rubble."

Jo bolted inside.

Webb clutched my shoulder. "I need to talk to Tripp. Take the stairs down to the basement. The elevators aren't working."

I darted in. "Sis, the elevators aren't working," I said loudly.

Her footsteps echoed as she pounded down at a rapid rate. I wasn't that far behind her, jumping several steps at a time.

An hour had passed since Abbey told us about my dad. I hoped we weren't too late.

In less than five minutes, Jo and I were in a hallway in the basement. To my left, things were clear. To my right, it was chaos, with five vampires all covered in stone dust as they'd formed a line, handing off large pieces of the building to one another. The vamp at the tail end tossed a large boulder into a hole in the wall that led into an interrogation room.

Jo plowed through the line, pushing each of the men out of the way until she reached Jonah. His curly blond hair was tied back with a leather strap. His blue eyes stood out beneath the dust covering his face.

"I hear his heartbeat," Jonah said. "It's weak."

Jo leaned into a small opening at the top of the pile of debris and listened. After a second, she briefly closed her eyes. "I hear it too." Then she started to lift rocks.

I was about to join the fray when my phone rang. I snagged it from the side pocket of my cargo pants. The number on the screen was a Montana area code and not Layla's. It was probably Conrad with news about Layla.

"Hey, man," I answered.

"Sam," the familiar female voice said, "this is Tabitha Aberdeen."

She didn't sound as harsh and mad as she had when I'd spoken to her earlier, but I panicked.

I pressed my fingers to my chest to get the piercing pain to subside. I was a tough mother-fucker. I could withstand anything. Hell, I had for years as a human and vampire, but everyone had a breaking point, including me. "What's wrong?"

"I only have a minute," she whispered. "You need to help Layla. You need to come and get her."

I choked on her last statement, but that wasn't the issue at the moment. "What did your husband do to her?"

"Nothing," she said, sounding horrified. "Something is off with Layla. She's been sick for the last three or four days, and today—"

"Who are you talking to?" Jack Aberdeen asked in the background.

"The doctor who saw Layla a few days ago," Tabitha responded to her husband. "I'll be out shortly."

A beat of silence ensued until his footsteps faded.

"What happened, Tabitha?" I asked.

"I have to go," she said.

"Don't hang up on me." I was ready to jump through the phone. "What type of sickness?" It had to be nonhuman if Tabitha wanted my help, but I had no idea what it could be.

As vampires, we didn't get sick. All the symptoms Layla had experienced had been a direct result of her drinking my blood, but enough time had passed that my blood was out of her system.

Unless what I'd suspected all along was true: Layla had vampire DNA, and she was experiencing tendencies like craving blood. She couldn't turn into one of us. She would need blood from her father. One, he was dead, and two, even if he had been alive, he wasn't a vampire, which was the key to make the change.

"I don't know. I can't talk. Just help her." Then she was gone.

I stared at the phone for a second before I redialed. The line rang and rang.

"Sam." Jo's voice punctured my sensitive hearing. "Get over here."

Growling, I tapped out a text to Conrad, hoping he could find out what was going on with Layla. Then I jogged over to my sister, climbing the mountain of debris just as she was crawling through the opening they'd made.

"Dad!" Jo's voice echoed in the distance. "Dad."

I was about to follow my sister when Jonah caught my arm. "Man, I want to warn you." His anguish gave me whiplash. "Roman isn't in there. He got away."

The blood in my veins gelled. If Roman had been able to escape, then he was gunning for Abbey. "Webb know?"

He nodded. "But Jo doesn't. Webb has a team looking for Roman now."

"Sam!" Jo screamed at the top of her lungs.

I dove into action, crawling through the tight and narrow opening. When I emerged on the other side, I took a breath to calm my racing mind and pulse. It felt as though my brain was on a collision course with a train and my heart was about to bulldoze its way out of my chest.

In the span of a few hours, the world had come crashing down.

Layla was in some kind of trouble. My father's life was on the line, and now Roman had escaped, which meant Abbey was in danger, and Layla could be as well.

7

———————

LAYLA

Jordyn and I were tucked into a booth in the back corner of a local restaurant in Big Timber. The lunch crowd was beginning to thin. Voices droned, glasses clinked, and the swinging doors to the kitchen squeaked.

I held onto my glass of Coke, debating whether I should ask the waitress if they had any Pepto-Bismol. My stomach still wasn't feeling all that great. I was glad the restrooms were down a short hall next to me. That way, if I lost the spoonful of chicken soup I'd slurped a minute ago, I could dart into the ladies' room quickly.

Jordyn picked at her Caesar salad as if looking for something interesting. We'd both been quiet on our way to the restaurant. I wasn't ready to deal with why I'd licked blood off a knife or why I craved the iron-flavored red stuff.

"Are we going to talk?" Her voice cracked.

I shuddered as I peeked around the tall wooden booth behind Jordyn. Since we'd sat down about fifteen minutes before, I kept eyeing the entrance in the distance like a damn soldier guarding a palace. I had no idea if Aunt Tab would spill her guts to Uncle Jack about me licking blood off the knife or if she would tell him that Sam had called. Knowing my uncle, he would hunt me down and probably lock me away for good. It was bad enough that he was pissed about the text from Sam.

She puffed out her cheeks. "Why did you lick blood off the knife? By now, Sam's blood should be out of your system."

I shrugged. "I have no idea. Something is wrong with me."

Jordyn set her fork down. "You need Dr. Vieira, then."

"I agree." I couldn't exactly ask a human doctor to test my DNA for a vampire gene. And if I didn't carry it, then Dr. Vieira would be the best doctor to diagnose why I was craving blood.

"Then we should head to Massachusetts. We can talk to Steven Mason about a job and Dr. Vieira can examine you. Two birds, one stone and all."

"Slow your roll, sis. I never said I would work for Steven." If I did, Sam would be around, and I didn't trust myself with him.

She leaned in, and strands of her brown hair brushed the tabletop. "Do you really want to stay in this town? Look around, Layla. Too many memories I would like to forget. Just driving into town, I imagined Mom going into the bakery down the street."

I smiled at a memory of Mom lighting up when she bought an upside-down pineapple cake from Weston's Bakery. "Is that why you were quiet? Or are you processing the knife-and-blood thing?"

"It doesn't matter," she fired back. "I'm ready to get on with my life. The ranch isn't the place for us if we want privacy. Fuck, Aunt Tab stole your phone. Uncle Jack read your text from Sam, and now Aunt Tab can tell her husband you licked blood. Think about the shitstorm over that one. We came here to relax and to make sure a war didn't break out between the Masons and our family. I get it. But our time here is up. We need to leave, and soon."

I couldn't disagree with her. But we didn't have enough money in our bank accounts to rent our own place. However, we did have enough cash to get us to Massachusetts. "We don't have a car."

She flicked her thumb behind her. "We have a truck outside."

"You want to steal Uncle Jack's truck?"

Jordyn sat back and removed her scarf. "We're only borrowing it." Her tone was matter-of-fact.

I took a swig of Coke. "Let me think about it."

"There's nothing to think about." Her voice rose in pitch. Jordyn hardly ever got mad, but when she did, she could blow the roof off a house. "If I have to drug you then drag you into the truck, I will."

I closed my eyes. If I wanted to get into the police academy, I had to apply. Not all applicants were selected. Plus, the application process took time, which meant I would be at the ranch longer than I would like.

"What about Rianne?"

She popped forward. "Rianne is on her own journey. She wants nothing to do with vampires. I'll miss her, but the military is the best place for her." She glanced around then regarded me. "I've been waiting to tell you this. Now seems like a good time."

Nerves pricked my stomach.

"Uncle Jack is resurrecting the family business and will be hunting shifters now too," she whispered. "So if he thinks you or any of us love vampires, the hunter might just become the hunted."

I stiffened and furrowed my brow. "Are you saying Uncle Jack will hunt us?" We didn't like each other, but I couldn't believe he would hurt us for befriending vampires. Sure, he would definitely disown us, but that was as far as he would go—at least I hoped so. Although Uncle Jack was a loose cannon.

She shrugged. "As much as he hates the bloodsuckers, I wouldn't put it past him."

If I had vampire DNA, then Jack might change his tune about me, but not about Jordyn. I was curious—if I had the gene, did that mean Jordyn and Rianne did as well? I shook it off. I was getting way ahead of myself.

I blinked and absently scanned the restaurant when a sharply dressed man caught my eye.

He took off his overcoat as he headed for the

bar while looking at me with a curious glint in his hazel eyes. It was as if he knew me. Suddenly, my mind drifted back to that night on the naval base when Roman stood proudly on the SUV, wearing a suit, of all things, to a fight.

I quivered at the thought and studied the man. He appeared to be in his late twenties with a close-shaven beard and thick short black hair cropped on the sides. Military man came to mind, but the way he was dressed screamed of a lawyer or rich businessman of some kind. There was a law office a block down.

Jordyn followed my line of sight. "Do you know him?"

"Nope." The last thing I needed was to hook up with a guy.

The cute brunette bartender took the man's drink order with a flirty smile as her big brown eyes lit up.

"So, sis, what's it going to be? Ranch from hell? Or hot sexy vampires?"

I snorted before I took a long pull of soda from the straw then picked up my phone from the tabletop. "I don't have Dr. Vieira's number."

She beamed from ear to ear. "Now, we're getting somewhere. Call Sam. He'll give it to you," she said all too smugly.

I snarled at her teasingly. "You're just dying to get us together, aren't you?"

She grinned like a Cheshire cat. "Layla, I know you like him. But you're frightened out of your mind. You're trying to do everything to avoid him." She twisted her lips. "Life's too short to worry about what our family thinks of you, of us. They don't own us. Maybe things would be different if Dad was still alive. Well, I take that back. We probably would've never met Sam and the others." She tucked her hair behind her ear. "I'm not saying rush back to him and get married, but you've got to explore how you feel. And right now, you're in denial."

I squeezed my eyes shut for a second. A dull throbbing began in my temples. My stomach swirled with nerves, and I knew I had to do something, especially after licking that blood off the knife like it was my favorite watermelon candy. I needed answers, ones that made sense. Answers that said I wasn't going crazy.

I opened the text from Sam.

"What does it say?" Jordyn snatched the phone from me. "'Baby doll, please return my messages. I want to make sure you're okay. Don't make me come to Montana.'" She giggled. "I guess I could see why Uncle Jack is having a cow. I would bet he's priming his flamethrower."

I bit a nail and swallowed as something dark and scary stole my breath. "You don't think Sam is on his way here now? The fact that Aunt Tab answered my phone would make Sam suspicious."

She slid my cell across the wooden table. "Only one way to find out. Call him. Or I will. At least tell him you're okay, even though it would be fun to see how Sam would fare if he stepped foot on the ranch."

A chill danced down my spine as I pictured Sam hanging by his ankles over a roaring fire. "You know as well as I do that he wouldn't stand a chance, no matter how powerful he is." I absently glanced around, and my gaze landed on the well-dressed man at the bar again.

He grinned and nodded.

What the hell? "That man is giving me the creeps," I whispered. "Let's get out of here."

It was time to get my life in order.

8

SAM

I paced outside my father's hospital room at our Boston medical facility. Jo and I had found him with rebar embedded near his heart about two hours before. I'd been ready to remove the rebar, but Jo had stopped me.

"He might bleed out," she'd said. "If he does, you and I wouldn't have enough blood to give him."

So we'd rushed him to our Boston medical facility in the chopper we'd arrived in. The good news—the rebar wasn't cobalt. The bad news—the metal severed a vena cava, which carries blood to the heart. And since he'd lost a ton, the vein wasn't healing as quickly, not even with the amount of blood Jo and I had given him.

Jo chewed on every one of her nails as she rested against the wall outside my father's room.

I twirled my phone in my hand, anger gripping my stomach like a vise. Fucking Roman and whoever was behind his escape would pay dearly. Roman needed to die. Otherwise, chaos would be a staple in our lives—in Abbey's life, and she needed to grow up without any fuckers like Roman whose sole purpose was to use her as his moneymaking machine.

A redheaded nurse chatted with a doctor at the nurse's station up ahead. I stared at her for a long second as Layla came to mind. Then I checked my phone. No update from Conrad yet.

The elevator dinged. I whirled around as Jo pushed off the wall. We were both on edge. Abbey had said my dad needed my blood and Jo's, but that didn't do the trick. Plan B was Dr. Vieira. We were waiting for him. He always kept blood reserves on hand for emergencies. Sometimes, especially in situations like this, the only way for a vampire to heal was with his own blood.

The elevator doors slid open, and Dr. Vieira rushed out with Abbey at his side.

Jo clutched her chest as she pushed out a relieved sigh, especially when she laid eyes on Abbey. The first thing Webb had done when he learned Roman had escaped was to get Abbey off the naval base.

Abbey's black ponytail swung behind her as she bolted for Jo. "Mom," she cried. "I'm sorry. My vision was off. I thought Grandpa needed your blood."

Jo lifted Abbey into her arms. "It's okay." She rubbed Abbey's back. "Grandpa is going to be fine."

I hated that Abbey carried the world on her shoulders. I hated that she had visions that were mostly nightmares of the future. I couldn't remember a time when Abbey saw a happy road ahead. Still, her visions had been off lately.

Despite that, I wished I had Jo's confidence. My sister had been on death's door several years ago, when one of our enemies drove a cobalt blade through her heart. Luckily, the dagger narrowly missed, though it severed a major vein. Since we were twins, Dr. Vieira had been certain my blood would heal her. In the end, my dad had been her savior.

Dr. Vieira was stoic and confident in his strut

as he carried a small cooler. "Is Dr. Greer with him?" He flicked his brown head of hair at the closed door leading into my father's room.

"Yeah," Jo and I said in unison.

Doc clapped me on the shoulder. "You look like crap. When was the last time you fed?"

"I'm fine," I returned. I was saving my blood-thirst for a certain auburn-haired goddess. Okay, I knew I couldn't go another day before the hunger set in, but I hadn't had time to think about any-thing else except saving those I loved.

Abbey slid out of Jo's arms, ran over to me, and grabbed my hand. "Come on, Uncle Sam. I know where the refrigerator is." Her blue eyes danced with a smile.

The minute her hand was in mine, a sense of relief coursed through me. I had to do everything in my power to ensure Roman didn't get his grubby hands on her. I grinned at Jo. "We'll be back."

Abbey led the way as if she owned the med-ical facility. I wasn't surprised. She'd been there several times when my sister hand-delivered sam-ples or was researching a topic for her college classes.

As we approached the nurse's station, the redheaded nurse, whose name tag read Beverly, smiled at Abbey. "Hey, sweetie. It's good to see you again, and I love your outfit."

My niece was always dressed in something colorful and cute. She wore a patterned top underneath a yellow sweater with jeans and suede boots.

Abbey blushed. "Thank you."

Beverly squatted down, her green eyes sparkling. "Dr. Greer brought in homemade chocolate chip cookies. They're in the break room," she said then rose. "You must be Sam. Abbey talks a lot about you." Lust oozed off the pretty nurse as she beamed at me.

I cocked an eyebrow at my niece. "Oh?"

"Abbey tells me you read her stories before bed." Beverly, flirty and hopeful, batted long lashes at me.

I wished I could say I was interested in the redheaded vampire, but I preferred an auburn-haired human instead. I couldn't get Layla out of my system. "I love to read her stories. So, I take it the break room is down the hall?"

"Yeah. Abbey knows where to go," Beverly said.

Abbey waved at Beverly before we kicked our legs into gear. "She likes you," Abbey said once we were in the break room.

Ignoring Abbey's comment, I went to the full-size fridge and pulled out a bottle of blood. Every staff member in the facility was a vampire, so the fridge was well stocked.

Abbey knelt down in front of the coffee, opened the coloring book, and snagged the crayons nearby.

The room was homey and inviting. There was a leather love seat to curl up on, a recliner that had my name on it if I'd had time to sleep, a TV, a small kitchen nook, and a private bathroom.

Abbey began coloring when my phone pinged. Her head shot up, her eyes filled with worry.

I glanced at my cell. "It's just a text message."

"From Layla?" she asked.

I furrowed my brow. "No. Why? Did you have a vision about her?" The last one Abbey had wasn't good. She'd seen Rianne Aberdeen, Layla's sister, killing Layla. Abbey had yet to tell anyone how. Layla had asked but then stopped Abbey from answering. The when and why, Abbey wasn't sure of. I thought to probe my niece, but she needed to be a kid and not relive her visions of death. It was bad enough that she was having nightmares.

Abbey frowned. "Not really." She gnawed on her lip. "I get glimpses of Layla when I sleep, but I can't remember the details."

I stared at my niece for a long second, wondering if she knew and didn't want to tell me, when my phone vibrated again.

I opened the text from Conrad. A picture of Layla graced the screen. Damn, she was hot. The way her auburn hair was piled on top of her head, her neck wrapped in a frilly scarf, and those plump lips painted pink took me back to her dream that night she stayed in the women's barracks.

I was the star of the show, but she had been the one to take the lead. How we both experienced the same dream was still a mystery, but that didn't matter. My cock jerked as I remembered how her lips felt around it.

I needed air or a cold shower. "Abbey, I'll be right back," I said as I stalked out.

I headed for the floor-to-ceiling window at the end of the hall, where it was quiet and out of earshot, and where I could safely adjust my dick.

Another text came through from Conrad. *Call me when you're free.*

I tapped Conrad's number as I gazed out at the Charles River. Orange and blue streaked the sky as dusk set in.

"I figured you would want to hear this instead of reading a text," Conrad said after he answered on the first ring. "The Aberdeens are resurrecting their family business."

That wasn't a shocker. Jack and Ray were probably out for revenge. After all, Roman had cut off Ray Aberdeen's thumb.

"Anything else? It seems Layla is fine."

"It looks that way. They just left a restaurant in town. It appears they're heading to the ranch. Do you want me to keep following?"

I scratched the top of my head. "Yeah. Her aunt sounded worried, and I want to be sure. So keep me updated." Her aunt wanted me to come to Montana. After I disconnected the call, my mind started working.

Layla could be in more trouble with Roman on the loose. Roman knew that I liked her, which meant he might try to hurt her to get to me. Maybe it was best that I got my ass to Montana. Conrad couldn't handle Roman and his thugs alone.

I spun on my heel and returned to Abbey, but she was gone. I glanced in the direction of my father's room, and Jo wasn't there. I jogged down and came to an abrupt halt when I saw Dr. Vieira talking to Dr. Greer behind the nurse's station.

Dr. Greer, who was a head taller than Dr. Vieira, rubbed the back of his neck. "We can always open him up and try to repair the vein."

"I'm confident his blood will do the trick," Dr. Vieira said, although he didn't sound optimistic.

"You know, Damon," Dr. Greer said to Doc. "In some cases like this, a vampire can give up. Steven might be at the end of his life."

I cleared my throat.

Both doctors jerked their heads at me.

"In what universe are you living, Dr. Greer?" I growled the entire sentence—not that either of the doctors was afraid of me. "My father never gives up."

Dr. Greer pinned me with his brown-eyed gaze. "Son, I'm sorry to say that some of us who have lived as long as your father do give up."

My fangs lowered as I sneered. "Not my father. Doc, did you give my dad the blood you brought?"

Dr. Vieira skirted the circular station. "Sam, Dr. Greer is right."

My nostrils flared. "I don't give a fuck who is right. Answer my question." My voice boomed. I wasn't accepting anything other than my father living. I wasn't ready for him to die—far from it. He and I hadn't had the best father-and-son relationship, but he was still my old man, and I hadn't had a chance to tell him that I forgave him for abandoning Jo and me in foster care.

Dr. Vieira glanced up at me. "Sam, take a breath. We'll do everything we can not to let Steven die. But you have to be prepared. As vampires, we might be invincible, but there comes a time when all of us will leave this Earth."

I snapped my spine straight. "Today isn't that day for my dad." I stalked down to his room just as Webb came off the elevator, looking as though he'd been through a wind tunnel.

I met him halfway. "What's wrong? Please tell me it has nothing to do with Roman." At that moment, I made a solemn promise to myself that Roman Brown would die by my hand and my hand only.

Webb tried to tame his disheveled brown hair. "The guardians found the van Roman was in at Boston Logan. Sawyer is trying to get flight data on every airplane."

Motherfucker. "I need to go to Montana. Layla's not safe. You know Roman will make his revenge personal."

Webb studied me, clearly unsure how to respond. "You think that's wise? *You* in vampire-hunter territory?"

"Conrad will back me up. I'll be two days, tops."

Webb scrubbed a hand along his jaw. "Roman will go after anyone who was there that night. So the entire Aberdeen family might be in danger."

I wasn't about to save every member of the family. Besides, Jack and Ray could handle themselves. For that matter, so could Layla. But after Tabitha's call, I knew something wasn't right with Layla, and I didn't trust Jack.

"I can handle myself," I assured him. "I'll keep you posted every step of the way. Plus, her aunt called me. She wants me to help Layla. Something is going on with her. She's been sick, but her aunt didn't elaborate."

"Mm," Webb said. "Go. Two days, tops. Check with Sawyer. See if our pilot is available."

The knot I'd had in my stomach for the last eleven days loosened for the moment as a flutter worked its way in. I couldn't wait to see the look on Layla's face when she laid eyes on me.

9

LAYLA

The bright afternoon sun beat through the windshield as Jordyn sped down the wide-open country road with minimal traffic. My brain rifled through everything in my life and what decision to make. Jordyn and Rianne knew what they wanted to do, but I couldn't decide. I wanted to be a cop, but first, I had to find out what was wrong with me.

I was tempted to tell Jordyn to head east to Massachusetts right that second. But it wasn't our truck, and as much as I would have liked to continue to piss off my uncle Jack, it was time I confronted him once and for all.

I kicked my feet up on the faded vinyl dash-board. "I've decided what I'm going to do first."

Jordyn gave me a sidelong glance. "What? Call Sam? You should before we get to the ranch."

I loved my sister dearly, but if she persisted in shoving Sam down my throat, I would jump out of the truck while it was moving.

"No," I snapped. "I have questions for Uncle Jack, and it's time he and I have a come-to-Jesus meeting."

She flinched, her big brown eyes lingering on me before she turned her attention back to the road. "Are you sure about that?"

I drummed my fingers on my leg. "One hundred percent. It's time. There's been over two years of tension in this family since Dad died, and I want answers."

"Like why they didn't hunt Dad's killer?"

I rested my head against the seat. "That and who the lady Dad had been dating was." *And why did my uncle hate me so much?*

She glanced in the rearview. "I think we're being followed."

I popped forward. "What?" I checked over my shoulder then the side mirror.

"That gray sedan has been behind us since we left the restaurant."

I wouldn't put it past Uncle Jack to have someone watching us, especially after reading Sam's text. "Maybe that dude at the restaurant was hired by Jack to keep an eye on us."

I should've been paying more attention when we left, but I had my nose buried in Sam's text, debating whether to respond to him.

She slowed to a four-way stop. "Let's find out."

The driver in the vehicle stayed about four car lengths behind us.

She turned right, which wasn't the way to the ranch. "Maybe I should've gone left. The only thing down this road is an old, abandoned sawmill. We might be trapped. What if Vera breaks her deal with the military vamps?" She made a U-turn. "If we want to confirm our suspicions, then let's do it in a more public place." Her knuckles were white against the steering wheel.

I wasn't as spooked as she was—I was irate. But I could understand why a sheen of sweat formed on her face. She'd been through hell with Sasquatch. And in my opinion, a wolf shifter was far scarier than a vampire.

No sooner than she pressed on the gas, the gray sedan came toward us.

"Slow down. I want to see who we're dealing with," I said.

She stiffened, easing up on the accelerator as we approached.

I turned my head slowly as both vehicles were side by side for a mere second.

The man from the restaurant grinned at us.

I wagged my forefinger to the side of the road. "Pull over. Let's see what he wants."

"Are you nuts?" she squeaked.

"Jordyn, the guy looks harmless. Maybe he's a lawyer and wants to serve us papers. Maybe Dad had some unfinished business."

"Two years later? I doubt that," she argued. "And disarming men in suits... they're the kind you should run from. The ones that don't look like they can hurt a fly, but when you get up close to them, they'll rip your intestines out. Um... remember Roman, who wore a suit to a fight?"

I shivered at the mention of him. I hadn't forgotten, either. I rooted around the floor in the back to see if there was a crowbar or anything I could use. "If anything happens, call for help."

"I don't like this." Her voice cracked twice.

The vehicle was turning around.

I came up empty as far as a weapon. "Stop the car, please."

She huffed, pumping the brakes. "Fine. I will kill you if you die."

"Noted." I jumped out and checked the truck bed for a crowbar or something to use. But all I found was hay. Then I marched toward the driver, who'd stopped and was staring at me.

Jordyn rushed up. "You're not doing this alone."

It would have been nice right about then to have had some sort of supernatural power.

"Get back in," I snapped at her. "I can handle this."

"You know I don't listen well. Besides, he won't be able to handle both of us."

The dark-haired man lifted his cell to his ear, then his lips moved.

"Who do you think he's talking to?" Jordyn asked.

I had no idea. As I crossed my arms over my chest, my heart punched my ribs like a jackhammer on steroids.

He climbed out of his vehicle with his phone to his ear.

Jordyn slid closer to me. "You go for his balls. I'll gouge his eyes out."

I laughed. I didn't know why that was funny. Maybe because the dude was broad and muscular and could squash us in a second flat. Or maybe because the last time I kicked a man in the balls, he barely reacted. Sam hadn't been fazed when my knee had connected with his manhood.

Grinning at us, the man handed me his cell. "Someone would like to speak with you."

My eyebrows shot to my hairline. "Tell whoever it is to pound sand."

Jordyn snorted.

The handsome stranger stood stoically with his arm still extended like he'd been flash frozen. His only movement was his eyes flickering from hazel to black then hazel once again. Great, we were dealing with a vampire.

"Layla," a husky voice that was deep and throaty and embedded in my brain forever shouted through the phone. A voice that sent heat straight to my nether regions, awakening a part of me that had been dormant since I'd left Sam. "Layla," he said again.

The man shoved the phone at me. "My boss needs to talk to you." If not for the urgency in

Sam's tone or the man's, I might just have walked away. I had too much other shit to deal with and jumping back into a world I wasn't ready for wasn't on the list. Hell, I would never be ready to see Sam or fuck Sam or be with Sam.

Yet, I'd learned one thing about the gorgeous vampire who'd rocked my world in the bedroom: he was persistent. If I didn't take his call, he would probably teleport to me—if he could.

I glued the cell to my ear. "What do you want?" My tone was brusque. "You know, you're a big pain in the ass. Can't you take a hint? I'm trying to forget you." *Liar. Liar. Liar.*

"I miss you too, baby doll," Sam said in his smooth, delicious voice. "I understand you need my help."

I ground my molars. "Who the fuck told you that?"

"Didn't you know?" I could picture Sam's smug grin. "Your aunt Tab and I are fast friends. She has me on speed dial."

I rolled my eyes as I regarded my sister, who must've heard Sam because her mouth was hanging open.

The man in front of me went back to his vehicle.

Tipping my head at Jordyn, I covered the phone's speaker with my hand. "Find out who he is." As much as I had my own issues with Sam, he wouldn't hurt us, which meant his man wouldn't either.

She strode over to the gray sedan while I walked around to the front of the truck. "My aunt called you?"

"She's worried about you," Sam said in a serious tone. "I am too. Why haven't you returned my messages?"

As much as I was trying to forget him, just hearing his voice settled the turbulent storm of nerves in my stomach. "What didn't you understand when I told you I needed some space?"

He growled. "I gave you space. Eleven days."

A light breeze blew, kicking up the brush along the sides of the road.

I swallowed thickly. "You're counting?" He was slowly worming his way into my heart. Maybe if I programmed it not to engage in any emotions, it would be easier. Relationships had never been my thing.

He made a weak noise of some kind. "Baby doll, tell me what's going on. Your aunt led me to believe that something is wrong with you? Although in the picture Conrad sent me of you, you don't look sick."

"Picture?" It was my turn to growl.

"I have to say, you're looking as hot as ever, baby doll."

I rolled my eyes even though the compliment made my heart flutter. "I had the flu. That's it."

"Then why did your aunt make it sound like you're still sick? What are you not telling me?"

I shivered more from the notion I could have vampire DNA than the cold gust of wind ruffling my auburn hair. "You really want to know?"

Silence reigned.

I looked at the screen. Sam was gone. Then I checked the bars in the upper right. The cell service was fine.

Then Conrad's phone vibrated in my hand.

"Hello," I said.

"Sorry." Sam sounded frustrated. "I'm in a bad spot. I might lose you again. You should—"

"Sam?" I checked the phone. Yep, the call disconnected. I stared at the screen for a second before I tapped on Sam's number. The line went straight to voice mail.

I was about to return to Conrad and Jordyn when Sam called back. "Hey."

"I have to make this quick before I lose you again," Sam said in a rush. "You should return to Massachusetts and let Dr. Vieira do a complete physical on you."

I wondered how much my aunt had told him or what Conrad had overheard at the restaurant, not that it mattered. "I appreciate your concern, but I have too much unfinished business here."

"Layla." My name in his gruff tone sounded like a threat and a prayer. "I highly suggest you rethink your plans."

I laughed. "Or what, Sam?"

He lost that demanding tone and chuckled. "I'll throw you over my shoulder and bring you back myself."

Another laugh barreled out of me. "You have to catch me first." The minute that line left my lips, I knew I was in trouble. Harley, Webb's assistant, had told me Sam loved a good game of cat and mouse.

I also knew he was confident, arrogant, and possessive and that I shouldn't be so cavalier about his idle threat. But I was finding he drew out a side of me that made me want to scream at him and kiss him at the same time.

"You can't run or stay away from me, Layla

Aberdeen." So much confidence infused his arrogant tone. "This is your last warning. You have forty-eight hours to get your sexy ass back here, or Conrad will tie you up and bring you to me." Then dead silence.

I glanced at the phone to find that the call had ended. I wasn't sure if he'd hung up or lost the connection for a third time. Either way, I was ready to fling the irritating piece of technology away when Jordyn ran over with Conrad on her heels.

"You must be Conrad," I said as I handed him his phone.

He tipped his chin down. "I am. Your sister has my info. If you need help, please call me."

Jordyn smiled as though she'd found a five-carat diamond. "He lives here." I didn't know why she sounded so surprised about that. Although to her credit, Conrad seemed as though he was from a big city like New York.

Regardless, I thanked him. Then I hopped back in the truck, flustered and ready to strangle Sam Mason after I fucked his brains out.

10

LAYLA

The tires crunched over gravel as Jordyn drove down the long driveway toward the ranch. Rain clouds skated in, and the sky was growing darker in the distance as the wind picked up.

I shivered as an ominous feeling prickled through me, and the hairs on my nape stood at attention. I heaved a sigh as Jordyn parked next to Uncle Jack's long-bed four-door diesel truck.

I scanned the property. "Things look quiet around here."

Jordyn cut the engine and pointed to the workshop in between the barn and the house. "It won't be for long."

My uncle was fiddling with something on his workbench, and if I had to guess, he was probably sharpening a dagger or one of his blades. Given that he was resurrecting the family business, I had no doubt he was gathering his weapons and making darn sure they worked. I was surprised he wasn't overhauling his flamethrower.

A feeling of dread set in. Between Aunt Tab calling Sam and talking to Sam myself, my brain was fried. I wasn't sure I knew what I wanted to say to Uncle Jack or where to begin. Maybe I should inform him that his wife was talking to a vampire.

I still didn't understand my aunt. In one breath, she wanted me to stay away from vampires. In another, she was reaching out to one of the most powerful vamps, thinking Sam could help me.

I chomped on a nail like a squirrel nibbling on a pine cone. "Can you believe Aunt Tab called Sam? If Uncle Jack knew, he would have a cow."

As if he heard me, Uncle Jack glanced our way. The ball cap he wore shadowed his expression, but I didn't need to see his face to know he was ready to unleash his fury on me. His stiff shoulders and posture said it all. Since my father died, I'd never seen my uncle crack a smile. I understood he was sad over the loss of his younger brother, but two years had passed.

What am I even thinking? My uncle's cruddy attitude was because of me.

"He would also shit bricks if Aunt Tab told him that you licked blood off the knife," Jordyn said.

"I can't see her doing that. She has to know that Sam would call me after she tattled on me. She also knows I could throw her under the bus." As much as I would love to see the look on my uncle's face if he learned his wife called a vampire, I wasn't the type to tattle.

He wiped his hands on a rag and strutted our way. His jeans were stained with oil. His boots had mud on the rims of the soles, and his belly stuck out beneath his flannel shirt.

I grabbed the door handle. "Time to get this over with." Then I could move on with whatever was next.

Jordyn caught my arm. "Wait. What's the long-term plan here? Sam wants you to see Dr. Vieira. Are you?"

I couldn't think past that moment, not with my uncle getting closer. From the look of his hard-set jaw and narrowed grayish-blue eyes, it was evident that I was in for one hell of a fight. "Maybe. I want to talk to Dr. Vieira first, but I don't have his number."

She took the keys out of the ignition. "I'll handle it. I'm sure Conrad will help."

I didn't have a chance to respond when Uncle Jack stood with his arms crossed over his chest in front of our truck.

Jordyn practically flew out, scurried past Uncle Jack with a quick hi, and disappeared into the house.

I lifted my chin as I climbed down, stepping on the running board before my booted feet touched the ground. "Is there something you want?" I asked, mostly to quiet my nerves.

"You and I need to talk." His tone permitted no argument.

The itch to flip him off was making me shake like a druggie that needed a fix, so I slipped my hands into my coat pockets. "Agreed. So, talk." I anchored myself at the edge of the truck's hood on the passenger side.

He removed his ball cap, swiped a hand over his thinning reddish hair, and placed the hat back on his head. "I thought you would come to your senses. But I was wrong, and I'm only going to say this once." He glared at me as though he was shoving a dagger in each one of my eyes. "If you continue to engage with vampires, then you don't have a place in this family." If not for his body language, I would think he was calm, cool, and collected with how even his tone was. "Are we clear?"

I should nod and agree and walk away. But one, that wasn't me. Two, I hadn't been around him and the rest of the Aberdeen clan for two years, so his threat that I didn't have a place among them didn't matter. Three, and most importantly, he had nosed around in my personal business, and that wasn't okay with me. It had been a mistake to come here to begin with.

I pressed my lips into a thin line. "No, we're not clear."

He flinched. "Come again?"

I squared my shoulders. "You invaded my privacy by reading my text message. That's not okay."

"What happened to you? What happened to the girl who got excited about hunting? Last I knew, you hated vampires, and now, you're sleeping with one." His voice grew in volume with each sentence.

My jaw practically came unhinged. "Who said I was sleeping with a vampire?" I muttered several swear words under my breath. I would strangle whoever told him. Given Noah's snarky comment that morning, I was beginning to believe Rianne had told Noah. The text from Sam hadn't indicated anything other than his concern for me.

His folded arms rested on his belly as he cocked an eyebrow. "Are you?"

Usually, my uncle didn't ask a question he didn't already know the answer to. I'd seen him grill his kids when they did something wrong. He wanted to hear the truth from them. But I wasn't his daughter.

"Is this why you're resurrecting the family business? Because you think I slept with a bloodsucker?"

"I suggest you choose sides."

My eyes widened so much that pain pulsed above my eyebrows. "Choose sides? So if I bat for the vampires, you will what? Hunt me down? Kill me?" If I did carry the vampire gene, I was beginning to believe that my uncles would send me to my grave.

His face reddened. "You will not be part of this family anymore. Either get on board or get out."

I wasn't planning on staying, anyway. "While we're on the topic of family, Aunt Tab told me you stopped hunting because you got spooked over my father's death—but you said it was because of finances and building a better life. I might believe the latter, but you're not one to get spooked. What's the real story, Uncle Jack?" I doubted, with his tough bravado, he would ever admit he was frightened. To his wife, sure. But not to anyone else.

His shoulders lowered slightly. "There is no story. Your father's death was a wake-up call for all of us. Frankly, I had to reevaluate what we were doing." He stared at the truck, seemingly reliving the grief over his brother.

"And now you're ready to hunt again?"

Blinking, he impaled me with a stern expression. "After what I saw on that naval base and from that Roman vampire, I realize it's time, especially after Rianne filled Noah in on a few things that happened."

I gaped. "She did?" I said more to jar the rock loose in my throat. Things made sense now. I held my stomach, suddenly feeling queasy. I didn't want to believe Rianne had betrayed me. Swallowing hard, I pushed my fingers into my chest. My lungs constricted, making it hard to breathe.

He scrubbed a hand over his mouth and down his chin. "It's time to do something with your life, Layla. Rianne is joining the military. Jordyn mentioned she's interviewing for a job at the tech company Carly works at in Chicago. You need to choose a path, and one that doesn't involve sleeping with vampires."

I fisted my hands at my sides. "Look, Uncle Jack, what I do is none of your business."

My brain had whiplash from such an eye-opening conversation. I was even miffed about why Jordyn hadn't told me about her job interview with Jack Jr.'s wife, Carly. My uncle's look-alike oldest son had taken off for Chicago right after he got married and not long after my father had died. Jordyn must've spoken to Carly.

He studied me with equal parts pity and derision.

Screw his pity. I made the decision to sleep with Sam, and I was not about to tremble or shy away from Uncle Jack's scrutiny. Since he already knew secondhand about Sam and me, I wanted to see his true reaction when he heard it from me. Besides, it was time to own my shit, to lay things out so he understood who I was. Then I could move the fuck on.

"You want me to choose sides? Well, my side is not here." I stabbed a finger toward the ground. "I appreciate you coming to our rescue in Massachusetts. To be honest, the only reason why I came here was to prevent a war from breaking out between you and the Masons. You want to hear me say I slept with a vampire? I did, and I have no regrets."

I swore steam blew from his nose as a muscle ticked in his jaw.

But I wasn't done yet. "That doesn't matter. What matters is stopping vampires like Roman Brown. I can see why you would want to hunt again." I lost my sarcastic tone and softened my voice, hoping I could at least make him understand we were on the same side. "Uncle Jack, spending time with the vampire military was eye-opening. Did you know that there are half-breeds out there because of an experiment gone wrong five years ago? Did you know that the Masons stopped their enemy from turning humans into vampires to build a super army?" I took a breath.

I couldn't discern yet whether he was hung up on my admission that I'd slept with a vampire. But I used his silence to continue. "I want the same thing as you. To live in a world where we can be free not to fear vampires and shifters and whatever other supernatural being is out there. That's what the vampire government is trying to do. They protect humanity." I paused once again, hoping for some reaction from him. But his expression was stone-cold.

"I understand you, Uncle Ray, and my dad had been arguing over a woman at the Deer and Elk not long before my dad died. Who was she? Was he dating her? Or were you arguing about my dad working for Steven Mason? Or my dad turning Sam Mason over to the CIA?"

He flinched out of his zombie state. "CIA? What are you talking about? Why would your dad turn a vampire over to them? That's insane. They would only...." He started pacing.

"Build super soldiers," I said.

He nodded.

Finally, something we agreed on. "You see? We can't let that happen. If we are true hunters who protect humans and our loved ones, then we need to work with those who want the same thing as us. We can't allow any part of the human government or rogue vampires to get their hands on someone like Sam Mason."

He stopped in his tracks and glowered. "What are you saying? That you plan on working with them? Or you just want to continue to sleep with one of them?"

I threw my hands up in the air. "Screw you. I'm trying to make you see the big picture." It was useless. I started for the house as anger tightened every muscle in me.

"You're just like your father, Layla," Uncle Jack said at my back. "He slept with a bloodsucker too. You both disgust me."

My limbs locked, and white dots blurred my vision. *Breathe, girl. Breathe. Walk away. Pack your things and get off this ranch. It's best for everyone.*

But I didn't listen to that little voice in my head. I spun around and stomped back to him like a soldier heading into war.

His smugness sent fury plowing through my

veins, and I itched to punch him square in his bulbous nose. "So the lady you were arguing over was a vampire?" I kept my voice even.

He flicked his head to one side. "You could say that."

I ground my back molars. "And let me guess: you banned him from the family because of that?"

"As I said, there is no place for anyone who's in bed with a vampire here."

"That was the reason he partnered with a former CIA agent to make money," I mumbled to myself. "You drove him to his death." I shook my head back and forth several times. "*You* disgust me."

"Your father made a choice, but that didn't mean I wanted him dead." He sounded horrified that I would accuse him of that.

I blew out a quiet breath as my head finally stopped moving back and forth. My stomach, on the other hand, was growing more nauseated by the second. "Who is this vampire my father slept with? Where is she? Did she kill my father?"

He tucked his hands into his jeans pockets. "All Ray and I have right now is a name. Kendra. He and I have been trying to find her since your father died. We don't know if she was the one who did it." He took a breath, and his pinched features relaxed. "We hired a friend of ours who does PI work."

A thousand volts of electricity jolted me into shock at how freely he'd just told me all that. Maybe there was hope for Jack. "Why didn't you tell me this a long time ago? I had to find out from a former CIA guy that my father had been dating someone. But he didn't know much."

"You and your sisters were distraught over his death. If I would've told you this then, would you have believed me?"

I shrugged. I probably would've thought he was nuts. But after sleeping with Sam, it wasn't difficult to wrap my head around the fact that my father had dated a vampire. "Is the PI still looking?" I would like to meet Kendra.

He nodded. "He is. He checks in every now and then with an update. He got a break about a week ago. He's not sure if it will pan out."

"If you do find her, I want to talk to her before you and Ray decide to seal her fate." I wouldn't hold out hope, though. As far as my uncles were concerned, Kendra was already guilty, whether or not she killed my dad.

His chest heaved before he pushed air out of

his lungs. "Worry about yourself. Do something with your life, Layla. Preferably not with vampires."

Oh, I would definitely do something with my life. But he wouldn't like it.

11

LAYLA

The next morning, I found myself hugging the toilet again. Something was definitely wrong with me. Jordyn speculated that I was sick because of Rianne's betrayal, finding out my father had been dating a vampire, and the entire fucked-up convo with my uncle. The stress had been monumental, for sure. I couldn't understand why Rianne had told Noah about Sam and me. According to Jordyn, Rianne and Noah had been drinking beers and watching a movie the night before last. I was going with her drinking too much and the liquor making her spill the beans.

Once I emptied the contents of my stomach, I jumped into the shower. The faster I could leave, the better. The only reason I hadn't left yet was Rianne. She'd decided to stay the night in Bozeman and party with Noah, or that was the gist of the text she'd sent Jordyn. I'd tried calling her, but she wouldn't answer. As time passed, I was becoming angrier and more stressed, hence my friendliness with the toilet that morning.

Aside from wondering about Rianne, I'd had time to think as I laid in bed last night. My uncle had been right about one thing—it was time for me to choose my path.

For the immediate future, my path was talking to Dr. Vieira. Conrad had given Jordyn Dr. Vieira's number. I'd called him but had to leave a voice mail.

The hot water felt great against the tense muscles in my shoulders and back. I couldn't help but think that my problems were just beginning. As I grabbed the shampoo bottle, something hit me out of nowhere, and I gasped. The plastic bottle fell, sounding like an explosion had gone off.

"Layla," Jordyn called before she practically ripped the shower curtain off its rings. "Are you okay?"

I nodded as I stood under the hot water.

Her brown hair was messy around her face. "You don't look so good."

"I thought of Abbey," I said, "and her vision of Rianne killing me." Call me crazy, but I got a foreboding ache deep down in my bones that something earth-shattering was going to happen.

"Why? Because Rianne confided in Noah about you and Sam? All Jack told you was that Rianne told Noah a few things. Jack never said what those things were. He could've assumed you slept with Sam because of Sam's text. You even said yourself that Rianne might've accidentally slipped. What does it matter, anyway? It's out there now." She picked up the bottle of shampoo for me. "Ease up on yourself." She closed the curtain. "And save some hot water for me."

I shook off the eerie feeling as I lathered the fruity shampoo in my hair and washed it as fast as I could. I was anxious to pack the small amount of clothes I had and leave, but not before confronting Rianne.

"By the way, any sign of your period?" Jordyn asked.

I peeked around the shower curtain to find Jordyn picking at something on her cheek in the mirror. "Where did that come from?" I hadn't thought much about my monthly friend, but if my calculations were correct, it should show up any day.

She turned to face me, leaning against the sink and smiling as if she knew something I didn't. "You were throwing up again earlier this morning. Store-bought pregnancy tests are not always accurate."

I flipped her off and went back to rinsing my hair as a boulder dropped into my stomach. "We've discussed this. It's not possible. Sam can't get me pregnant. Besides, I licked blood off a knife. That is not a sign of pregnancy."

"True, but you're still not feeling well."

"As soon as we talk with Rianne, we'll head to the airport."

Jordyn and I had decided to fly to Massachusetts instead of driving. We'd debated whether to steal the beat-up truck we'd borrowed the day before but nixed that idea. The less shit I had to deal with when it came to my uncle, the better.

I'd tried to talk to Aunt Tab yesterday, but she avoided me like the plague.

After I rinsed, I stood under the hot water for a minute longer, taking deep breaths and trying to clear my mind. But it was no use until I got answers. I snagged a towel that was hanging over the shower rod, dried myself off, squeezed the water out of my hair, and wrapped the towel around me. I pulled the shower curtain back to find Jordyn sitting on the sink, filing her nails, when something occurred to me.

"Jack mentioned you had an interview with Carly's company in Chicago. Is that true?" I'd been so hung up on Rianne, my father, and Kendra that I'd forgotten that small tidbit of information.

"No. I told him I might. Carly and Jack Jr. were FaceTiming Uncle Jack and Aunt Tab the other night when I went into the kitchen. Carly was talking to them about her job and how she was looking for help on her tech team at Intech. I just said I could do that job. Before I knew what was happening, she and I were on the phone, talking one-on-one. I did send my résumé in because she asked me to. But I haven't heard anything. And before you freak out, I was going to tell you, but since you just joined the living yesterday, I haven't had a chance. Besides, I would rather work for the vampires."

I wanted to believe her, but truth be told, a

tiny part of me didn't. Still, I knew when Jordyn was lying or trying to get around the truth. She always looked anywhere but at the person, and her eyes were glued to mine.

"You don't know yet if Steven has an opening. Right?" I asked.

"I don't. But we have a plan, and that makes me happy." She hopped off the counter. "Maybe Dr. Vieira will call you back today."

"Does it matter? We'll see him soon enough." Not that I was looking forward to seeing Sam gloat over the fact that he'd given me forty-eight hours before he chased me and brought me back to Massachusetts. At that point, I didn't care who chased who or who was right. My health came first.

Jordyn undressed. "I'll be quick."

I wound my way out of the en suite bathroom and into the bedroom. I dressed quickly, letting my hair air-dry. I was dying to see if Aunt Tab was home. I wasn't letting her off the hook without explaining why she called Sam. I stuck my head in the bathroom. "I'll meet you in the kitchen."

"Okay," she said.

Before I left the bedroom, I called Rianne. The line went straight to voice mail. Then I sent her a text: *Call me. I know you told Noah about Sam and me, and that's not the only reason I want to talk. It's important. I also want to know how your meeting went with the recruiter.* I wasn't leaving the state until Rianne and I settled things.

Once I hit Send, I wound my way through the house, listening intently. It was dead quiet, although our bedroom was secluded from the rest of the house. Plus, my cousins were probably in school. I was praying my uncle wasn't home.

As I crossed the carpeted floor from the hall into the media room, my aunt asked someone, "Cream?"

I had no idea how my uncle liked his coffee.

I inched closer to the arched doorway leading into the kitchen. Daylight sprayed in from the large windows, giving the rustic media room a warmer vibe than the cold feeling that had plagued the house since I'd arrived. The clang of a spoon against glass filtered out.

I held my stomach, willing the nerves to take a breather as I stopped along the wall of family pictures.

"Jack and I were out last night," my aunt said, "so I'm not sure."

I blew out a breath, relieved that she was

talking to someone other than my uncle. As the tightness in my stomach eased, I marched into the kitchen.

Aunt Tab was sitting at the island. Her face wore a smattering of makeup. Her salt-and-pepper hair was styled nicely into a chignon bun, and she was wearing a blue scooped long-sleeved top over a pair of jeans.

When I swung my gaze to her friend, I did a double take, blinked, looked again, then lost my breath. Suddenly, my heart was on a fast-moving train that was about to run off the side of a mountain.

Sam Mason rose from the barstool like a Greek god and gentleman. He raked his forest-green eyes up and down my body, lighting up like a Christmas tree.

Damn if all my limbs didn't go weak.

I swept my gaze over him, slow and sure. His white button-down shirt stretched across his broad chest, and the rolled sleeves showed off equally muscled forearms and that massive watch he wore on his right wrist. His faded and tattered blue jeans hugged every inch of his toned thighs, and to complement his outfit, he was sporting black military boots, spit-shined and all.

But what had my lady parts singing a tune was the way his ebony hair was pulled into a low ponytail, highlighting the strong close-shaven beard that had grown in since the last time I'd seen him.

I shouldn't be checking him out. I should be freaking the fuck out. He was in a vampire hunter's house.

I rushed out of the kitchen, trying to get air in my lungs. Maybe I was dreaming.

Sam said to my aunt, "She looks pale."

I searched the media room—for what, I didn't know. With my heart in my throat, I inched back into the kitchen and tried to speak, but nothing came out.

"There's coffee," my aunt said in a calm tone I had yet to hear from her.

My guess—Aunt Tab was under Sam's spell. She had to have been.

Sam waltzed up to me, grabbed my hand, and guided me to sit on a stool at the end of the island. "You don't look so good, Layla. Tabitha is right. You need to be seen by a doctor."

I was sure my complexion was stark white because it felt like the blood had stopped flowing through my veins. "You." I cleared my throat. "You can't be here," I managed to say as I sat on the edge of the stool, ready to run in the event my uncle walked in.

Aunt Tab sipped her coffee. "Jack has gone to Billings today."

I licked my dry lips. "Noah and Rianne should be home soon." Or maybe not. Maybe Rianne would avoid me altogether. Though that wasn't how my sister operated. She lived for confrontation.

Aunt Tab shook her head. "He and Rianne are meeting Jack in Billings."

I wanted to ask why, but when I swiveled my head ever so slowly at Sam, I lost all thought. I couldn't believe the arrogant vampire was sitting next to me and, to repeat, in a vampire hunter's house. My aunt didn't even seem frightened, which was messing with my brain as well. Granted, she wasn't afraid of vampires, but she sure as hell had to be scared of what could happen if her husband came home.

Sam returned to his seat, which was to my left, while my aunt was to my right.

"What are you doing here?" My face was scrunched every which way. "And you two seem like best friends." I wagged a shaky finger between them.

Sam smiled from ear to ear, and butterflies took flight inside my stomach. "I told you on the phone yesterday. Your aunt and I hit it off."

If I recalled when I walked in on her talking with Sam the first time, she'd been biting off his head.

I clasped my hands in my lap, digging my nails into my skin to be sure I wasn't dreaming. "Aunt Tab, I'm confused. You tell me vampires are no good for me, but you called Sam and invited him here. Explain."

She beamed at Sam before she regarded me. "You need help, Layla. Sam has been kind enough to explain what happened to you while you were on the naval base. I'm glad I called him. They have a doctor on staff who specializes in blood cravings."

Horror had me baring my teeth at Sam. "You did what?"

Sam smirked, and those damn sexy dimples emerged. "She needed to know that you accidentally tasted one of our bottles of blood and it made you sick. I explained to Tabitha that some brands are sweeter than others. My sister likes the orange crème variety."

I wrinkled my nose, deciding whether to laugh

or not. Sam lied for me, and that said a lot about his character.

"Sam says that the blood is so addictive that some humans crave it all the time. You must've drunk a lot of it, though," she said.

Sam lifted his coffee cup to his lips and kept those luscious green eyes on me. "She drank enough."

The shock of him being there was stifling my ability to think, even more with his made-up story about vampire blood. I was convinced he'd compelled her. But I wasn't complaining.

"Sam thinks you might have vampire DNA," Aunt Tab said matter-of-factly.

Okay. I stabbed a thumb at my aunt while I glanced at Sam. "Did you compel her?"

My aunt jerked back. "Of course not. You know I take our potion to prevent vampires from doing that."

Sam shook his head. "See? I didn't."

I was in an alternate universe. But since she brought up the topic, I had to ask, "Well, do we have vampires in our family?"

She bit her bottom lip and looked around the beautiful kitchen my mom always loved.

A chill skated down my spine the longer Aunt Tab didn't speak.

Then she sighed. "Your father had planned to tell you."

I almost slid off the barstool, my lungs burning for air. Maybe that was the reason my uncle Jack hated me or the family shunned my sisters and me for so long.

Sam was riveted to Aunt Tab as if fascinated. I bet he was. He and I had something in common.

Aunt Tab blinked. "There is no history of vampires in the Aberdeen family, but there is on your mom's side of the family."

I shot up like a jack-in-the-box. "No way. She would've told me." My dad would've told me. I refused to believe that my parents kept this bombshell from me.

"Now, things are making sense." Sam sounded relieved for some reason.

"I don't know the specifics, except that it was such a long time ago," Aunt Tab said.

I grabbed my head, hoping the dull throbbing didn't get any worse.

Aunt Tab gave me a pitying look. "My understanding is your mom shared that piece of her family with your father on her deathbed."

I shook my head furiously. "I find it unbeliev-able that my mom kept this shocking revelation from my dad."

Sam cleared his throat. "Maybe she knew the ramifications of what could happen if the Aberdeens learned about her family. And maybe, Layla, she hated vampires as much as your father."

I wanted to scream at the top of my lungs. I clutched my chest as my breathing increased. So that was the reason I was craving blood. That was the reason I acted the way I had after tasting Sam's blood. I had the vampire gene.

Breathe, Layla. Breathe.

I eyed the green-eyed vampire, who was still affecting me in ways I didn't care to accept. "Do you think that your blood was the spark that set me off because I'm descended from vampires?" I didn't know if he could answer that, but I had to make sense of what was happening to me.

"It would explain a few things," he said. "But you can't turn."

I let out a wild laugh. "Maybe not, but I don't want to live the rest of my life wanting to lick blood off a knife or drink it from a bottle like you." I whipped my gaze at my aunt. "That's why my uncles hate my sisters and me. Right?"

Holy fuck above all fucks in the world. Rianne was going to flip out like a wild gymnast who had lost her mind. And Jordyn would probably laugh.

The puzzle pieces were coming together. "Does Jack know this?" I asked Aunt Tab. He had to have known. Yet, he told me several things the day before but failed to mention that critical piece of information. Then again, he'd been too hung up on me screwing a vampire.

"They don't hate you girls," she said. "But they haven't come to terms with it. They felt your father should've known this about your mother when he married her."

I had to agree with my uncles. "I need to find proof." More for my sanity than anything. I'd been raised to hate bloodsuckers, to kill them with every fiber of my being. Now, I was one of them—or at least descended from the undead creatures.

Aunt Tab frowned. "How? Your mom doesn't have any family."

If she kept secrets from my dad, then maybe she did have a sibling or two or an aunt or someone who could corroborate this outrageous revelation.

"Aunt Tab, do you know anything about a vampire my dad was dating before he died? Uncle

Jack says her name is Kendra." Maybe she was my mom's sibling or aunt. Maybe my father didn't sleep with Kendra, but my uncle had gotten that impression.

Sam chuckled. "That is an interesting twist."

I was tempted to tell him to leave, but I had Aunt Tab talking.

"I don't," she said. "But your father was trying to uncover proof of what your mom told him. Maybe Kendra was someone who knew your mother." Aunt Tab rose from her stool. "That's all I know. Sam, I think it's time for you to leave and take Layla with you."

I knitted my eyebrows. "I'm not going any-where." Before I walked in, I'd been ready to fly out of there. "Not until I find out more about my mom." I wasn't sure how. I didn't even know where to start. Hell, as I thought more about it, I didn't need to stay in Montana to do research. Still, in my mind, it was life-and-death for me. I had to know. I had to understand who I was and what I was becoming. Sam couldn't help me, and the only thing Dr. Vieira could do was a physical, which was necessary but not urgent.

Sam's phone vibrated along the island, and he tapped on the screen. "There's a car coming down the road," he said casually, as if he didn't have a care in the world.

Aunt Tab went stark white as she ran to the window.

I swore vampires had no emotions whatsoever. That wasn't exactly true. Sam had a few, but lust and arrogance were far from concern or worry about another's plight.

"Does Jack or Ray or anyone you know drive a black SUV?" Sam asked Aunt Tab.

Even though I was still trying to process what I'd just learned, his description of the kind of vehicle made me freeze. The last black SUV I'd seen belonged to Roman Brown. But it couldn't have been. He was in a vampire prison. Plus, the car had been damaged when Sam had ripped the C-4 vest off Jordyn and flung it over the SUV.

Aunt Tab pressed her fingers to her mouth. "No one in the family drives that type of car."

Sam pushed to his feet, and it was the first time I'd seen an iota of fear wash across his face, almost making him whiter than the snow on the mountains that surrounded the ranch. "I need to make a call." He swaggered out before I could ask him what was wrong.

Then my mind cleared for a second. Sam

wasn't frightened of anything, not even my uncle. Unless... the shifters. They'd made a deal with the vamp military not to touch us. Maybe they'd reneged, and they were coming after my sisters and me. As powerful as Sam was, he couldn't face a pack of wolves on his own. Or maybe he wasn't alone. After all, Sam didn't go anywhere without two or three others from his SEAL team.

Aunt Tab snapped her fingers. "Layla, do you know who it is?"

I blinked several times. "Not really. But get the weapons out of the closet in the mudroom just in case." We always had weapons readily available.

Aunt Tab started for the mudroom. "I'll handle our guests. Make sure Sam doesn't do anything stupid. Go." She flicked her hands toward the door.

One thing I liked about Aunt Tab was her courage, even though she was shitting bricks inside. I only knew that because her shoulder twitched in tough situations, and it was moving a mile a minute.

12

SAM

I quickly walked around the house, scanning the property far and wide. If I knew Roman, he was probably on foot, although he was the type who got his rocks off on making a flamboyant entrance.

Then again, I doubted he wanted to show himself so soon after escaping. Still, I had to be cautious. I didn't have my team behind me, and frankly, we never went anywhere without backup. But this wasn't a mission. I could handle myself, and I had Conrad, who, according to Webb, was a bad motherfucker.

I tapped Conrad's name on my phone as I sharpened my hearing and vision.

The line rang once, twice, three times before Conrad picked up. "Sam, do you need my help?"

"Why did it take so long to answer?" I zeroed in on the two-story building that appeared to be a six-car garage—a perfect place for anyone to hide.

I stomped through the grass, heading in that direction. A cluster of cumulus clouds slid over the midmorning sun, and a hard wind blew. I sniffed the air. No sign of humans or vampires, although the strong stench of horse manure was overpowering.

"Sorry. The driver of the SUV stopped to ask if I needed help. I tried to probe him for info, but he didn't bite. He's by himself. I'll get my binoculars and take a hike around. By the way, he pulled over. Looks like he's making a call."

That didn't sound good. I whistled when I entered the garage, which was actually a weapons room.

"What is it?" Conrad asked.

"I'll explain later. Is the vehicle government issue?"

"License plate doesn't indicate that."

I picked up a sweet-looking dagger that had the Aberdeen crest on it. "Get in your car and leave."

"What? Are you nuts?"

"You probably made him suspicious. Just get out of sight but stay close." I twirled the dagger in my hand as though the leather grip belonged there.

"If I were you, I would get your ass off that property. No good can come from you being in the house of a vampire hunter. And may I remind you that the Aberdeens take no prisoners?"

I remembered my old man telling me something similar. "They're not a family you want to run into on a dark road in the middle of the night." I had yet to ask more about that.

At the thought of my father, a sense of dread blanketed me. I needed to call Jo and find out whether he was awake yet and how he was doing.

"Duly noted," I said to Conrad. "I'll be at most another hour. Ping me if you see anyone else." I ended the call and was examining the multitude of weapons when a door somewhere in the garage creaked open.

Her cherry scent gave her away. "My aunt will handle our guest," Layla said.

I spun from the workbench and lost my train of thought as my bloodthirst reared its ugly head. I could sense the sweetness of her blood. Hell, I still hadn't gotten her taste out of my mouth. I licked my lips, my gums throbbing endlessly, my fangs ready to devour my goddess. "What do you mean, your aunt will handle him?"

She gave me a ball-squeezing smile. "Look around, vampire. We kill your kind."

I chuckled. "Is that line supposed to scare me? Or these weapons?"

Daggers, flamethrowers, swords, guns, stakes— the list went on, and that was only what I could see. I was sure there was more artillery behind the row of cabinets lining one side of the building.

She swung her curvy hips as she closed the distance between us, twirling her finger around my groin. "And can you control your dick, please?"

Man, I was desperate to feel those massive tits pressed against my chest. I was desperate to be inside her, to feel my taste buds explode when I drank from the very spot I was looking at on her inner thigh. "Around you, baby doll, never."

She glanced at her thighs then up at me. "Don't even think about biting me."

Her lust whipped around me like a fast-moving storm, and I welcomed it. I wanted to feel it over and over again.

She sighed as she stood before me, sliding her gaze up and down my body.

Leaning in, I whispered in her ear, "You want to fuck me as bad as I want to be inside you."

She whimpered, a sound that cut through my resolve. I was learning that when it came to Layla Aberdeen, I had none.

I combed my fingers through her silky strands and groaned. *Fuck control.* My fangs clicked into place.

Another sweet noise escaped her as she angled her neck.

I licked her carotid artery, feeling the blood pumping through it.

She latched onto my belt, dipping her fingers just inside the waistband of my jeans. "Why are you here, Sam?"

To fuck you. To taste you. To do things to you that we haven't even begun to do. My fangs grazed over her earlobe.

She shivered. "And don't say because my aunt invited you. I'm sensing you're here for another reason."

I nibbled on her ear. "I am. You." No lie in my statement. But she was smart to think I had another reason too.

"Sam." She gripped my cock. "You're leaving something out."

My brain shut down as I pushed my groin into her, hoping she would do more than squeeze my erection. I nuzzled her hair, inhaled deeply, and moaned.

Before I could process her next move, she had a dagger in her hand. Letting go of my dick, she pointed the blade at my heart. "Now, the truth."

A deep, satisfied laugh burst free as I pressed my chest into the blade. "You won't hurt me."

She narrowed her eyes as she dragged the dagger down my chest, slowly, methodically.

My cock was harder than marble.

I grinned like a damn proud asshole as I watched her chest rise and fall, imagining my mouth around her tits.

She traced the tip of the blade over my cock. "This isn't a butter knife, you know."

I cupped her tits and groaned.

Her eyes became hooded. "You should be afraid, Sam."

I tried to pinch a nipple through the fabric of her sweater and bra. "Baby doll, my cock is your playground. You won't do anything to ruin that."

"Arrogant vampire."

I yanked on her damp hair, pulling her head back so she could look at me. "Did you miss me?" With her in my grasp, I realized just how much I'd missed her. That knot that had grown since she'd sped off twelve days before had now loosened. Oh, yeah. I was still counting.

Her hungry blue eyes were dilated. "Miss you? Not a chance, vampire." She grabbed my wrist, sliced a small opening, and stared at the blood oozing out.

I guided her head to my wrist. "You're dying for a taste."

She licked her lips, and my cock jerked. Man, I was about to lose my shit in my jeans.

She shook her head. "I can't."

"Hurry before it closes." I sounded like a beggar.

"Something is wrong with me. Why do I want blood?"

My fangs descended as I pulled the dagger from her and slit a deeper cut into my wrist. "Drink. We'll worry about why later."

She didn't hesitate as she latched onto my skin and suckled then moaned as if ready to orgasm.

I knew I was. *Motherfucker.*

I smoothed my free hand over her hair before I

kissed her head. "That's it. Take all you need, baby." I was such a goner.

But our bubble of lust popped instantly when tires crunched over gravel.

Layla jerked back, horrified.

I tugged her to me and kissed her quickly, licking my blood off her mouth.

She resisted for a split second then molded her body into mine.

The engine grew louder, so I broke the kiss. "There. No more blood."

She swayed on her feet, and I caught her. Then she wiped her hands on her tight jeans, shook off the aftereffects of what had just happened, and skirted the workbench.

I followed her out through the open garage door as the SUV parked alongside my rental car.

"This SUV reminds me of what Roman was driving the night he cut off my uncle Ray's thumb," she said in an even tone.

Her aunt came out of the house, glanced at us, then addressed the man dressed in what looked to be a government-issue suit. His brown hair was slicked back with hair gel, and he wore a boatload of aftershave.

I winced at the smell, which didn't mix well

with horse manure. "Do you normally have guests who look like the FBI or CIA?" I asked Layla.

Just the thought of the CIA had me clenching my fists. The former CIA agent, Wyman, was still our guest on the naval base. So he couldn't have contacted his former employer, even though his goal had been capturing me then turning me over to them.

I discarded that thought. The CIA wouldn't know I was there. This trip had been a last-minute decision. Maybe this dude was working with Roman. Maybe Roman had sent him to scope things out for him.

"Did you come alone, Sam?" She kept her gaze trained on the man, who was handing Tabitha a business card.

"Yeah. Conrad has my back, though."

"I should see where Jordyn is," she mumbled as her pulse skyrocketed.

"Sensing trouble?" I asked.

"Something isn't right."

"His heart rate is normal." The man looked our way, smiled, and nodded. "But I'm glad you're on alert." That told me she didn't trust anyone, and I liked that about her, even though she probably didn't trust me, either. But in my opinion, lack of trust kept a person alive.

She gave me a sidelong glance. "It's the shifters, isn't it? They broke the deal with you about coming after us?"

I shook my head. "Not at all."

"I'm Lester Worthington," the man said to Tabitha. "Is Jack Aberdeen home?"

"I'm afraid not," Tabitha said. "Can I tell him what this is about?"

"I'm interested in buying a horse," Lester replied.

He didn't strike me as a horse type of dude. "Your uncle sells horses, right?"

She nodded.

"He seems legit." I still wasn't lowering my radar.

Layla sighed, grabbed my hand, and pulled me into the workshop and out of Tabitha and Lester's view. "Tell me the other reason you're here. Then you need to leave before my uncle comes home. I can't protect you, Sam."

I touched my heart. It was endearing that she thought she could protect me. "You care about me?"

She rolled her eyes. "Whatever."

"I came to take you back to the naval base. You're not safe here anymore."

She widened her big blue eyes. "So if it isn't the shifters, then it's Roman." She clutched her chest. "Isn't it?"

"He escaped yesterday. He blew his way out with C-4. As a result, my old man is in bad shape."

She walked around in a circle, biting a nail. "I'm sorry about your father, but I can't leave just yet, Sam."

I grasped her arm. "Listen to me, Layla. Roman is going to hunt down every person I care about."

She rolled her shoulders back. "I'm not afraid."

Her bravery was turning me the fuck on, but I needed to protect her. "I know you're not. But you need to see Dr. Vieira. He's the only one who can help you figure out why you're craving blood. He can do a complete genetic workup. He knows what to look for. A human doctor doesn't."

A car door shut, and the engine rumbled. I guessed Lester was leaving. Nevertheless, I poked my head out. Her aunt waved at Lester as he drove away.

I returned to Layla. "You're right. I need to get

my ass out of here."

My phone rang. I wanted to ignore it but couldn't. I plucked it from the pocket of my jeans and answered. "Webb. Everything okay?"

"We might have found Roman. He got on a flight to Chicago."

"What's in Chicago for him? Do we know?" I asked.

"We're looking into it. We'll have boots on the ground later this afternoon. Still, watch your six."

"Always," I said. "How's my dad?"

"He's not awake yet, and neither is Ben," Webb said. "Did you convince Layla to return with you? Dr. Vieira just informed me that Layla left him a message."

I eyed Layla's ass as she left to meet her aunt halfway. "She's craving blood. She learned this morning that there are vampires on her mom's side."

"No shit," Webb said. "I bet that's driving a stake through the family bond."

Jack had probably pissed his pants when he found that out. "I have to run. I'll fill you in later." I was about to dump my phone in my pocket when it pinged with a text from Conrad: *Get your ass out of there NOW!*

13

LAYLA

My aunt plucked her phone from her apron pocket, and the color drained from her face. Then she whipped her attention to Sam, who was strutting up to us. "Jack is on his way home."

"I believe he's already here," Sam said.

I spun in all directions as I caught sight of the SUV passing my uncle's truck on the road in the distance. My heart punched my ribs like a boxer jabbing lefts and rights in succession.

Jordyn chose that moment to bounce out of the house, eager and ready to leave. But she stopped short on the top step of the porch when she laid eyes on Sam. "Oh my. How long have you been here?" She ran up to Sam and touched him. "Are you really here?"

"Uncle Jack is turning down the driveway," I said harshly, not directing it at her. My nerves were gearing up for a fight.

It took Jordyn a second for the red flags to go off in her head. When they did, she squeaked.

Sam, cool and calm, said, "No worries, ladies. He'll want to hear what I have to say."

Jordyn tilted her head at Sam. "I don't think so. But this should be fun, just the same."

"Sam, get in your car now before Jack kills you." Aunt Tab's voice was teetering on the edge of a screech.

Laughing, Sam shook his head. "Why on earth are you ladies afraid Jack can kill me?"

All of us gave him a look that said "it's your funeral." Still, I knew Sam would desecrate my uncle with a wave of his hand or some type of destructive elemental power he harbored.

Jack's truck wheeled down the driveway as if in slow motion. Aunt Tab was stiff as a board next to me. Jordyn stood on Sam's right with her hands in the pockets of her black jeans. I was on his left and could almost feel the energy coming off of him. He oozed power and mayhem, though he kept his fangs tucked away.

The minute I could see my uncle clearly, his expression turned dark when he realized that Sam Mason was standing on his property. Uncle Jack slammed on the brakes, jumped out of his truck faster than I'd ever seen him move, opened the back door of his truck, and pulled out his flamethrower. "I wasn't able to use this on you or your kind in Massachusetts, but I'm ready now. What the fuck are you doing here?" He kept his distance from Sam, which didn't mean squat. That flamethrower could spit fire much farther than the ten feet separating them.

Sam raised his hands.

My uncle engaged his weapon, and fire spit from it. Man, he had balls, but that was never in question. Anyone who wasn't welcome on his property paid the price.

I wanted to say to Sam, "See? I told you so." He might have had all the power in the world to squash my uncle, but with the weapon my uncle was holding, Sam would light up like the fireworks on the Fourth of July.

Aunt Tab squealed. "Jack Aberdeen, put that away."

My uncle sent a loathing glare at his wife. I was certain she would pay later for telling him what to do.

I slid in front of Sam who in turn laughed. "Uncle Jack, Sam is here because Roman Brown escaped. Sam thinks Roman is on his way here. So he came to warn us."

"Bullshit," my uncle spat.

Sam gripped the sides of my shoulders. "Baby doll, I adore that you want to protect me. But I've got this." He guided me to stand next to him.

"Your funeral," I said.

"Layla's right, Jack." Sam held up his hands again. "Roman has escaped. I thought it was best to warn you in person just in case you could use my help."

"I don't need your help, vampire." My uncle held the flamethrower steady and with precision. "Tab, I want you to call Ray. Tell him to bring the cavalry."

The tension was sucking the fresh air out of everyone except Jack and Sam, who stared each other down.

But Sam didn't look angry or ready to hurt anyone. "Jack, you know I can take that weapon from you before you can even blink," he said too confidently.

"Tab, I told you to call my brother. Don't just stand there!" Jack barked.

"No," she volleyed back. "You wanted Layla gone, so she's leaving with Sam. He's here to take her back to Massachusetts."

I exchanged a wide-eyed look with Jordyn before I turned to my aunt. "May I remind you that..." I couldn't bring myself to throw her under the bus, so the only other thing I could do was meet my uncle head-on. If he burned me alive, so be it.

Sam reached out and caught my hand. "What are you doing?"

I shrugged him off. "Get your ass in your car and leave. I'll handle my family."

The stubborn vampire didn't move as his green eyes vacillated to silver then back to green.

"I said go." I stomped my foot.

A deep crease formed between his eyebrows. "I'm not leaving without you. It's best if I protect you."

Without taking my eyes off Sam, I said, "Jordyn, leave with Sam. I'll meet you in town. You know where." I wasn't about to divulge that piece of information. Knowing my uncle, as soon as Sam left, he would gather the troops and hunt him down.

I hated to believe that the images I had of Sam hanging by his ankles over our firepit would come true. But somehow, my intuition was pinging me left and right that Sam was in danger if he didn't get his butt on a plane and out of Montana.

"Let me get my bag," Jordyn said. "I'm all packed and ready to go, anyway."

"Packed?" Uncle Jack asked. "Where are you going?"

I finally broke my stare with Sam. "She's not staying here, either."

"I thought you had an interview with that company in Chicago that Carly works for?" Jack asked.

"I told you I hadn't heard from them yet," Jordyn said, sounding elated. "But I'm going to talk to Steven Mason about a job."

"What?" Jack and Sam asked in unison.

My sister smiled as though she'd won a beauty contest. "Steven was hoping you would work for him, Uncle. But we know that won't happen. And frankly, while we're telling the truth around here, I want you to know that not all of them are as evil as this family made us believe. The military vampires protect those who can't protect themselves, and they are better than we ever could be."

My uncle's complexion went beet red.

I pursed my lips at my sister. "Move." We didn't need to incite him any further.

Jordyn disappeared into the house while Sam ambled over to his car. "Layla, make it quick. My plane leaves at eight tonight."

I had plenty of time. It was only approaching noon. Nevertheless, I didn't want to spend another minute there if I didn't have to. I also didn't want to leave the area until I could talk to Rianne. I had to see her before I got on the plane.

"Where's Rianne?" I asked my uncle.

Jack kept his sharp focus on Sam as he waited at his car for Jordyn. "She'll be here within the hour."

Jordyn barreled out of the house. "I have your bag, too, Layla."

I wanted to laugh. I hadn't packed, but I guessed that was the reason Jordyn had been nonexistent since I'd left her while she showered. Then something dawned on me. I had no transportation to meet Jordyn later. No matter. I would coax my aunt into giving me a ride.

Jordyn tossed the bags into the back seat of Sam's rental car. "I'll text you, Layla."

Sam hesitated, staring at me.

I prodded him with my eyes. "Go."

When he finally acquiesced and slid behind the wheel, my uncle lowered his flamethrower.

Aunt Tab, my uncle, and I didn't say a word until Sam's car was speeding down the road.

"When were you going to tell me my mom had vampires in her family?" I asked my uncle.

"That's what you have to say to me? I expect an apology first. How dare you bring a blood-sucker onto this property." He threw his flamethrower in his truck.

"I didn't ask him to come here." I gave Aunt Tab a quick glare.

Aunt Tab stuck out her chest defiantly. "I did."

My uncle faltered as his blue-gray eyes became slits. "I didn't hear that."

My aunt fastened her hands to her hips. "You most certainly did, Jack. Stop all this secrecy and bullshit with Layla. The only thing she's done wrong was to take that job with that former agent. So she screwed up. You have, too, in your day. Let's not pretend you're perfect."

I was dumbfounded as I watched the fury grow on Jack's face. The more Aunt Tab spoke, the redder he became.

"I'm tired, Jack." Aunt Tab threw up her hands. "You give up the business, then you're back in it. Frankly, I want nothing to do with hunting vampires. And before you even say a word, I invited Sam here to help Layla. You know as well as I do that she needs help. If anyone can help her, it's the vampire military. They have access to do the research on her mom's family. And if she does carry any vampire DNA, then the naval doctor is the best doctor for her."

It had become crystal clear why Jack had treated me like the enemy since my father died. My head spun at Aunt Tab coming to my rescue despite her husband. She really did mean what she'd said about helping my sisters and me. I also realized that Sam must've told her how Dr. Vieira could help me. Not only that, Sawyer, the SEAL team computer geek, had mad tech skills. He could help me find out more about my family. Maybe even Kendra. After all, Uncle Jack wasn't having any luck.

Jack quietly slipped into his workshop with his tail between his legs, though I highly doubted that was the end of Jack and his hunting, despite Aunt Tab's wishes.

"That went well," I said.

Sighing, Aunt Tab watched her husband with a sad expression. "He just hasn't been the same since your father died."

"Aunt Tab, my dad's death has affected all of us."

"Sure, but Jack feels responsible."

I crossed my arms over my chest. "Because he kicked my father out?" It was good to know that Jack felt remorse.

She nodded. "I'll take you to meet Jordyn. I'm afraid that things are about to get messy."

"What do you mean?" Surely, my uncle wasn't stupid enough to think he could take on the vampire military.

"Your uncles want the vampire who cut off Ray's thumb."

"So does the vampire military," I mumbled.

She draped an arm around me. "Layla, I'm sorry about taking your phone. I'm sorry I haven't been a better aunt to you. I promise I'll help in any way I can, but you need to promise me you'll get on that plane tonight with Sam."

"I'm not leaving until I talk to Rianne."

"I know she said some things to Noah, and she shouldn't have. But don't be too hard on her. She's your sister."

"Do you know why she told Noah about Sam and me?"

"Not my story to tell. You and she have to work that out."

I hugged my aunt. "Thank you for sticking up for me."

She squeezed me to her.

"Will you be okay?" I'd never known my uncle to lash out at his wife using his fists, but stranger things had happened.

She let go of me. "Of course. Believe it or not, Jack listens to me."

"Keep in mind, I know a few scary vamps that would gladly help. Just saying."

We both laughed.

I finally felt as though I had a purpose, but a small voice in my head said to tread lightly.

14

SAM

I was ready to mutilate Jack Aberdeen.

"Sam," Jordyn said behind me, "Layla will be fine."

When we left the ranch, we hadn't gone far. There was no way I was leaving Layla completely alone with Jack. On Jordyn's advice, Conrad and I had parked on a dirt path off the main road. Then we hoofed it back toward the ranch and stayed far enough away but close enough that I could see without being detected.

"I know she will"—I didn't take my eyes off Jack, who was talking to Layla and Tabitha—"because I'm not leaving until I know she's fine."

"My uncle isn't going to hurt her," Jordyn said.

"Are you sure about that? Because with vampires on your mom's side, I'm betting his revulsion for Layla is as strong as his hatred for me." He'd been one second away from lighting my ass up with his wife and two nieces in firing range.

Ripping out his heart would be too kind.

"Ninety-nine percent sure," Jordyn said, her eyes widening.

Conrad came down a small hill. "I think I heard the aunt is taking Layla into town."

The women went inside the house.

I texted Layla: *Hurry the fuck up.*

She replied immediately: *Chill, vampire. I'll be there soon.*

If she wasn't, I would plow in and bring down the house.

Jordyn tapped on my shoulder. "Let's go. We're meeting her at the Deer and Elk just outside of town." She sounded a little jumpy. "I'll be in the car."

Conrad brushed dust off his black pants. "Now that Jack knows you're here, this town definitely isn't safe for you. Get to the airport. I'll pick up Layla from the Deer and Elk."

"I can handle myself." I appreciated that he had my back, but I wasn't one to hide or run.

Conrad glanced toward our cars. "Word around town is that Jack has a new weapon. I don't know the specifics."

"You mean the flamethrower isn't doing the job?" My tone dripped with sarcasm. Still, the drug Layla had used at the nightclub came to mind. "We know he's testing out a drug, or he was two years ago. I doubt that's it since most drugs won't kill us unless it's an endotoxin." At the moment, I couldn't worry about a new weapon. "Look, man. You should think about getting out of town. Come back with me."

He scratched the underside of his chin. "My job is to keep an eye on the Aberdeens. I can do that without getting caught. I don't stay in one place that long, anyway. Besides, until your father tells me otherwise, I can't leave my post. Any word on his condition?"

"He's still out but alive. I'll head to the Deer and Elk." As much as I would have loved a good sparring with Jack Aberdeen, it wasn't the time. I was certain he and I would go head-to-head at some point in the future. "Hang here until you see Layla leaving."

Jordyn had the phone to her ear when I climbed behind the wheel. "Rianne, why are you ghosting Layla and me? Answer our freaking calls. We're on our way to the Deer and Elk. Sam is in town. Meet us there as soon as you can." She snarled at me, looking a little like Layla at that moment as she tossed the phone in her lap.

I laughed, starting the engine. "Don't kill the messenger." I imagined she was still coming to terms with having vampires in her family.

She clicked her seat belt into place. "I'm not irritated with you. I'm mad that I don't know who my family is anymore, and it's kind of sad too. Rianne seems to have joined the darker side, and my mom had vampires on her side. That's a hard nut to swallow."

"Explain about Rianne," I said.

She toyed with her phone. "I don't know why, but she told Noah about you and Layla sleeping together. It was probably a slip of the tongue. She and Noah had been watching a movie and drinking. I think she had one too many beers and told him accidentally."

"And it got back to Jack, I'm guessing?" I would've loved to have been a fly on the wall when Jack found that out.

"Yeah, and that kind of set Jack off because my father dated a vampire before he died," she mumbled. "Another piece of our history that is coming to light. I feel numb and sad. I don't know where Rianne's head is at. It's like Layla and I are now banished from the family."

I wheeled onto the main road. "I'm usually not good at giving advice, but I would be numb, too, after learning all that. I had a hard time when I woke up as a vampire, and not by my choice. It had been a life-or-death situation. I feel ya." As a foster child, I knew what it was like not to have anyone care about me—except Jo, of course. "Your aunt cares about you and your sisters."

She whipped her gaze at me, pursing her lips. "When did you and my aunt become best friends?"

I chuckled. "We're far from that. But she's worried about Layla." I sped down the road faster than the speed limit, keeping my focus ahead of me. "What's this about you talking to my dad about a job?" Her brazen delivery of that information still had me shocked.

She stared at her phone in her lap. "He was interested in my dad working for him. I'm an Aberdeen with skills. Why not? I could be a scout like Conrad or help in some way."

We had a few humans working for our government, but Conrad wasn't a human.

"My father is fighting for his life right now because of Roman." A stabbing pain clutched my chest.

She sucked in a deep breath. "I'm so sorry. Is he going to make it?"

I gripped the steering wheel with crushing force. "Let's hope so. Otherwise, I'll go on a rampage until Roman is dead."

Silence followed us for a few miles. The mood in the car was as dark as the storm clouds rolling in.

She rubbed my arm. "What can I do to help?"

"You can light a fire under Layla's ass and tell her to hurry up." It was best if we took off before the weather turned nasty.

She tapped out a text to Layla.

Silence followed us the rest of the way to the Deer and Elk, and within twenty minutes, Jordyn and I were crushing empty peanut shells beneath our feet on the sticky floor inside what looked to be a dive bar.

The burly bartender glanced up from the glass he was wiping. "Have a seat anywhere."

The place was dead as a doornail.

Booths and tables were scattered around in front of the U-shaped bar. A doorway with a lighted sign above it led the way to the restrooms, and Sam Tinnesz belted out "Legends Are Made" from a jukebox that sat in the corner adjacent to the entrance.

A petite blond waitress, who was cutting lemons and limes, popped off the bar. "Jordyn Aberdeen, is that you?"

"Linda Getty," Jordyn said. "It's been a long time."

The two women hugged briefly.

Then Linda sized me up, lingering too fucking long on my crotch. "Who's this tall drink of water?"

I was about to say "none of your business" when Jordyn answered, "A friend of Layla's."

Linda finally looked up at me with too much lust swimming in her brown eyes. "You have a name?"

I didn't want to say and didn't have to when the bartender called Linda.

She huffed. "We just opened. I have to finish

what I was doing. What can I get you two to drink?"

"Coffee for me," Jordyn said.

"I'll take a draft beer of any kind."

She bounced away while Jordyn and I commandeered one of the booths.

"She and Layla went to high school together," Jordyn offered. "Not a match made in heaven, if you know what I mean."

Linda went by the wayside when a deep belly laugh pierced the stale air as two men strutted in. The shorter of the two was dressed in business casual—black pants, blue shirt, and loafers. The taller one was taking off his suit jacket as he ponied up to the bar. Then he smoothed a hand over his brown crop and glanced around. When his gaze landed on me, his dark eyes widened.

Jordyn followed my line of sight. "Do you know him?"

I acknowledged Lester Worthington with a nod before he hung his suit jacket over the back of the bar chair and said something to his friend.

"Some dude who showed up at the house earlier. He's interested in buying a horse."

"I missed a lot while I was packing."

Linda deposited our drinks. "Is Layla meeting you here?"

Nodding, Jordyn picked up her cup as the two started chatting about Layla.

That was my cue to contact the pilot. "I'll be right back." I was never one to sit idle and make small talk. And waiting for Layla was driving me mad.

A strong breeze whipped by the minute I stepped outside. The storm clouds had grown darker, and a sudden eerie feeling dropped to the pit of my stomach. Inhaling, I crossed the gravel lot as the scent of rain invaded my nostrils. Man, I hated flying in a storm. I could withstand a bomb, but I just couldn't get excited about falling out of the sky in a metal tube. Webb and a few of my comrades had survived a plane crash a few years back, but they'd had parachutes strapped to them.

I tapped the number for the pilot. He answered on the first ring. "I was just about to call you, Sam. The weather isn't looking good. I suggest we leave as soon as possible."

"Ten-four, man. I'm waiting on one person who should be here shortly. Give me an hour." After I hung up, I strutted over to my rental, which was parked alongside a black SUV that I was sure was Lester's, since there wasn't another one like it in the parking lot.

My suspicious nature had me checking out the inside. A folder with the Aberdeen name on it lay on the back seat, and a small black case with the name Camden Industries etched into the plastic was next to the folder. The first thing that came to mind was a gun case. I couldn't help but think of what Conrad had mentioned about Jack having a new weapon.

Maybe Lester wasn't buying a horse but selling Jack a weapon, though I doubted whatever was in that box would kill a vampire. The only sure ways that someone like me could die was by fire, a cobalt stake to the heart, and losing my head. Even the cobalt stake had to be embedded until my heart burned to ash.

I called Tripp.

He answered on the first ring. "Are you on your way home?"

"I should be shortly. There's a storm coming in." I scanned the inside of the SUV again. "I need you to have Sawyer look into something for me."

"Anything wrong?" Tripp's voice dropped an octave.

"Not sure." I didn't see anything else that

would lead me to believe Lester was lying about buying a horse.

"What's going on?" Tripp asked.

"Have Sawyer do some digging on Camden Industries when he has a chance."

"Sam?" A familiar female voice trickled on the wind before Rianne came into view from around the SUV.

Where the fuck did she come from? I scanned the lot and didn't see anyone with her. "I have to run," I said to Tripp. "I'll call just before the plane takes off." Then I hung up.

Rianne smiled as she raked her brown gaze over me. "I didn't believe Jordyn when I heard her message that you were in town."

I kept my senses open as I looked down her dirt-covered jeans to her mud-encrusted boots. "Have you been mud wrestling?"

"I was helping my uncle with something," she said, staring at me as though she was trying to bore a hole in my skull.

I did another sweep of the lot but didn't see anyone else with her. I also didn't smell another human nearby. "Have you been here long?" I sniffed the air just the same. I couldn't even pick up her scent, although the wind was whipping around pretty strongly, and a thick aroma of cooking oil wafted in the air.

She flicked a thumb at the bar. "I parked behind the club."

There were plenty of parking spaces in front.

As if she knew what I was thinking, she said, "My cousin knows the bartender."

That still didn't satisfy my suspicions. "I have another call to make. I'll meet you inside."

She tucked her hands into her coat pockets and hesitated as if struggling with what to say.

"What is it?" I asked.

She swiped a hand over her brown hair. "If you're calling Layla, she's not coming."

Every muscle in my body froze. "Say that again?" My fangs were ready to shoot out, and not because of her statement but the disdain in her tone. I angled my head, opening my empath senses. Fear lay beneath the fake bravado she was trying to portray.

She squared her shoulders. "She won't be going anywhere with you." Her voice was calm, in stark contrast to her rapid pulse.

"Is that what Layla told you?" I wouldn't put it past Layla to run from me, but I knew without a doubt that she hadn't changed her mind within the last fifteen minutes. If she had, I would stake my own heart.

"Something like that. Sam, just get in your car and go." Her voice cracked on the last three words.

I closed the distance between us, and she stiffened. "Are you warning me?" At least she wasn't threatening me like she had the first time I met her.

She lowered her gaze. "I'm telling you to go home. Let my family handle Layla."

My fangs lowered, quick and deadly. "How in the fuck will your family handle Layla?" I fisted my hands at my sides. With the hard wind and the storm about to dump a ton of rain, it was the perfect opportunity to fuel my elemental powers. I pulled my energy from nature, which meant I was more powerful than Rianne was ready for. If she thought my compelling abilities were scary, she had no idea how powerful I could be in nature's storm.

I leaned in, and she faltered, her back hitting the tail end of the SUV. "What's really going on?"

She craned her neck up and stuck out her chin, defiant and brave, or at least she was trying to show me she was. "We're ending any chance you have to corrupt my sister."

Before I could grip her throat or compel her into oblivion, a series of rapid sounds pricked my ears before I felt a sharp, stabbing pain in my back. Then another. Then another. Suddenly, fire whipped through my body. I felt as though I was burning from the inside out. Rianne's face blurred.

I shook it off as I slapped my hands on the SUV on either side of her head. The need to cause destruction saturated my veins, but I was about a gnat's ass away from collapsing.

Rianne pushed me, and I stumbled back easily.

Then a male voice, deep and mocking, muttered words that were garbled.

I straightened and shook off the effects of the drug as best I could. I wasn't going down without a fight.

Rianne scurried away. "Noah, you need to pump a lot more into him. He's powerful."

I roared like a lion who was primed to fight off his attacker then whirled around—and not too gracefully, either. The man before me looked like an Aberdeen, only younger, and aimed a dart gun at me. He laughed like he'd won the fucking war.

"Is that all you got?" I uttered, but I sounded like I'd had one too many bottles of bourbon.

He shook his dark head of hair. "Vampire, you have no idea how powerful I am."

I opened my arms. "Then, asshole, give me all you got." I was about a second away from collapsing. I wasn't sure if I would come out alive, only because I could feel the cobalt doing a number on my insides. "Because when I wake up, you'll regret what you've done."

The brave motherfucker marched closer with the gun, ready to pump more darts into me. "Oh, you might wake up, but when you do, you'll have a front-row seat to your own death."

Rianne rushed up to him. "Noah, shut the fuck up."

I roared like the animal I was and tried with all the energy I had to conjure my elemental powers—to no avail.

Before I could take a step, Noah fired three more rounds into me. "There, that should do it."

I blinked once, then everything around me went black.

15

LAYLA

My aunt pulled into the Deer and Elk. "I'm glad we had a chance to talk. I would love for you to stay longer, but I know you need to see that vampire doctor."

Even though my aunt and I were on better terms, my decision to leave would still be the same. It was best if I created distance from Jack. I wasn't even sure if I could be around Rianne.

"Jack said earlier that Rianne and Noah were on their way home, but I thought she would've shown up by now. Do you know anything? Did she enlist like she wanted to? She won't answer my calls or return my texts."

She raised a shoulder. "No idea. But if I find

anything out, I'll let you know." She gave me a weak smile. "Layla, I hope that doctor can help you."

I grabbed the door handle of her Suburban. "I do too."

"Do you have any cravings for blood?"

I rubbed my lips together. "Not right now." I didn't want to tell her I'd sucked on Sam's wrist. But boy, once I did that, the world righted itself.

She tucked my hair behind my ear. "I do hope you find what you're looking for in life, Layla. And again, I'm sorry I wasn't there for you. But I am now. Call me if you need anything."

Despite us talking and her sticking up for me, I wasn't sure I could trust her. "Thanks." I spotted Sam's rental. "I better go. Sam will send out a hunting party if I don't show myself soon." I bet he was a nervous wreck. He didn't strike me as the type to sit idle, especially when he wanted something.

"He seems like a good vampire," my aunt said.

"He's kind of an ass." But he was my ass.

She laughed. "Dare I say"—she glanced around—"you two make a great couple. Sam seems to need someone who is tough like you."

I laughed hard. "This coming from a vampire

hunter's wife. Don't let Jack hear you say that." I climbed out then stuck my head in the car. "Be careful, Aunt Tab."

She shifted into gear, ready to drive away. "You do the same."

I shut the door and watched her as she wheeled out of the gravel lot. A fat raindrop fell from the sky. Then another. I pivoted on my heel and went inside.

Music pumped from the jukebox. Two men were sitting at the bar. One of them looked a lot like Lester, the guy who had been at the ranch earlier. I couldn't quite tell from that angle, though, since he was facing the collection of liquor bottles behind the bar.

Aside from the two men, the bar was empty of patrons. It was early afternoon, and the place didn't start hopping until later in the evening. Still, I didn't see Jordyn or Sam anywhere. I ducked back outside. Sam's rental car was parked next to a black SUV. I returned inside. Maybe Sam and Jordyn had gone to the restroom.

I started in that direction when I heard Sam's name.

"I was surprised to see Mason at the ranch." That was Lester talking.

My heart sank as I debated whether to confront Lester or not.

My decision was taken away when Linda Getty—blond, big boobs, curvy waist, and my nemesis in high school—swung her hips as she ambled up to me. "Wow! You look fantastic. What's your secret?"

So much for listening to Lester. "Are you the same person who hated me in high school?" I wasn't teasing at all.

She rolled her eyes. "We were teenagers then. We did stupid shit."

I grinned as I thought back to one incident when I'd stolen her clothes during gym class when she was in the shower. She'd run around school in a towel, looking for me. I blinked away the flashback. "Have you seen Jordyn? She was with a tall dude, black hair, green eyes."

She feigned fanning herself. "Where did you find him? Does he have any friends?"

Loads, but I wasn't about to share that with her or tell her how I'd met him. "Is my sister in the bathroom?"

"Last I saw. Your guy friend left, and then Rianne came in and said something to Jordyn before they rushed out. Maybe thirty minutes ago."

I flinched. "Rianne was here?" Jordyn must've gotten ahold of her. "Do you know where they were going?" I doubted she did, but I had to ask just in case she'd overheard them talking. Linda was nosy like that. "Was Noah with them?"

"I have no idea. I assumed they were meeting you because Jordyn told me you were on your way. As far as Noah, he didn't come in."

My mind scrambled to think of where they could've gone. Maybe Sam had car trouble. But he would've called Conrad. Or maybe Sam was with Conrad. I plucked my phone from my coat pocket and called Jordyn. The line rang several times before her voice mail kicked in. I rushed outside and searched as far as I could as I called Rianne. Again, my sister wasn't answering my fucking call.

My pulse quickly shot up. Damn, I didn't have Conrad's number. I darted around to the back of the building. No one. Just two cars. My heart rammed against my sternum.

I called Sam's phone as I circled the building and went over to his car. Everything looked normal. My bag was in the back with Jordyn's. That wasn't good.

I leaned against the SUV when Sam's voice mail picked up.

"Sam, where are you?" I squeezed my eyes shut as I ended the call and tried to think of my next move or what could've happened to them. They wouldn't have left without alerting me.

Maybe Sam's impatience prompted him to return to the ranch with Conrad. After all, I didn't leave as quickly as I'd wanted to because my aunt and I had been talking.

The sound of an engine rumbled as a gray sedan pulled into the lot.

"Conrad," I said as I pushed off the SUV and hurried over to him.

Before he even opened his door, he knew something was wrong. Maybe because I had panic written all over my face or maybe because I was standing there in the rain, looking like a wet dog.

He rolled down his window. "What is it?"

"Sam and Jordyn aren't here."

Conrad turned toward Sam's car then back to me. "Hop in."

Once inside, he handed me a towel he had on the floor behind the passenger seat. "Let me do a sweep of the premises."

I caught his arm. "You won't find them. I promise you, they're not inside."

He tilted his head. "Layla, you know I'm a

vampire. I can compel information out of people if I have to."

"Well, don't put anyone in a comatose state." Just thinking of how Sam had done that to Rianne made me shiver.

"We normal vampires can't do the shit Sam Mason can. But we're still effective in extracting information." Then he left me alone.

I sat there, twisting the towel in my hands. Then I checked my phone when it rang. Rianne's name brightened the screen.

"Hey." My voice was strained. "Where are you? Is Jordyn with you?"

"She is," Rianne said evenly.

I couldn't gauge her mood. "Again, where are you? What's going on?" Something wasn't adding up. "Please tell me Sam isn't with her." Maybe Uncle Jack kidnapped Sam.

A deafening silence stretched through the line.

"Rianne," I warned in a tone that bordered on a scream. "What did you do?" I didn't want to assume anything, but the sinking feeling in the pit of my stomach told me that something wasn't right. Rianne tended to act before she thought things through, a flaw of hers that had sometimes gotten us into trouble. "If this is about you telling Noah I slept with Sam, I'm not mad." I felt more betrayed than anything. "I know you were drinking. Mistakes happen."

She laughed in a way that raised a thousand red flags. "I'm doing this for you. Humans can't fall in love with vamps."

"What?" I screamed. "Who the fuck says I'm in love with him? What have you done? I want to know right now!"

"Please, Layla." Condescension wove those words together. "You are. You just don't want to admit it."

I inhaled through my nose then blew it out through my mouth. Conrad's Old Spice cologne lingered in the car and eased some of my nerves. "What happened to you? Noah brainwashed you."

"I'm my own person, Layla. And we don't belong with vampires."

It was my turn to drop the bomb of the century. "Dad dated a vampire."

"Bullshit," she said.

I puffed out my chest as though she could see me. "Talk to Uncle Jack."

Her heavy breathing crackled through the line

and competed with the *ting, ting, ting* of the rain pelting the roof of the car.

"Where's Sam, Rianne?"

She sighed. "He's fine for now."

"Sam saved your life. Have you forgotten that?" I was hoping I was penetrating through her stubborn brain.

"He also fucked us up."

I dug my nails into the palm of my free hand. "No, he didn't. We were the ones who started the shitshow and took that job. Don't blame everything on Sam. And how soon you forget that your hotheaded attitude caused Sam to compel you like he did." My teeth were locked together. "You realize that if anything happens to Sam, you and the entire family will die."

She laughed. "That won't happen."

Her confidence was irritating the crap out of me. I clutched the phone tightly. "Rianne, if Sam dies, you're dead, and so is everyone who takes part in his death. Have you forgotten the power that his sister holds, or his dad, or the vampire Navy SEALs? Are you thinking straight?"

"Call Webb or Tripp!" Jordyn shouted in the background. "Hurry, Layla!"

Things were spiraling and quickly. I felt as though I had whiplash.

"Tape her mouth shut," Noah said to someone.

Hot, blinding fury blurred my vision. "So you're going to hurt our sister?"

"Jordyn is fine," Rianne said in an icy tone.

I silently counted to three, attempting to calm my racing heart and the rage pouring through me. "Does Uncle Jack know what you're doing?"

"He will soon enough. Besides, he wants all vampires dead. So Sam isn't special."

Jack did want all of them dead, but I believed my uncle didn't want to fuck with Steven Mason. If he did, he would've hunted Steven already. He would've burned Sam at the ranch earlier—Jack had no problem doing that when a bloodsucker stepped foot on his property. I doubted the Aberdeens were frightened of Steven. But the more I thought about it, the more I believed there was a reason the Aberdeens had never hunted the Masons. Sure, he and Uncle Ray were diving back into the business, and Uncle Ray wanted revenge on Roman and those like him. Hell, Sam would probably support my uncles in their quest to hunt and murder Roman.

"Think about it, sis. Our family has had every opportunity to wipe out the Masons. Ask yourself why we haven't."

I glanced around outside. Conrad seemed to be taking a long time.

"It's time someone takes a stand in this family, no matter how powerful Sam and his sister are," Rianne said. "No one should have that amount of power, anyway."

I couldn't see much through the pouring rain. "What happened to you? In a matter of days, you went from hating Jack and wanting to stay in Massachusetts to this." Noah had to have been feeding her some great lines of bullshit. "I guess now isn't the time to tell you that Mom comes from a vampire family." Bomb number two. If that didn't do the trick, I couldn't help her.

She squeaked out a noise. "Bull crap. You're lying."

"Ask Jack or Aunt Tab," I fired back.

"That's bullshit," Noah barked. "My dad would've told me."

I sneered. "Hey, asswipe. Your father doesn't tell you everything." I was sure of that. My uncle didn't want anyone to know that his brother married a woman who had vampire blood running through her veins.

"Fuck you," Noah said.

I could hear Jordyn mumbling in the background.

"If you so much as harm Jordyn, either of you, I will make it my mission to see that you both suffer." I couldn't believe those words were coming out of my mouth and directed at Rianne.

"We both know, Layla, that you would never hurt me." Her smugness was maddening, even though she was probably right. "And I would never do anything to Jordyn."

The blood running through my veins came to an abrupt halt. She didn't include me in that statement. I was beginning to think Abbey was right. "But you would hurt me?" I held my breath.

"This isn't about you, Layla," Rianne said. "It's about ridding this world of vampires."

There was no reasoning with her. "Let Jordyn go. There's no reason to keep her tied up."

Noah belted out a laugh. "There most certainly is."

My curiosity peaked. "Do tell, fuckwad." The hate I had for Noah before multiplied tenfold.

"She loves the bloodsuckers, like you. You

both need to suffer," Noah said, as confident and sure as the rain battering against the windshield.

The driver's side door opened, and Conrad climbed in.

I raised my finger to my lips.

"Tell me where you are, Rianne," I demanded.

"You'll figure it out," she said before she hung up.

I was tempted to throw my phone through the windshield. Instead, I screamed at the top of my lungs.

Conrad winced.

When I was done releasing all my pent-up anger, I searched his car. "Do you have any weapons in here?"

He scrubbed a hand down his face, wiping the water from it. "Of course. But tell me what's going on."

"Head back toward the ranch, and I'll fill you in."

Maybe Abbey's premonition about Rianne killing me was about to come true. But not before I put up a good fucking fight.

16

LAYLA

The rain pounded down, each drop pinging off the metal of Conrad's vehicle. I felt as though I was standing under one of the waterfalls at Niagara Falls.

Conrad parked about half a mile from the abandoned farm where I knew Rianne and Noah had Sam and Jordyn. The same place with the firepit, where we tortured vampires.

I couldn't believe I was about to face off with my sister. My fucking sister. I had no idea how her attitude had changed so quickly, how I had missed something so important in the time I was laid up with the flu.

"Stay here," I said to Conrad. "I want to scope out the situation first."

He swung out his arm. "Not so fast. You're not going in alone. Sam would gut me."

Lightning streaked across the sky, followed by a peal of thunder. The windshield wipers swished back and forth quickly. My heart went *boom, boom, boom*. The damn thing slammed into my rib cage, sounding louder than the force of nature outside.

Conrad glanced out. "Not sure you want to be out there."

I wanted to be miles up in the sky and on my way to see Dr. Vieira because since slurping Sam's blood earlier, I was thirsty for more. But I wasn't about to dissect the reasons or speculate. I was done with that.

I grabbed the door handle. "We can't wait for the weather to let up. If I know my cousin Noah, he'll burn Sam before we can blink."

"I'm not suggesting we wait for the rain to stop. But before we go in, I need to call Webb," Conrad said. "We need someone to know what's going on."

I let out a nervous laugh. "You mean someone

needs to know where to find our bodies." I was half teasing.

A wild laugh broke out in my head as that premonition Abbey had of Rianne killing me brightened like a neon sign in the dead of night. I clutched my chest to will my heart to slow the fuck down.

Conrad lifted his phone off the console between us, found Webb's number, and tapped on it. Then he put the call on speaker.

The line rang once before Webb's deep voice came through. "Conrad? What's wrong?"

Freaking vampires had that sixth sense even through the phone.

"Hi, Webb. It's Layla. You're on speaker, and Conrad is sitting next to me." My hands trembled. "Sam has been kidnapped by Rianne and one of my cousins." I swallowed the pail of sand in my throat. "I talked to Rianne. So I know Sam isn't dead yet."

"How did they capture Sam? Do we know?" Webb asked calmly.

"Not sure."

"I suspect Rianne used that drug that killed the shifter," Webb said. "We learned from

Wyman that he got his supply from your father before he died."

I captured a nail between my teeth, not concerned about where the drug had come from. "We need to act fast. I'm going in."

"Like hell you are." Webb's deep voice echoed over the rain coming down in sheets.

"Are your uncles involved?"

I wanted to argue with him, but again, we didn't have time. "I want to say no. As much as Jack despises vampires, there's a reason he hasn't gone after the Masons. On the other hand, Sam and Jack had a tense encounter earlier today. Jack had been ready to set Sam on fire."

Conrad's hazel eyes widened. "So what do we do?"

Webb sighed heavily. "Conrad, where are you?"

"We're not far from the Aberdeen ranch," he said.

"Send me Jack Aberdeen's number," Webb commanded.

Conrad obeyed while Webb was still on the phone.

"I don't want either of you to engage until I talk to Jack," Webb said. "Is that clear?"

Conrad acknowledged Webb with a firm yes as I stared out at the windshield. I couldn't see much past the rain.

"Layla, are we understood?" Webb's scary tone wasn't frightening me.

I didn't work for Webb, nor was I one of his soldiers. "I can't stay put. Jordyn is in trouble too."

"May I remind you that Abbey predicts Rianne will kill you?" Webb asked.

Conrad reared back. "No shit."

I clasped my hands together as though praying, and I should have been. "And all of you said Abbey's visions were off."

"That may be so, but do you want to test that theory?" Webb asked in a calmer tone.

I stretched my neck, hoping to relieve some tension. "Rianne won't harm me." I didn't sound confident at all. Rianne's tone on the phone had given me the chills, but she'd also made me furious. I had no idea what she would do to me. Noah was the one we had to tread lightly around, though.

Webb groaned out his frustration. "Maybe not, but accidents do happen. Abbey never said Rianne would kill you intentionally."

Damn vampire had a point. "Webb, I have to

try to reason with Rianne. I can't sit here and do nothing. Call Jack. Conrad and I will scope out the scene, and Conrad will report back to you." I was done talking. Besides, Webb and his team couldn't get there in time. So we had to do something. I wasn't about to put my faith in my uncle, no matter how much I believed he didn't want to piss off the Masons.

Webb half laughed. "Conrad, make sure no one dies. I'll be in touch." Webb's name vanished from the screen.

Conrad dumped his phone in the inside pocket of his coat. "Are you sure you want to do this?"

"One hundred percent." I had to knock some sense into Rianne, make sure Jordyn was okay, and above all else, save Sam.

We hadn't known each other that long or expressed our endless love for one another, but he couldn't die. I believed if he did, I would too. The mind-blowing idea that he and I were connected sounded absurd, but I felt it down to my toes. The gorgeous vampire and I were linked. I couldn't explain it. Didn't want to try to understand it either, but something was pushing me to save him.

"Here's the plan," Conrad said. "I'm going to

circle the perimeter of the property. I want you to go in slowly. I don't know your sister or what she's capable of, but I want you to go in with eyes and ears open. Don't for one second let your guard down because you see Jordyn or Sam in a compromised position. Talk to Rianne or something to distract her. If we are only up against Rianne and your cousin, I should be able to stop them. If there are more people than we expect, I'll figure something out. I do have a buddy who's local, but he doesn't like to deal with your family."

I didn't either.

Conrad bent over slightly and fished under his seat before producing a black canvas pouch that held four daggers. He handed me one that was in a leather sheath. "Not sure if this will be enough or not."

I tucked the dagger into my boot, even though I wasn't thrilled about using it on my family members. "I believe there is a third person with them. I don't know who, though."

"Let's find out," he said.

With that tentative plan, Conrad and I headed out. He took off in one direction, and I jogged down the dirt road leading into the abandoned farm. I sloshed through the mud and puddles as the rain soaked me to my bones, but I couldn't feel much beneath the panic, shock, and nerves that kept my adrenaline spiked.

I had no idea how to reason with Rianne. She didn't listen on the phone. I doubt she would in person. And Noah was going to be a bigger problem unless the third person was Jack—or worse, Ray. Then again, Noah wouldn't bark orders to Jack or Ray or even to his older brother, Jack Jr.

I was guessing Brodi, Noah's seventeen-year-old brother, was the third person. He was the black sheep of the family, and Noah had a way of pulling his chains.

I swiped at my face, trying to clear the rain from my eyes.

Lightning cracked. Thunder boomed.

I pumped my legs harder. I wanted to get it over with. But somehow, even if I was able to save the day, I had a feeling there was more strife and mayhem to come.

By the time I reached the edge of the property, I couldn't breathe. My lungs burned, my legs ached, and I could barely see anything in front of me.

Damn rain.

I spotted a light filtering out of the boarded-up house in between the raindrops. I cleared my eyes and took inventory of the property. As I scanned left, then right, then did another sweep, I lost my breath.

17

LAYLA

I squinted to be sure I was seeing clearly.

For fuck's sake.

I darted over a low wire fence like a gazelle running from a lion. My pulse beat for freedom as I stepped in mud, almost getting stuck. I gave it everything I had and ran up to the firepit. The good news—no fire. The bad news—Sam was handcuffed to the top bar, dangling over the pit, his ankles shackled in cobalt and several darts embedded in his back.

Holy hell. I prayed he wasn't dead. There would be so many repercussions if he was. One, the vampire military would descend on Montana as if fighting an enemy army. Two, Jo Mason would go on a killing rampage. Sam's twin sister scared me more than any of the others in her circle of vamps. She came off as reserved and quiet, but underneath, I knew without a doubt that she could wield more power than Sam. Finally, and most importantly, my heart would split into a million pieces. I couldn't lose Sam. I liked what we were building. I liked the possessive, strong, cocky alpha male. He fit my personality to a tee. We might argue or banter or claim we hated each other, but the truth was far from it.

Sam was right when he'd said I was his. Up until that point, I'd been fighting my own feelings about him, afraid to admit I was falling for a vampire. More importantly, there was a metaphysical connection tying us together, and if that connection snapped, I was afraid we would both die.

I inhaled, shivered, then frantically searched for the platform we used to hoist a victim. Another crack of lightning made me squeal, seeming far too close for comfort. I trudged through the tall grass, looking for the wooden platform, but it was nowhere to be found.

I shook Sam. "Sam, wake up. Sam." I was trying to keep my voice low. If he awoke, he could probably free himself. After all, he was one of the most powerful vampires around. His elemental powers alone could help him. Or I prayed they could. I dug my nails into his leg. "Sam." That time, my voice was hard and a bit louder.

But I was striking out. With Sam not in any immediate danger at the moment, I picked up two large rocks from the firepit. I had to improvise. Rocks wouldn't kill anyone unless I hit them in just the right spot to cause a fatal head injury.

I started for the dilapidated house when heavy breathing sounded from behind me. I sucked in air. Sam was awake. But when I whirled around, my hopes died.

Noah aimed the dart gun at me. "I'm glad you made it, cousin. You're about to find out what we do to vampire lovers."

Laughing, I sized him up. Noah was wearing a ball cap, rain gear, rubber boots that climbed to his knees, and a grin that reminded me too much of Roman Brown. "Where are Rianne and Jordyn?"

For all I knew, he'd drugged Rianne into doing as he said.

The sound of thunder made me jump.

He laughed. "The supposed tough one in the family. You're afraid of your own shadow."

Rianne stepped out of the copse of trees to the

right of Sam. She must've been watching me trying to help him.

She ponied up to Noah, and like him, she was dressed for the storm or a bloodbath. "Noah, take it down a notch. I'm not in this to hurt my sister."

Could've fooled me. "Why do I get the feeling you were planning this all along?" I asked.

Rianne pushed the dart gun down so Noah was aiming it at the ground. "We didn't know Sam was coming to see you."

"But the minute we did," Noah said giddily, "we jumped into action. You know we're always ready to burn vampires."

I needed to take an extremely long shower to get the scum of Noah off me.

I lasered my gaze on Rianne. I was still dumbfounded by her change in attitude. "Did you enlist in the air force? Or was that a ploy?"

"I've decided to join Uncle Jack," Rianne replied. "It's time I take a stand and follow my true calling."

Rain slid over my eyes and cheeks and into my mouth. "Yeah, and what is your true calling?"

"Not sleeping with vampires," she chided.

My mind was blown. "Who are you? I think Noah brainwashed you."

The bill of her ball cap kept most of her expression in shadow, but that snarl she was wearing said it all. "No. He made me see the light. What happened to you while in Sam's company made you weak," Rianne said. "He made you a nutcase. I mean, who is to say you're not pregnant?"

Noah jerked back. "For fuck's sake. Can that happen to you?"

Rianne glared at me. "Think about it, Noah. If it's true, and my mom had vampire blood in her, who's to say Layla doesn't have the right blood type to get pregnant?"

I snorted. "If I do, then you do too." That wasn't entirely correct. My sisters and I could have had different blood types. Still, to infer I had Vel-negative blood just because there was a vampire or two in our lineage was a stretch. "Rianne, please rethink what you're doing," I pleaded.

She stood taller. "I know what I'm doing. I'm ridding the world of one of the most powerful vampires. When I'm done, his sister is next."

Noah grinned like he was proud of her. "I've been waiting for Rianne to wake up and join the family."

"Sam saved your life," I reminded her. "Are

you forgetting that? You were all over him after he did."

She flinched slightly.

Yeah, I hit a nerve. That was my opening to push harder. "Rianne, please."

Noah dug into his coat pocket. "Wow, you're really into the bloodsucker." He pulled out a lighter and flicked it. "Time to say goodbye." Then he threw it in the firepit.

I screamed at the top of my lungs as I ran toward Sam.

My vision blurred as two things happened simultaneously. I bumped against Rianne as she blocked me, and Sam woke up.

His green eyes glowed as he examined himself. When he did, he growled so loud that I was sure the coyotes and any other animals ran for the mountains.

A ring of fire circled the pit as flames flickered upward, grazing his boots.

Outwardly, Sam was calm as the ocean on a warm summer day. Inside, I would bet my life that he was raging like the storm around us.

He closed his eyes and dipped his chin to his chest as though preparing himself to break free.

Noah aimed the dart gun at Sam.

I pushed Rianne hard and ran past her. I had no idea how to help Sam, but I was hoping the rain would drench the fire. At the moment, it wasn't anywhere near roaring like it should have been.

Just as I gripped Sam's ankles, Rianne pulled out a dart gun. "Get away from him, Layla."

With two dart guns—one pointed at Sam and the other me—we didn't stand a chance. If I passed out, Sam would burn.

I swallowed the dryness in my throat. I raised my hands and slowly backed away.

Rianne lowered her gun, seemingly relieved that she didn't have to shoot me.

"Sam, I don't know what you're doing, but please get on with it," I said, keeping my eyes on Rianne and Noah.

Noah fired the gun, and the dart landed in Sam's thigh.

Sam's eyes shot open, and silver overpowered the green as his fangs descended. He let out a guttural growl, and within seconds, the earth beneath our feet was shaking so hard, the ground was splitting in two.

"What's happening?" Noah asked as he

looked at his feet. Then he quickly pointed the gun at Sam's head and pulled the trigger.

The dart landed on Sam's forehead.

A sound I'd never heard before came out of Sam's mouth. He sounded like one angry fucking bear.

I dropped to my knees and started digging and throwing dirt on the fire. "Rianne, if you know what's good for you, help me. If Sam dies, we're all dead. His sister will make sure of it." I had no other tactic but to scare the heck out of her. Rianne wasn't frightened easily, but I had to try.

The embers danced in the wind as I threw more dirt on the fire.

Sam swung his legs forward then backward. When he did, he clipped Noah's chin. Noah fell as the gun dropped from his hands.

I crawled to my feet and lunged for the gun when Rianne beat me to it. I shoulder checked her as we both tumbled to the ground.

"Why are you doing this?" I asked as we rolled around.

"I hate them!" she shouted above the whistling wind and whipping rain.

A loud explosion split the air, giving me the opportunity to shove Rianne off me. I stumbled to my feet but lost my balance and fell backward. Before I could stop myself, my head hit a rock.

Air punched from my lungs. The sky above spun, and pain dug its claws into me. I blinked several times, breathing in, hoping to fill my lungs with necessary air.

Voices droned around me.

Rain fell.

Thunder boomed.

I blinked again, inhaled painfully, and oriented my vision as I tried to sit up, but Noah rammed his foot into my chest and pointed the fucking dart gun at me. "Say good night, cousin."

"No!" Sam shouted. "I'll kill you, human, if you so much as touch her."

Noah let out an evil laugh. "Too late, vampire." Then he pulled the trigger.

It felt like pinpricks on my chest before warmth traveled through my veins.

I removed the dart and threw it at Noah. "Fuck you, cousin. You will not get the best of me." I planted my hands in the muddy ground, pushed myself up, and swayed. The drug was in my system, but hopefully not enough to knock me out.

Noah laughed again. Rianne watched in

horror as though frozen. I couldn't tell if she was regretting her actions or she was actually frightened. But fuck everyone. I stomped over to Sam on shaky legs, not as gracefully as I would've liked, but I made it, nonetheless. I grabbed the structure that Sam was hanging from and tried to move it.

Jordyn ran up, screaming like a bad actress in a horror movie. "I will gut Noah, but first"—she turned to Rianne—"you're not my sister anymore."

Conrad jogged up and dove into action, tearing the structure down.

Before I could help Sam out of his handcuffs, something sharp pierced my neck.

Shouts tore through the storm. Screams hurt my eardrums.

The only voice I registered was Sam's. "Layla, no!"

Then the voices died as I plummeted into the abyss.

18

SAM

I paced Layla's hospital room in our medical facility in Boston. It seemed pacing and hospital rooms were becoming the norm for me. My father was in the next room but still not awake. Ben was in the same situation as my father in the infirmary on the naval base. Alia Costner had been correct. Things did happen in threes.

I pulled on my hair, mumbling swear words and more swear words. I was ready to go on a murdering spree. If Layla's life hadn't been on the line, I would've slit Rianne's, Noah's, and the other cousin's, whose name failed me, throats. Four fucking days since that shit show, and I was still seething and ready to sever heads.

I settled at her bedside, shoving both hands through my hair. Other than her ashen skin tone and chapped lips, she looked more beautiful than I'd ever seen her. Her auburn hair was down around her shoulders. Her freckles seemed to twinkle in the muted light of the room, and her long lashes curled slightly. For the first time since I'd met her, she seemed peaceful and free from her demons.

I trailed my fingers along one of her high cheekbones. "Come back to me, baby doll. We have a lot to do, you and me." I closed my eyes, enjoying her scent of cherries that seemed to be a balm to my frayed nerves. I hadn't slept. I couldn't eat. I could barely keep down blood. But that didn't matter. Layla was with me, and I prayed to the gods she would wake up soon.

Vanilla tickled my nostrils as Jordyn rested against the doorjamb. "Sam, can I come in?"

Aside from the medical staff, no one was allowed in, not even Jordyn. I didn't care that she was Layla's sister or that she was innocent in the plot to burn me alive. I didn't trust her. Rianne had all but turned on a dime, and I wasn't foolish enough to think that Jordyn couldn't do the same.

Above all else, I wasn't in the mood to deal with people unless Jo or Dr. Vieira had news about Ben or my dad, and even then, that news had to be good. That was the extent of what I could handle. I considered myself a badass motherfucker with a high threshold for pain, but when it came to someone I cared about, the steel walls around my heart crumbled. My insides felt like someone had shoved them into a food processor. My brain wasn't thinking straight, and my heart literally hurt.

"Go away, Jordyn," I snapped. Again, I didn't blame her.

"Please, Sam," Jordyn cried. "She might not wake up."

I bared my fangs at the brown-haired human. "She'll wake up." I had to believe that, although she had been shot in the neck, and I worried that the drug had been too potent. But according to Jordyn, Noah had filled the darts with a lower dosage just for Layla. The fucker.

I scrubbed a hand down my face. I couldn't lose her. We were just getting started. But Layla's fate was in her own hands. The ER doctor at the Montana hospital suspected her head injury was the reason why she wasn't waking up. She'd hit her head hard on a rock. Add in the drug, and she could be out for days.

I hadn't told the ER doc about the drug. It was best to avoid the questions it would raise with the human authorities. Instead, I'd brought her to the medical facility as quickly as I could. Dr. Vieira and Dr. Greer would know what to do. I worried that the cobalt in the sedative would wreak havoc on her. But if she had been shot with a lower dose, maybe it wouldn't be too much of an issue.

As soon as we'd gotten there, Dr. Vieira and Dr. Greer went to work. They flushed Layla's system, did a CT scan on her head, and had been checking her blood for traces of cobalt and the drug. The good news—her CT scan was clear. Her test results showed barely any cobalt or drug in her, so it was up to Layla.

I'd prayed for days that maybe she wasn't human. Perhaps she had vampire DNA. If she did, she had a chance. Humans who carried the vampire gene did have some supernatural abilities. Dr. Vieira speculated that might have been the reason Layla was still breathing.

"You're pale, Sam, and you need to sleep." Jordyn was on the verge of tears. "Let me stay with her for a while to give you a break."

"I don't need sleep," I shot back.

She sniffled. "She's my sister, and I'm on your side."

I narrowed my eyes, and when I did, I saw nothing but profound sadness and felt nothing but heartache from her. She was right, though. I had to be white as a ghost. I hadn't had any blood since the morning before. On top of that, I needed some sleep. And it wasn't as if Jordyn could take Layla out of the medical facility. Guardians stood watch at every entrance and on every floor, and a human wouldn't get by them.

"I *am* hungry," I said.

She inched in one step. "Thank you."

I sauntered up to her, baring my fangs. "If anything happens to her, you know I'll wipe your family off the face of this Earth."

Tears clouded her eyes. "I will help you." She skirted by me and went over to Layla. "Oh, Sam, any word on her DNA results?"

Dr. Vieira was also running a DNA test, since we knew Layla's mom had vampires somewhere in her family lineage.

"Not yet," I said before stalking out.

The minute I was in the hall, I sighed heavily and swayed.

Footsteps plodded toward me as my vision blurred. I needed a case of blood.

Jo rushed up and grabbed my arm. "I got you, brother." She ushered me to the break room, where she helped me onto the couch. "I want you to get an hour of sleep at least. I'll watch Layla for you." She pulled two bottles of blood from the fridge, popped the top on one, handed it to me, and placed the other on the coffee table before she sat next to me.

I downed one in less than a second. The minute the blood exploded on my tongue, I felt instant relief as my vision sharpened.

She smiled as her silver eyes sparkled like diamonds in the rough. "Better?"

A shudder racked my body. "Much. You look happy. What's going on?"

She swiped a hand up the back of her black hair piled on top of her head. "Ben is awake. The shifter blood seemed to do the trick."

I pressed my fingers into my chest and pushed out the air in my lungs as a ten-ton weight lifted off me. "For real? That's fantastic news. And Pops?"

She tucked her hands into the lab coat with her name embroidered on the chest. "He's not awake yet, but tests show that the vein is healing slowly. And as it turns out, Abbey was right. Dad needed our blood."

I grabbed the second bottle and twisted off the cap. "I don't understand. We gave him ours."

"You're right. But Dad also needed his own blood. Dr. Vieira mixed all three, and that did the trick. We think it's working because the mixture is super strong with lots of iron and platelets, which is the key for Dad since he's an older vampire."

I didn't care how it worked as long as my father was healing.

"I'm so glad that Dr. Vieira keeps our blood in supply for emergencies," Jo said.

He'd been doing that as protocol since becoming the attending physician for the vampire Navy SEAL team many moons ago.

I closed my eyes, praying that three was a charm and Layla would also wake up. Unfortunately, blood wouldn't heal her since she was human—unless... My eyes flew open.

"What is it?" Jo asked.

"I need to speak to Doc." I hopped up. "Is he in the lab?"

She hurried behind me. "Yeah. He's working with the lab tech on Layla's DNA testing."

For the first time in four days, hope blossomed and happiness loomed. I couldn't get down to the second floor quickly enough. I opted for the stairs to keep myself moving.

Jo was right on my heels. "Sam, tell me what you're thinking."

"I will when we're with Doc." It was better to say it once. If I articulated it too often, I would get my hopes up, only to be shot down.

I rushed into the lab minutes later. Dr. Vieira was examining something under a microscope while the lab tech, a pretty blond vampire named Giselle, typed on a computer.

They both looked up at me, surprise evident on their faces.

I skirted two lab benches before I was standing across from Doc. "If we suspect Layla has the vampire gene, maybe blood would do the trick. She is super pale. I know you said she doesn't have any internal injuries, but I can't help but think that blood is the answer. She seems to react to my blood for some reason. She craves it, actually."

Jo stood beside me. "Sam, Layla's been through a lot. Before the showdown in Montana, she'd been sick with the flu. Her body needs time to heal. She'll wake up when she's ready."

I loved my sister, but I was ready to bite off her head. I didn't want to hear the standard medical jargon about how the body will heal on its own and blah, blah, blah.

A beat passed as dead silence zipped around the lab, bouncing off glass cabinets and the scores of lab equipment scattered around the room.

Dr. Vieira exchanged a knowing look with Giselle, who was one lab bench over but in line with Doc.

"What is it?" I asked. "Did you find something?"

Dr. Vieira grabbed the back of his neck and rubbed. "Sam, you might want to sit down for this."

I could feel my eyebrows drawing down. "I'm fine standing up. Hit me."

Dr. Vieira cleared his throat. "Layla is pregnant."

I squeezed my eyes shut, opened them, and shook my head. "I'm sorry?"

"You heard me," Doc said. "Layla doesn't carry the vampire gene, but she's Vel negative."

Motherfucker. I blew out one breath then another. "You're right. I need to sit."

Jo's mouth was on the floor.

Giselle beamed as she rolled her chair over to me quickly. "This is great news."

In whose fucking world is that great news? I dropped down and bent over, breathing in and out, in and out.

Jo finally snapped out of her frozen state and rubbed my back as she mumbled all kinds of words I couldn't make out. Hell, my brain was on a collision course with a Mack truck.

Sitting up straighter, I pushed my fingers through my hair. "Have you known this since you started testing her blood? I mean, what made you test for that?" His reasons didn't matter. The cat was out of the bag and had clawed out my eyes.

Doc grinned as if proud of me. "Sam, you know I run a full gamut of tests with patients. I don't leave any stone unturned. Anyway, we ran her blood type a few times just to be sure and repeated the pregnancy test several times. Her pregnancy hormone, hCG, is on the rise. She's not that far along, but this is great news. Your father will be elated."

I laughed like a nervous Nellie. "Layla won't be." I wasn't sure I was on board, either.

Dude, you have no choice. You can't take that steamy, sexy, hot-as-fuck night back no matter how many magical powers you might have or witches you might know. The last part made me laugh again. I doubted Alia Costner had any magical witch spells to help me with this one.

"This is insane," I muttered. "Is that why Layla's craving blood? Because she's pregnant?"

"She shouldn't be," Doc said, a ton of questions written all over his face. "She should have a normal pregnancy like any other human woman who gets pregnant by a vampire."

"So why does she have a hunger for blood?" None of it was making sense.

Jo, Giselle, and Doc looked at each other, confused as well.

Dr. Vieira scratched his neck. "You know nothing about the Mason family is normal. Maybe the fetus does require blood. Jo, start a small IV drip with Sam's blood. If Layla shows any signs of a severe reaction, stop it immediately. I'll be up later to check on her."

I growled, wanting to punch something. "I need air." I skirted benches and equipment.

"Sam, you need to go with Jo," Doc said, raising his voice. "I don't have any more of your blood here, so we'll need to connect a line from you to Layla."

"I need a minute." I slapped a hand on the door and pushed so hard the wooden structure flew open, hit the wall, and punctured a hole in it.

Man, Layla was going to have a cow when she found out.

19

LAYLA

I squirmed as my eyelids fluttered open to the sound of beeps and dings. I swiveled my head one way and then the other. Sam sat in a chair beside me, sleeping with an IV that was tethered to me stuck in his arm. I closed my eyes again then opened them. *No. No. No. Why is there a line of blood from him into me?* I grabbed the needle and ripped it out. Blood immediately dribbled onto the stark-white blanket, soaking through.

Footsteps, sounding like a horse in a gallop, grew louder before Jordyn came running in. "You can't do that."

Like hell I can't.

Sam shot off the chair like a cannon being fired in war. "Get Dr. Vieira!" Sam shouted at Jordyn, like it was her fault.

Clenching my fists, I snarled at the green-eyed vampire.

He growled back as the room began to shake.

I mashed my lips together. "Really, vampire. You have to use your elemental powers on me?"

He flinched, and his eyes bulged. "I didn't do that." He removed the IV from his arm, gathered my needle, then placed it on the table beside my bed. Then he traipsed over to the window.

Sun glinted off the tall buildings in the distance.

"Maybe it's a small tremor from an earthquake, then," I offered.

"Boston doesn't have earthquakes," he said. "There's construction going on across the street. I'm sure that's what caused it." He returned to my bedside, his long legs eating up the vast space.

My gaze took a long, slow hike up and down his body while I tried to reboot my brain. Damn, if he wasn't a sight for sore eyes. His Navy SEAL T-shirt stretched across his muscled chest. His jeans were slung low on his hips, and his black hair was tied back into a low ponytail.

I licked my chapped lips. "Why are you giving me blood? Did I lose that much? I only hit my head."

He examined me like a doctor. His lush green eyes had way too much emotion in them that I couldn't quite figure out. He was holding something back.

"Oh my God. I have the vampire gene, don't I?"

No response as he continued to cast an unnerving look at me.

"Sam, you're frightening me. Am I dying of cancer?" My mom had died of breast cancer. "Did the doctors find something?" *Please say no.* "Does the drug in those darts have some sort of poison in them?"

It seemed as though someone had cut out his tongue as he loomed over me.

"Talk, dammit!" I shouted, and the bed moved. *There must be some heavy construction going on across the street.* "Something bad happened, didn't it?" The only thing that came to mind was Rianne. "Please tell me you didn't harm Rianne."

He sneered.

I closed my eyes briefly, counting to three. I

swore if he hurt her, I would break his neck. If he killed her, I would claw out his heart, cut off his dick, and poke out his eyes, in no particular order.

"She was fine when we left Montana." His Adam's apple bobbed. "She's lucky I didn't break any of her limbs."

"Then spill already!" I screeched like a cat who'd been stepped on.

He scrubbed a hand down his scruffy jaw. "You know what Tabitha told you about your mom's family, vampires and all?"

I knew it. "I'm going to crave blood for the rest of my life? That's why you were giving me your blood."

His features were stonelike. "Nope. The baby needs my blood."

Time stopped. My breath halted in my lungs. My vision blurred, and my pulse pounded in my ears as the heart monitor beeped like crazy. I opened my mouth to speak, but I was at a loss for words.

He grabbed my hand, brought it to his lips, and kissed my palm softly.

I snagged my hand from him even though his tender actions had made my stomach flip like a gymnast performing her mat routine. "Could you please repeat that?" My voice wasn't my own.

"I'm as astounded as you are," he said. "We're going to be parents."

A bark of laughter, and not a happy one, tore from my lips. "Like hell we are!" I shouted as heat whipped through my body to clutch my cheeks. "It's impossible. I don't have that rare blood type."

He cocked an eyebrow with an award-winning smirk that could land him in the beds of a thousand women, and my freaking belly flipped and fluttered again.

Damn vampire.

"Apparently, you do," he said. "There's a lot your parents didn't tell you."

Dr. Vieira waltzed in, lighting up like a kid on Christmas morning. "Good to see Sam's blood helped. Your color has returned." He stood on the other side of my bed, adjusting the stethoscope around his neck. "How are you feeling?" His brown eyes held warmth and excitement.

"Please tell me I'm not pregnant." Tears were on the verge of spilling. I wasn't one to cry, but I couldn't be pregnant. I wasn't prepared for kids. I wasn't ready for a vampire kid. *Holy fuckety fuck.*

Dr. Vieira swapped a knowing look with Sam. "Tests don't lie."

I popped forward, tensing every muscle in me. "Then run it again!" My heart slammed against my rib cage. "I am not pregnant!" The machines behind me sang like a canary on a warm sunny morning. "I can't be pregnant. Not by a vampire."

Sam's eyes flashed silver. "While I get you're in shock, I have feelings too."

I laughed, sounding like a crazy woman. "I'm supposed to care about your feelings? What about mine? Do you know how crazy it is for me, a vampire hunter, to be pregnant by a vampire?"

That was one for the books. My family would surely carve out my intestines—and the baby, for that matter. My father would roll over in his grave. My uncle would hunt me down and kill me for sure. I could never go home. I could never make amends with Rianne. The news of my pregnancy would seal her fate to do as Abbey's vision had warned.

Holy shit. Abbey's vision *would* come true. I shook my head like I had Tourette's syndrome. I couldn't worry about that. I had bigger fish to fry, like strangling a sexy vampire who appeared to be cool with this breaking and fucked-up news. Or at least he wasn't freaking out like I was.

Dr. Vieira checked the heart monitor that was still beeping like mad. "You have to calm down, Layla. You're going to pass out."

So what? Maybe I could reboot time, and when I woke up, I wouldn't be pregnant. "Human and vampire," I mumbled. "It will never work." I felt my face twisting into something that probably resembled the devil. I was ready to foam at the mouth and spit all kinds of venom at Sam Mason. It was his fault. He'd lured me into his bedroom with his supernatural charm, sweet-tasting blood, and witchy magic.

No one lured you, girl. You wanted him as badly as he wanted you. I hated that small devilish voice in my head.

"Why not?" Sam's face was redder than a tomato. It was clear he was holding in his rage, and maybe underneath all that was anguish. I couldn't tell.

The bed moved, and a glass fell off the table beside my bed and shattered on the tiled floor.

Dr. Vieira eyed Sam. "No elemental powers in this facility."

Sam glowered at Dr. Vieira and me. "*I am not*

using my powers. Construction is going on across the street."

Satisfied with Sam's answer, he turned his attention to me. "Layla, I want you to take a breath. Your heart rate is still extremely high."

I did as he instructed. My heart was jumping like a kid on a trampoline. "Is that why I've been craving blood? The baby?"

Dr. Vieira sighed. "Not 100 percent sure. But it seems that way. The fact that you haven't had a severe reaction leads me to believe that the fetus needs blood. I haven't come across a pregnancy where the mother needed blood as a source of food."

I honestly didn't know what was worse, carrying the vampire gene or being pregnant with a vampire baby. "Wait. If my memory serves me correctly, I wanted Sam's blood before we slept together." I dipped back into my memory of the elevator scene. I'd bit him so he wouldn't bite me. That didn't count. Then I bit him again during the heat of passion, but I hadn't been jonesing for his blood.

"No," Sam said. "You began to crave my blood when we pulled up to that rental house of yours."

The lightbulb brightened as I nodded.

"It doesn't matter," Dr. Vieira chimed in.

"It does," I countered. "I'm trying to understand. How could I want blood the day after sex?" I said that last word without any shyness in front of the reserved doctor.

Dr. Vieira smiled. "In our world, Layla, you'll learn that some things don't have an explanation, especially when magic is involved. And you'll hear me say this many times: nothing is normal when it comes to Sam or Jo."

I giggled out loud, remembering Jordyn mentioning that Sam could have magic sperm. I guess he truly did.

Sam cocked his head. "Care to share?"

"Not really." Maybe someday, I would tell him that. For the time being, I let my head fall back against the pillow. "There was no magic involved in my parents not telling me I had that rare blood type. I want you to rerun the test. My parents would've told me."

"Maybe so," Dr. Vieira said. "But tests for blood types aren't usually routine unless a person needs a transfusion, and in some cases for pregnant women if there's an issue."

I could buy that. Blood types weren't a regular topic of conversation, and if they had known, they wouldn't have shared that with anyone. My father knew he would be ostracized from his brothers. Besides, we hunted vampires, so the chances of me having sex with one were remote. "I want an over-the-counter pregnancy test or five. I want to see for myself. It came back negative once."

Dr. Vieira and Sam flinched.

"So you suspected you were?" Dr. Vieira asked.

Jordyn sashayed in. "Not really. We did it for shits and giggles."

I raised an eyebrow at her. If I knew Jordyn, she had been standing outside, eavesdropping. Regardless, my sister looked like death. Dark circles traced the outline of her brown eyes. Her skin was ashen, and her T-shirt was wrinkled and too big for her petite body.

"So do my sisters have the same blood type?" I asked.

"Not all siblings will, and not all children carry the same one as their parents," Dr. Vieira explained.

Jo poked her head in. "Look who's awake." She beamed as her silver eyes sparkled. "You and my dad must be in sync."

Sam's tension vanished. "Pops is awake?" His

voice hitched. Then he kissed me on the forehead, which was odd. "I'll be back." Then he and Jo left.

Jordyn stepped into Sam's spot. "Dr. Vieira, can I talk to my sister alone?"

A shiver racked my body at the seriousness in her tone.

20

LAYLA

Dr. Vieira fiddled with the machine behind me while Jordyn gnawed on a nail. A nervous energy bounced off her, and whatever was bothering her was making me jittery. My trust factor was dwindling by the minute. I couldn't handle any more betrayal—or *anything,* for that matter. Pregnant? I couldn't be.

"Layla, I want you to take it easy. You've been through a lot," Dr. Vieira said. "And now that you're expecting, your body will be changing by the minute. So you need to rest."

Several swear words blared in my head as I gritted my teeth, held back tears, and tried like hell to breathe. It was no use. The heart monitor was singing. "I'm dreaming. I have to be." I blinked several times. But each time I oriented my vision, the scene was still the same.

Dr. Vieira jotted notes on a small pad he'd pulled out of his lab coat. Jordyn studied me as though she had a million questions.

"What's wrong, sis?" I asked.

"I've been trying to figure out how things went to shit in a matter of hours. How come Jack didn't tell us about our mom? Or Dad dating a vampire? Why did Rianne flip her humanity switch to something evil? And now, you're pregnant."

I guessed that was the reason she looked like crap. "Who was working with Rianne and Noah?" Not that it mattered. But I wanted to add him to my list of people to strangle. "Jack?"

"I'll let you two talk," Dr. Vieira said. "I'll be back to check on you later."

"Wait," I called to Doc as he was halfway to the door.

"I'll have my lab tech bring up a pregnancy test," he said.

"Thank you, but will I need blood for the next nine months?" I asked.

He returned to my bedside, his soft brown eyes flashing with concern. "It's hard to say. I haven't dealt with an expecting mom who required blood for the baby. I would caution you, though. If you have a desire for blood, I suggest Sam's. The processed kind we drink has additives in it that won't be healthy for the baby."

I tried to laugh but made a weird sound instead. We were talking about blood as a food source, which was so wrong, at least for me as a human. "Am I supposed to cart Sam around with me all the time?" I snorted.

Jordyn giggled.

Dr. Vieira wore a serious expression. "I always keep a small supply of all the SEAL team's blood on hand for emergencies. But I'll be sure to have more of Sam's. In the meantime, as long as you two are physically together, you'll be fine." He gave me a warm smile before he left.

I swallowed just thinking about drinking from Sam. There was something erotic about the act.

Once Jordyn and I were alone, she shut the door before sinking into the chair.

We locked eyes and didn't say a word for several minutes.

"Talk to me. What happened after I passed out?" I asked.

She tucked her legs underneath her and resumed gnawing on her nail. "It was chaos. Sam was so enraged. I'd never seen Brodi and Rianne so scared. Noah, on the other hand, was ready to butt heads with Sam. Moron, if you ask me."

Noah had the same brashness as Jack. Like father, like son.

She held her nail between her teeth. "After you collapsed, Sam tore his restraints off and almost attacked Brodi, but Conrad stopped him. Sam's elemental powers were out of control. Fire everywhere. The earth shook and split and..." She shuddered. "The only thing that stopped Sam from going on a killing spree was you. You came to for a second and called his name."

"And Rianne?" I asked.

She shrugged, tears in her eyes. "She took off. After Sam whisked you away to the local medical center in Big Timber, I tried to call her, but she didn't answer. I've been trying for the last four days. Nothing." She swiped at a tear.

I was ready to bawl my eyes out with her, and not only because of Rianne. It was everything.

She picked at something on her sock and blew out a breath. "I think we're living in hell." A tear slipped down her cheek. "Carly called me about that position at her company, Intech. They want to interview me."

"Go. See what it's all about. You can still talk to Steven at some point."

"I can't leave you," she cried.

"It's just an interview. Right?"

She nodded. "Are you sure?"

"Absolutely. I'll be fine, and I'm not going any-where." I wanted to talk to Sawyer to see if he could help with finding Kendra. I believed she might be the key, since my dad was trying to find proof of what my mom had told him about her family. "I want you to be happy, Jordyn."

She sniffled. "Honestly, I wouldn't even have considered the job, but after what Rianne has done, I don't know. It might be good for me, at least for now." She let go of my hand and sat back.

"Go! Meet with Intech. I'm going to see if I can find something about our mom or Kendra. I think the vampires here can help. We need an-swers." I was sure I wouldn't find them right away. If my dad couldn't find any proof in the two years after my mom passed, I was in for a long ride. Hell, Jack hadn't been able to find Kendra, either, so maybe she was dead. Above all else, I needed a distraction from Rianne and what she'd done and my impending pregnancy. "So did Carly say when you would interview?"

She rubbed her lips together. "I need to call her."

"Say hi for me." I'd always liked Carly, a petite woman with a lot of fire in her attitude. She knew how to put Jack Jr. in his place.

She picked at something on her jeans. "I will. I might still chat with Steven if he's taking visitors."

I adjusted my body so I was sitting up a little more. "Jordyn, let that go for now. Focus on this interview. Speaking of which, I thought of something. With Roman on the loose, it might be dangerous for you to go alone. Maybe we can ask Webb for a bodyguard for you? Or I can come with you."

She smiled. "I doubt Sam is about to let you out of his sight. That man has it bad for you. And you need to rest. Not to mention, if Roman kidnaps anyone, it will be you. Remember, he held me hostage to force you to do something for him. This time, I'm sure his plan is to hurt Sam where it counts, and that's you."

I wasn't blind. I knew Sam had feelings for me. But I wasn't ready to deal with those emotions from him or how I felt about the sexy vamp, either.

"Remind me again what Intech does," I said, wanting to think of anything but where I was or my own fucked-up situation.

"They develop computer programs for the human government sector," she said.

"Right up your alley," I replied. She'd always been great with computers. She'd gotten hooked when she'd taken a coding class in high school. "Life is changing by the minute, huh?" I muttered.

"Understatement of the century," she replied.

I clutched my stomach. "Jordyn, you can't tell Rianne I'm pregnant."

She sighed. "I know, and you know I won't."

Even though I believed her, in the heat of a moment, anyone was capable of slipping.

21

SAM

I was heading toward my father's room when Jo cornered me. I'd taken a detour when I left Layla. I wouldn't have rushed out as quickly as I did, considering we had a list of things to talk about, especially with a kid on the way, but I needed air. Her scent had been driving me mad, and my bloodlust was at an all-time high. And I wanted to see my father.

Jo shoved me down a hall beside the empty nurse's station. A gurney, a supply cart, and some other medical equipment littered the area. She kept pushing me until we were near the emergency exit door.

Then her silver eyes morphed to glistening

violet as her emotions fluctuated between nervous and happy. Her edginess drenched me as if I'd spent the day in soaking rain. "Dad's powers are weak, so he's unable to read our minds at the moment."

I knitted my brows together. "Okay. You forced me down here to tell me that? Is that why you're anxious?"

She sucked in her bottom lip. "No. If word gets out you're going to be a father, our enemies will converge like a swarm of killer bees. The Aberdeens being one of them."

"A little late for that. Jordyn knows. And by the way, the Aberdeens know Layla and I slept together." It was highly unlikely that Jack or any of his clan would infer she was pregnant just because Layla and I had sex. Still, stranger things had happened. "I dare Jack or any of those fuckers to do anything to hurt her again."

"Regardless, this baby just might be the reason the Aberdeens start an all-out war with us, which could mean Abbey's vision comes true. Bottom line, Sam—we need to start planning how to make sure we keep this a secret. It's not just the Aberdeens we need to worry about."

I scratched the back of my neck, where a nagging pain was beginning to throb. "Can you give me time to think? I just found out I'm going to be a dad. It's kind of overwhelming."

She pushed out a heavy breath. "I'm sorry I'm coming at you with guns blazing. Why don't you take Layla up to my house in Maine for a couple of days? Clear your mind. Talk. Plan. Relax."

"I can't just pick up and leave, Jo. I have a job. Roman's on the loose. Then we have the shifters. Ben. Pops. And Layla. Hell, the Aberdeens." Rianne could have been on her way to Massachusetts with that bastard, Noah.

She wrapped her slim fingers around my wrist. Jo stood about five-ten, so she didn't have to crane her neck that much to look me in the eye. "You cannot put anything else in front of that baby. That is your priority. Do I have to remind you what happened to us when Edmund Rain found out we existed? You and I don't want to put anyone through that."

All the shit that happened to us. I shuddered but understood why she was jumpy.

"Layla needs round-the-clock protection," Jo said.

I couldn't stop the laugh from coming out of my mouth. "Have you met Layla?" She was stubborn and would fight tooth and nail if I tried to suffocate her. But her safety was my priority. "She's not about to let anyone babysit her." Frustration laced my words.

"Then you better find a way to protect her and the baby," Jo said matter-of-factly. "I'll let George know you two are coming." She rose up on her toes and kissed me on the cheek. "We have a lot to do."

"Whoa! Wait one minute. I never agreed to go to Maine."

She stuck her hands on her hips. "You look like shit. You haven't slept, and what better way to get Layla's undivided attention? Besides, I'm sure Webb and Tripp will inform you if they find a lead on Roman."

I could use some relaxation with Layla's naked body wrapped around mine for hours on end. *Heaven. Pure unadulterated heaven.* I gritted my teeth before my cock took on a mind of its own. "Fine."

"Are you ready to give Dad the great news?" She tugged on my hand.

"Hey, sis. One thing. I can't do this without you."

Her eyes glossed over. "I'm not going anywhere, and I would never let you do this alone. I'm over the moon that you're going to be a father, a great one. I'll be honest, though. I'm somewhat jealous that I can't have kids, but that would never get in the way of my happiness for you and Layla."

I hugged and squeezed her and didn't want to let her go. "Promise me, Jo. If anything happens to me, you'll take care of my kid and Layla."

She eased back as her hands slid up to my biceps. "Nothing will happen to you."

Man, if it hadn't been for the perfect storm the other night—as in pouring rain, Layla, and Conrad—I wouldn't have been standing there. I wasn't a sentimental guy, nor was I naive enough to believe I couldn't die. But all the talk about the next nine months and our enemies was giving me a bad fucking feeling and the headache of the century. I kissed her on the top of her head. "Just promise me."

She tapped her heart twice, a signal we started when we were kids that meant she had my back and loved me. "I promise I'll protect them with my life."

I returned the gesture. "Time to tell Pops."

A minute later, I grinned when I sauntered into my father's room. He was sitting up. His green eyes were bright. The color had returned to his cheeks, and he beamed when he saw me. As far as I knew, he didn't know about Layla's pregnancy, but he sure was acting as though he did. Then again, being so close to death usually had a profound effect on a person.

I ponied up to his bed across from Webb. "Did I hear Roman?" Maybe I wouldn't be going to Maine.

Webb stood with his feet shoulder width apart, his hands cupped in front of him. His brown hair was pulled into a low ponytail, and he was wearing his all-black uniform. He had weapons strapped to his legs and around his belt, and his dull blue eyes and dark circles were evidence he was as tired as I felt.

"We lost Roman's trail," he said. "Sawyer's working around the clock, tracking the airlines, flight plans, and passenger lists. I have a team on the ground in Boston and one in Chicago. He'll turn up."

Roman was too arrogant not to show himself. "Has Sawyer had a chance to check on Camden Industries?" I knew the answer, but I had to ask. Roman was our priority, not a man who wanted to buy a horse.

"Not yet. Roman first," Webb said.

"It's probably nothing, anyway, but I just want to be sure," I said. "Also, any luck in contacting Jack?"

Webb's jaw tightened. "He hasn't returned my call."

"Webb, leave Jack Aberdeen to me. He might respond better if I call him," my dad said.

I was curious whether Jack had been involved in the scheme to burn me alive, or if Noah and Rianne acted alone. Considering Jack hadn't been there when I was dangling over the fire, I suspected he didn't know what his son had been up to.

Jo sidled up to Webb and hooked her arm in his. "Honey, we should have lunch with Abbey. Dad, I'll bring her in later. We'll give you and Sam some time to catch up."

"Steven, I'll keep you posted," Webb said. "Glad you made it through. You had all of us worried." Then Webb gave me a funky grin, a new look for the hardcore Navy SEAL. Nevertheless, I knew it was about Layla.

Once Dad and I were alone, I dragged the lone chair in the room from the corner to his bedside.

My father stabbed a finger at the retreating Webb. "What's with his goofy grin?"

My heart punched my ribs, and I was nervous as hell to answer him. I wasn't sure why. I had never been afraid of anything other than losing my sister. But now I had a kid on the way, someone else to worry about. I had *two* other people to protect.

The conversation I'd had with Jo began to weigh heavily on my mind. "I'm glad you're back, Pops." I tapped my chest. "You gave my heart a run for its money."

"I love you too, Sam. I understand you almost lost your life." A muscle ticked in his jaw. He was a second away from reading me my rights before he dumped me in the brig.

"Before you start yelling, I know it was stupid of me to go to Montana alone and walk into a vampire hunter's lair."

"Why did you?" His tone was even.

I crossed one leg over the other so my ankle was resting on my knee. "Layla. I felt she was in danger after Roman escaped."

"Son, you need to learn to think with your brain and not your heart before you jump into action. I don't care how powerful you are or think you might be. Our enemies will always find a way to bring you down. Are we understood?"

I leaned forward, elbows on knees. "We are." Though with a baby on the way, I wasn't sure how well his advice would work. Layla and my kid were my number one priority, and I would die protecting them.

"Why the despondent look?" he asked.

Here goes nothing. Doc thinks my dad will be happy that Layla's having my child or that he's about to be a grandfather, but I'm not so sure. I sat back, inhaled, swallowed, and pushed my fingers through my hair. "Layla's pregnant." A weird feeling traveled through me when I said that. I couldn't put my finger on the sensation, but it was a cross between a cold chill and a pain in my gut. Certainly not a good sign, but I suspected my convo with Jo was contributing to the thoughts and feelings consuming me.

He closed his eyes then slowly fluttered them open. "Say that again?"

I knew he heard me. But I responded just the same, "Layla is pregnant."

His green eyes drilled a hole through me. "Your child? Impossible."

I jerked back. "Come again?"

He pursed his lips. "Son, are you sure it's yours?"

Anger bit me in the ass, and I wasn't sure why. "Why would you think it wasn't mine?" I'd done the math from the time we had sex to the present, and from everything I'd heard and learned from Layla, Jordyn, and Tabitha, Layla hadn't left the ranch except for the day Conrad followed them to a restaurant in Big Timber. I supposed she could have bedded someone right before we'd met, but I doubted it. "She's Vel negative too."

He gave me an incredulous look.

Might as well continue to shock him. "Layla's mother has vampires in her heritage."

"Impossible," he said again. "Our government looked into all the Aberdeens, including their spouses."

"You weren't always on the Council of Elders. Your predecessor missed something, then."

He rubbed his shoulder. "Maybe, but that's a huge miss. Did Layla know she has that blood type before you and she—"

"No, and I flat out asked her." After we had sex, though. In the heat of the moment, blood types certainly hadn't crossed my fucking mind.

"She was adamant she had the average human blood type."

Silence stretched between us for a beat.

"How is Layla taking the news?" he asked, seemingly still perplexed.

I laughed. "She's in denial. I'm kind of with her too."

"Her family *cannot* find out," he said through gritted teeth. "Cannot," he reiterated. "Fuck, this could also be Edmund Rain all over again."

I bobbed my head. "Jo agrees."

His green eyes bled to silver. "And you, son? You better get your ass on board. Not only is Abbey in danger... that unborn Mason will be too."

"And how do you propose keeping the baby a secret when she starts showing? I'm not locking Layla up for nine months. So don't even think about that." My old man's way of keeping us under his thumb was lockdown. Jo and I hadn't even been able to leave the naval base when we'd become vampires.

"We at least have to keep her from the Aberdeens when she starts showing," he said.

"She's not going anywhere near them again," I bit out.

Dad rubbed his other shoulder, appearing tired all of a sudden as he scrutinized me.

"You love her, don't you? Otherwise, you wouldn't have gone to Montana."

"That's not true," I said easily. "We protect humans, and with Roman on the loose... Layla could be his target."

"Are you trying to convince me or yourself?"

I shrugged. "I've never been in love. But she's beautiful, feisty, and stubborn, and I can't seem to get her out of my head."

He chuckled. "Sounds to me like you're on your way." Then he scratched his jaw. "Sam, there are a few things you should know—"

The door swung open, and a fireball with black hair, blue eyes, and a look that screamed she was excited to see my dad flew in and jumped on the bed. "Grandpa!"

Abbey's excitement put me at ease.

Dad gave her a hug. "I'm okay, sweet pea."

"I know." She cozied up to my father, kicking out her legs. "Layla is awake, too, and she's having a baby. I can't wait. I'll have a cousin."

Dad and I laughed.

I wished I had her enthusiasm, but if my gut was right, gloom and doom were headed our way.

22

LAYLA

I'd been sitting on the floor in the bathroom attached to my hospital room for two hours. After Jordyn had left to call Carly, Dr. Vieira's lab tech, Giselle, had brought me a handful of over-the-counter pregnancy tests.

I hugged my knees tighter to my chest, tears flowing like water from a faucet. The atmosphere was cold and sterile, and the air had an alcohol scent to it that was making me sick to my stomach. Oh, wait. That wasn't it. The pregnancy tests were the reason.

I'm pregnant by a vampire. A fucking vampire.

I rocked back and forth. I wanted my mom so badly. I was willing to dig her up just to yell at her for not telling me about the bloodsuckers on her side then ask for her advice. *Oh fuck.* I was losing it.

I stared at the blinding-white tile, crying like a damn baby. I hadn't bawled my eyes out since my dad's funeral. I tried to make sense of how my life had changed with one stupid decision. If I could rewind back to the day my sisters and I had agreed to the job, I would walk away. I would've told Wyman no then joined the police academy. *Ha, the police academy.* That was a pipe dream.

Knuckles rapped on the door, severing my pity party. "Layla." Sam's husky voice made my heart flutter.

What the hell? The man was irritatingly sexy. *How can I go from self-pity to butterflies and giddiness over a vampire?* "Go away." My voice was barely a whisper.

"Baby doll, please?" He sounded as desperate and messed up as I was. "You know I can open this door easily."

I rolled my eyes, even though he couldn't see me. "Then open it." I wasn't ready to stand on wobbly legs or have the room turn like a washing machine on the spin cycle. My brain was rather fuzzy, whether from the impossible pregnancy, my head injury, or Rianne. *Argh!* I wanted to scream, run, and disappear. I wanted to strangle my dead father, shoot my uncle Jack, kill Noah, knock some sense into Rianne, and disappear again.

The knob turned once. The lock was flimsy, so anyone could open it, even Jordyn. Tears spilled again. I really didn't want her to leave me, but I couldn't stand in her way. Hell, if Rianne was happy in her mission to join the family business, I wouldn't stop her, either. I would, however, cut her off at the knees if she hunted Sam and me.

I was getting ahead of myself. Maybe Rianne regretted what she'd done to Sam and that was why she'd taken off. *Or she's scared.*

Meanwhile, I was stuck with a vampire.

Stop whining and rise up like the woman your parents raised you to be—tough, confident, determined. Take no prisoners. You can handle anything. Famous words from my mom to her daughters.

I wasn't sure I could handle a child who would eventually become a vampire.

The popping sound severed my thoughts when Sam tore the doorknob off. He swaggered in like an ethereal being, six plus feet of sexiness on a damn stick. *Shut the fuck up, brain. Get your mind out of the gutter.*

That crooked grin of his along with his forest-green eyes, which seemed darker in the light of the bathroom, sent waves of heat to my belly. Who was I kidding? My lady parts were drooling to have him inside me.

Shut the hell up, brain! I'm supposed to be mad at him. He did this to me. A crazy laugh thundered in my head. *It takes two, darling.*

He swept his gaze over the sea of boxes surrounding me.

Sam picked up one pregnancy stick. "Mm." Then he examined another.

My arms were numb from hugging my knees to my chest. "They're all positive."

"I see that." He joined me on the floor and kicked out his muscular jean-clad legs. He seemed out of place in the small bathroom.

Silence ensued as we each fixated on something ahead of us, which for me was the toilet paper. I smiled as a memory surfaced of when my sisters and I were just barely teenagers with rebellious streaks.

"Come on, Lay," Rianne whined. "I want to TP her house. She's such a bitch."

"Yeah," Jordyn had chimed in. "It will be fun. And I don't like Kari, either. She stuck a dead rat in Taylor's locker."

I would have given anything to go back to happier days when life was simpler than it had become. A tear slid down my face. I hated that Sam was witnessing a weaker side of me. But the tears wouldn't stop. "Jordyn is heading to Chicago for a job interview, Rianne hates me, and I want my mom." I sounded so pitiful. I had no idea why I was telling him all that.

"I wish I would've known my mom."

The pain in his voice made my own heart hurt, but underneath that—shock. The vampire had feelings, strong ones, for his mom. Not that Sam hadn't given me glimpses of a softer and caring side of him. He'd all but begged me not to return to Montana. He'd shown up to protect me for fear that Roman would kidnap me. He'd texted me nonstop and tried to check on me. He would die for his sister. He didn't just talk a big game. His actions definitely showed who he was, despite whatever stupid shit that came out of his mouth.

His hand slid over to settle on my thigh. I had yet to take a shower. I was still in an ugly hospital gown. Blood was caked in my hair. I probably smelled like a dead cat, and I needed a pedicure.

He rubbed a path up and down my leg. "Want me to take a shower with you?"

I snorted, and spit sprayed out. "Are you in my head?" Surely, he couldn't read my mind. That wasn't his specialty. "And how can you think about sex?"

"Who said anything about sex?" He sounded appalled that I would say such a thing.

My eyes widened at his profile—sharp jaw, patrician nose, and a five-o'clock shadow that was more than a shadow. My hand was on the move before my brain caught up with my actions. As soon as I touched his face, he leaned in and moaned.

Oh, for all that was holy. The man—the vampire—would be my undoing.

I traded his jaw for the hand he had on my leg. I interlaced my fingers with his, and minutes ticked by as a calming silence hung over us. As much as I had no idea what tomorrow or the next nine months would bring, I knew one thing—I would forever be tied to Sam, and at that moment, I was beginning to realize that might not be so bad. He was protective. He loved hard, at least according to Harley. Oh my. When the strawberry blonde found out I was pregnant, she would be giddy.

"How's Harley?" I asked.

He whipped his gaze at me. "We're pregnant, and you want to talk about Webb's assistant?"

"Let's get one thing straight, vampire. I'm pregnant. Not you." Just articulating that out loud made me shiver. "She's my friend. Friends ask about each other."

Before I could take a breath, he lifted me up onto his lap as though I was light as a feather. He curled my hair behind my ear before his calloused fingers danced down my neck to settle on my carotid artery.

"Are you hungry?" Normally, his eyes changed from green to silver when hunger struck or his emotions changed. But he was still in human form, no fangs or anything.

"I want to taste you." He traded my neck for my inner thigh and circled a spot he wanted to sink his fangs into. "But here." Then his fingers lightly brushed my clit. "And here."

I quivered as lust consumed me then I flattened my palms on his face. "Why am I drawn to you?"

He propped his head against the wall, grinning. "You tell me." I thought he would answer with some snarky remark about his blood or being a god among gods, but his tone had a curious lilt to it.

I brushed my fingers over his lips. "I like these on me. Your eyes are mesmerizing, especially when they change colors." I shifted my gaze back and forth, studying him and thinking.

He smirked, and his dimples emerged.

I gently poked my finger into one of them. "It's these babies. And I'm a sucker for asshole men."

He cupped my breasts. "You say the sweetest things. So you're only attracted to me for my dimples and asshole ways?" He fake pouted. "Not my dick?"

I sucked my bottom lip in between my teeth as I grabbed his cock through the fabric of his jeans. "Maybe."

"Careful, baby doll. I have no problem fucking you right here."

"Tease," I returned.

In a flash, he was on his feet with me in his arms. Then he set me on the small counter to the right of the sink. "Not much to take off." He lifted my hospital gown.

I swatted at him. "I haven't had a shower."

He snarled, raising an eyebrow. "You're assuming I'm about to eat you."

It was my turn to pout. "You're not?"

He chuckled as his fangs lowered.

My stomach dipped as butterflies flapped their wings, and I opened my legs like a puppy who wanted her belly rubbed.

He leaned in and licked a path from my collarbone to my ear. "Tell me what you want, Layla. Tell me you want me as badly as I want you."

I gripped his silky hair then guided his head down to my breasts, where he tugged a nipple with his teeth. Damn hospital gown was in the way.

I whimpered. "We shouldn't do this here." With the exception of Jordyn and me, I would guess that everyone in the building was a vampire, which meant sharp hearing.

He ignored me as he kissed his way down to my inner thigh.

I opened my legs as wide as I could.

Then Jordyn called my name, and Sam froze.

I sighed. "I'll be right out."

The door was ajar since Sam had torn the knob off. Jordyn peeked in. "Oh. Never mind. I'll wait out here."

Obviously flustered and with beads of sweat on his brow, Sam straightened. "You and I are leaving town for a couple of days." He eyed the door. "Alone."

I opened my mouth to speak, ready to tell him he couldn't order me around, when he snarled at me.

I flipped him off. "You don't own me, vampire."

A slow wolfish grin emerged on his face as he brushed his lips over mine. "How many times do I have to tell you? You're mine, Layla." Then he rubbed my stomach in gentle strokes. "Baby or not. You. Are. Mine." He emphasized each word in his last statement.

Delicious shivers racked my body at the huskiness in his voice and the conviction in his tone.

We locked eyes. The sounds around me diminished as a dull noise pounded in my ears. I swallowed what felt like a ball of fur, searching for some snarky retort that I couldn't find. So I bit his lip, drawing blood.

He chuckled. "You and I are going to have a great time in Maine."

I stuck out my chin, staring at the blood. "Not happening. I'm going with Jordyn. She needs me with her." *Liar*.

He didn't bat an eye. Instead, he palmed the back of my head as he leaned and brushed his mouth over my ear. "Stop fighting what you're feeling. Your lust is gripping my balls. Your desire is off the charts, and your heartbeat is racing with excitement at the thought of you and me alone. Do whatever you need to do today, but come morning, your sweet, gorgeous ass will be in my Jeep... with me." After a hard and fast kiss that took my breath away, he left, melting me into a pile of mush.

I adjusted my gown and closed my legs as Jordyn came in, brown eyes bright and appearing less downtrodden than earlier. "See, he loves you. You two make a great pair."

The need to flip her off was strong, but the banter of love that Sam and I had was rather fun. The next nine months would certainly be a test of patience and every other emotion. We would either kill each other or fight to protect one another. For the time being, I guessed it wouldn't hurt to have some alone time with him. Just the thought of screwing his brains out had me hot all over. Regardless, we did need to be on the same page with the baby. And a getaway to sleep and think sounded like heaven.

Jordyn eyed the boxes that littered the floor. "Are you a believer now?" She picked up one and then another. "Yep, you're definitely preggo." She tossed them in the trash then sat on the lid of the toilet seat. "I talked to Carly. I fly out in the morning. I also talked to Webb. He's agreed to have Conrad meet me at the airport in Chicago. He'll be my bodyguard."

"That's great news," I said, trying to inject as much sisterly excitement as I could into my words, when in truth, my brain was concentrating on the baby and how in the heck I'd been cursed with Vel-negative blood.

"I heard something interesting before I came in here. Jo was talking to Dr. Vieira about women who have gotten knocked up by vampires. He asked her to check out the archives at the library they have here in Boston. Maybe they have records on Mom's family, the Drakes."

Excitement stirred. "I'll talk to Jo." After all,

she was studying genetics and hematology, if memory served me correctly.

A small weight fell off my shoulders, making me feel like I had a sense of purpose rather than just being Sam's baby mama. What continued to nag at the deep recesses of my being was not knowing what Rianne and the Aberdeen clan were up to.

"Jordyn, please. You cannot say anything about the baby to anyone."

She huffed. "You told me that already. I won't."

There was no question in my mind that if the Aberdeens learned about the pregnancy, a war would erupt.

23

SAM

The next day, Layla and I were speeding up I-95 in my Jeep. I couldn't get to Maine quickly enough. The medical facility had been suffocating. I hadn't slept. My mind kept wandering to my screwed-up situation. How to protect Layla. Where Roman was. Who else would come out of the woodwork when they found out I was having a kid? The list was piling up.

I'd kept debating whether to steal Layla away or push forward and help my team find Roman. But I wasn't going to figure anything out unless I had some space to think, although two days with Layla wouldn't help me sort anything but where to fuck her. Maybe that was all I needed for the world to right itself on its axis.

I pressed on the gas as I wound around the coastline. Waves crashed along the shore. Light glinted off the Atlantic as the sun rose high in the sky.

I envisioned Layla running naked along the water, and my cock sprang to life and pulsed endlessly to be inside her. If I didn't get some relief soon, my balls would be blue. Hell, they already were. Closed in a vehicle with her next to me made taming the wild beast who was clawing his way out difficult. I'd almost pulled off the highway for a quickie in the back seat.

Thankfully, we weren't far from Jo and Webb's house.

She groaned in frustration as she set her phone in her lap. "Rianne isn't answering."

She'd been trying to get ahold of her sister since last night. I understood her irritation. If I'd been in her shoes, and Jo had some notion of jumping to the dark side, I would have been tearing shit up. "Layla."

She whipped her head my way. "Don't say it, Sam."

"Can you read minds now? You don't know what I'm thinking."

"Argh!" she practically screamed in frustration. "Maybe not, but I've been racking my brain about how I missed the signs with Rianne. I tried to reason with her, but she seemed so far gone. I don't think she'll come around. I want to talk to her one more time. If anything, I just want to make sure she's okay."

I reached over and placed my hand on her thigh. "Don't beat yourself up, baby doll. Webb went through something similar with his sister, Kate. She betrayed him and tried to kill him. She went after Jo first." Jo had gone through hell and back five years ago.

Layla's big blues bulged. "What happened?"

"Long story and not mine to tell," I said as I put two hands on the wheel.

"Obviously, Kate didn't succeed. Webb is alive. Where's Kate now?" she asked as intrigue washed over her.

I slowed around a curve and wasn't sure if I should tell her. I didn't want to sour her mood even more. But she would insist. "No longer here."

She sucked in a sharp breath. "As in dead?"

I nodded.

Her shoulders slumped as she gazed out the passenger window. "Just when I think I have it bad, someone always has it worse."

"Layla, let's try and relax for the next two days and not think of your sister trying to annihilate your boyfriend."

She half laughed. "You're my boyfriend?"

I gave her a quick glance. "You don't agree? How about partners? Enemies? Fuck buddies? Pick one or two."

"Partners." She snorted. "That's a weird one. I'm going with enemies."

That suited me fine, as long as she was with me.

"Just don't ever call me your baby mama because I will cut off your balls and feed them to the sharks." She stabbed a finger toward the ocean.

I roared with laughter, and the tension in my shoulders subsided. "Duly noted, baby mama."

She whacked me on the arm, giggling, a sound so sweet it gripped my balls. I was looking forward to spending time with her. Maybe we *could* make a relationship work, despite the problems we were about to face.

Roughly two minutes later, I pulled into the

driveway of a two-story, shingle-sided cottage hideaway with the Atlantic as its backdrop.

"Holy shit!" she squealed. "This place is amazing."

The house had four dormers on the front and a large wraparound porch on three sides. Even on a cold day in February, the property was spectacular. I'd always loved it there. Too bad the flowers weren't in bloom. The rosebushes that climbed the trellis on the side of the house had brown leaves hanging from their vines. Blades of green grass poked through the light dusting of snow, and the water fountain, the centerpiece of the yard, was dry and shut off for the winter.

Before I could turn off the engine, Layla climbed out, ran down the path, and stopped at the edge of the stairs that led down to the ocean. Then she held out her arms as if to say, "Come and get me, Atlantic Ocean." Man, my heart skipped like a kid in a schoolyard at recess. To see her happy made me one delighted motherfucker. Then she angled her face toward the sun, high in the sky. The hunger to kiss her until we couldn't breathe, to taste her in more ways than to satisfy my bloodlust, to wake up next to her and fuck some more, was making my cock harder than the circle of rocks around a bed of dormant flowers. Morning sex was by far the best in my book. I was dying to lick Layla awake.

I finally got out and stretched, inhaling the mist of salt in the air, when the glass door creaked and George cleared his throat. Webb's dear friend and father figure was a tall and lanky century-plus-old vampire who had taken care of Webb over the years. He also lived at the house when Jo and Webb weren't there.

"Glad you made it." He sauntered down the porch steps.

I opened the trunk. "Did you think we wouldn't?" I handed him Layla's bag.

"That accident north of Boston has traffic stopped for miles," he said.

"We must've just missed it, then. Are you staying?" I was sure Jo had warned him that I needed alone time with Layla.

"Not here, but with Stan in town."

"How is the sheriff?" Most of the occupants of the small coastal town were vamps. Occasionally, some of the homes were rented to humans during the summer months. But during the winter, the only humans around were the ones who stopped at the diner in town on their way north or south.

"Stan is still ornery." He peeked around the car. "It's Layla, right?"

"Yep, and she's a firecracker."

He clapped me on the shoulder. "I don't doubt that, Sam. I couldn't see you with any other type of woman. You need someone to match your arrogance."

I laughed wildly and freely, and it felt fucking good as we started for the house. "You know me well."

"A vampire hunter, though," he said with concern. "I assume her family doesn't know about the baby. Webb told me, by the way."

It wasn't a big deal with George. He would and had protected Jo and me with his life. "Hell no. I'm hoping they never find out." That was a tall order. Nothing ever stayed hidden for long.

Jordyn could slip up if she spoke to Rianne. Layla could too. And as I knew all too well, we could have moles within our organization—not that we did or knew of, though.

The thought of erasing the memories of anyone who found out sounded like a great idea. But that wouldn't matter when Layla started to show.

"Congrats," he said as we reached the porch steps. "It's a miracle, if you ask me. I didn't think I would see any of my vampire friends become dads."

"Trust me, I didn't think I would ever be one." I always saw myself fighting, killing, and fucking for eternity.

"Fate has plans for you," George said. "Big plans." He sounded as though he knew my destiny. But he didn't have the ability to read minds or see the future.

"Do you know something I don't?" I was only half teasing. Maybe Abbey had imparted her vision of my future to Jo.

He chuckled. "Not a thing except that you're a Mason. That means right out of the gate, that baby will have powers you're probably not ready for."

It was my turn to laugh. "Hopefully, the little guy will take after me."

We both chuckled just as Layla's scent announced her before she rounded the corner of the house and stiffened.

Layla sized up George as though he was a threat. "Who are you?"

I grinned at how she was ready to go into battle, her electric-blue eyes narrowing, her fists ready to swing.

George, ever the gentleman, smiled warmly. "I'm George. I live here mostly year-round and take care of the house for Webb and Jo. You must be Layla."

She lowered her shoulders, unclenched her fists, and returned a smile. "I am. Nice to meet you."

While the two got acquainted, I went inside. I was ready for a beer or ten and definitely blood. Their voices droned as I dropped my bags on the honeyed wooden floor in the foyer then ambled through the open floor plan to the accordion glass doors that opened to the Atlantic. The gentle waves slid over the sand in the push and pull of the ocean as the tide came in. On a sigh, I skirted the speckled tan granite island and beelined for the fridge. Beer, blood, soda, containers of food, and a drawer of fruit packed the inside of the fridge to its gills. I'd just snagged a bottle of blood when my phone rang, the screen lighting with Tripp's name.

"What's up, man?" I asked.

"Are you alone? Or are you still in the car?" His lieutenant's tone said he had bad news.

A boulder dropped into the pit of my stomach. "We just got here."

"Find a quiet spot where no one can hear you," he said.

I took the bottle of blood and walked out onto the sprawling two-tiered deck. "You're clear to talk."

"You know we've been monitoring the airports for Roman."

Excitement barreled through me. "You got a lead?"

"Not exactly," Tripp said. "We spotted Rianne at O'Hare airport in Chicago. Passenger list says she's on her way to Boston."

Motherfucker. "Are you sure? Maybe she's meeting Jordyn in Chicago."

"I'm afraid not. According to one of the passenger lists, she's on the plane now, heading to Boston. She's probably coming to the naval base." He sounded as frustrated as I felt.

If it had been me, I would have done the same thing, whether to beg for Layla's forgiveness or follow through and finish what I'd started.

I took a long swig of blood, the thickness cooling the burn in the back of my throat and the anger simmering inside me. *Fucking Aberdeens.*

"Layla has been trying to call her since we left Boston with no luck."

"I'll alert Stan to keep his eyes open just in case she shows up there," Tripp said.

"She doesn't know where Layla is, and the only thing Jordyn knows is that the house is in Maine. Speaking of Jordyn, any word from Conrad about meeting up with her yet?" Conrad was assigned to guard Jordyn and was meeting her at O'Hare. With our luck, Jordyn would run into Rianne. I had no idea how that reunion would go, although if it was anything like that night at the firepit, Jordyn would probably strangle Rianne. Regardless, blood was blood, and while I believed Jordyn was on Layla's side, I couldn't trust her completely. Hell, I hardly trusted anyone to begin with.

"Conrad checked in. All is good with Jordyn. He's in the lobby of Intech, waiting for her."

"Layla will be relieved to know that. Also, is there any other Aberdeen with Rianne?" If it was Noah, I would gladly tell him where we were, just to yank out his tongue and then his heart.

"The passenger list doesn't show any Aberdeen but her," he said. "If you want Layla's undivided attention while you're there, I highly recommend you shut off her phone."

Or throw it into the Atlantic.

Tripp cleared his throat. "Sam, aside from the baby, is she worth it?"

I stared at the whitecaps cresting the water as the wind picked up. "Fuck yeah. I know it's crazy to be into a vampire hunter." If I royally pissed her off, she could axe me in my sleep. "But, man, I had this desperate need to protect her even before I found out she was pregnant." I swore if she died, my soul would die with her.

"Sam Mason has fallen for a woman." I could picture him grinning like an ass.

"Are you trying to bust my balls? You know payback is a bitch."

He chuckled. "As much as I enjoy seeing you tear yourself apart over a woman, I need you to answer that question out loud. You and she need to be on the same page, man. Does she feel *you're* worth the fight?"

Layla's actions so far said yes. But family ruled, and a niggle of doubt lingered in the back of my mind. "Man, that's the purpose of this quick getaway. We'll come to terms on things."

"I hope so. I need your head in the game, because if my instincts are correct, we're in for a rough road ahead. Not to mention, finding Roman is front and center."

So was my kid, but I knew we needed to take Roman out. If he found out Layla was carrying a Mason baby, he would go to the ends of the Earth, not only to use her to his advantage but to profit off my child as he'd planned to do with Abbey.

Blowing out a breath, I tossed a look over my shoulder. Layla and George were in the house, engrossed in a conversation. "Keep me posted on Rianne. I'll check in later."

"Watch your six." Then he hung up.

I downed my drink as my mind drifted out to sea. Darkness was coming. Like Tripp, I could feel it, and I had to do everything in my power to protect my loved ones.

24

SAM

I hung outside, listening to the whoosh of the waves crashing along the shore. They seemed as furious and frustrated as I felt.

If Layla found out Rianne was on her way to Boston, she would tear out of here like the Flash. Man, as much as I understood her need to reason with Rianne, she wasn't our priority anymore, and I couldn't risk Layla getting kidnapped.

As much as I didn't want to snag her phone, I had to until we could at least agree on a plan forward regarding her family, the baby, and our next steps. We couldn't just run into harm's way without thinking.

I tilted my face toward the sun, absorbing as

much of it as I could. My elemental powers were fueled by the sun and nature, and I needed to be stronger than ever for the road ahead.

"Sam." Layla's siren voice buttered my nerves, melting our problems for the moment. "Are you okay?"

I am now. The woman could probably lull me into her arms just with her seductive tone.

She sidled up to me, and her arm brushed mine. Electricity hurtled up my arm and exploded through every fiber in my body. "Your shoulders are hunched. You're tense. Who called? Is it bad news?"

With my blood running through her veins, I imagined she could feel what I felt. I tucked her into me, and she leaned her head on my chest. "It's all good. Just Tripp checking in." I forced my emotions into a safe, locked it, and lost the combination for the time being.

She fished her phone from the pocket of the jeans molded to her curvy hips. "I want to check in with Jordyn and make sure she made it safely to Chicago."

I eyed the cell like it was a bomb about to explode. "She did. I asked Tripp about her. I think she's in her interview now."

"You're worried about Jordyn?" She batted puppy dog eyes up at me.

I kissed her on the head. "Of course. Don't sound so surprised. I do have a heart."

She rubbed a hand up my chest. "Sometimes I wonder, though," she said with a giggle.

I plucked her phone from her. "Do me a favor? No phones while we're here. Dr. Vieira ordered you to rest, which means no drama."

A crease dented the smooth skin in between her eyebrows. "No. What if Rianne calls? And I want to talk to Jordyn."

I set the bottle on the deck's rail. "Tripp feels that Roman can track us." It was kind of a lie but mostly true. Roman had my number, and if he wanted to find Layla's, I was sure he could. I couldn't believe I hadn't thought of that before. "I'm turning mine off." I proceeded to shut mine down. After pocketing it, I ghosted my lips over hers. "Leave Jordyn a message. Tell her you'll call her later. If anyone needs us, Tripp and Webb know to call George."

She stuck out her chest, obviously ready to unleash defiance as though I'd just scolded her.

I showered kisses along her cheek until I was nibbling her ear. "I have something in mind for us that will help you relax, and I don't want any distractions."

She shivered. "What is it?"

Man, I wished the weather was warmer so we could dive into the ocean naked. "Do I really have to explain?"

She nodded as she audibly swallowed. "I want details, vampire."

Smirking, I inched back.

Her cheeks were flushed. Lust dripped off her, and her long lashes swept down as her eyelids grew heavy.

"Let me talk to George. You leave Jordyn a message. Then, baby doll"—I tugged her to me —"I'm going to bury myself inside you until morning."

A soft mewl escaped her sultry lips.

I was sure I left her dripping wet as I went inside.

George was in the kitchen, rinsing a glass. "I'm heading out. I made a pot roast for you. And if you run out of blood, there's more in the fridge in the garage."

"Thanks, man. I'll be fine. The way shit is going, I won't be here long."

He raised a dark eyebrow. "Anything I can help with?"

I filled him on part of my convo with Tripp. "I'll probably leave tomorrow night instead of the two days I planned."

"Given what Webb has told me about Roman Brown, I have a feeling it's about to be Edmund Rain all over again. Then there's her family." He whistled. "Take the time to build your energy. Your elemental powers need to be ready."

I didn't need any daggers, swords, or guns. "I agree, man. Only my gut tells me that whatever Roman has up his sleeve will put Edmund Rain to shame."

"Stan and I will keep our eyes open for any newcomers in town. I'll call you in the morning." He grabbed his keys off the table in the foyer, gave me a nod, then left.

I shoved my fingers through my hair, pulling out the leather strap. Settling at the accordion glass doors, I watched Layla as I sharpened my hearing, listening to her caller. For a second, the blood halted in my veins until I realized it was Jordyn speaking.

"My interview went great," Jordyn said. "Carly's

boss offered me the job. They gave me some time to think about it. Carly suggested I stay for the week. She wants to show me around and meet some of the people I would be working with. Oh, and she says hi."

Layla and Jordyn had filled Webb and me in on Intech and Carly, who I learned was married to Jack's oldest son.

"I hear some apprehension," Layla said. "If it's me you're worried about, don't."

"Sure, I'm concerned about you, but it's a big move," Jordyn replied. "I like Carly. I don't know that I'm ready to work for her or live here. I'm not exactly happy with our family at the moment."

"Does she know what happened at the ranch?" Layla asked.

"You know Jack Jr. left Montana as soon as they married because he doesn't want Carly involved in hunting vamps."

"Yeah, but they've been married for two years," Layla said. "Maybe he finally told her."

"If she knows, she didn't say anything to me," Jordyn said. "Besides, remember Uncle Jack quit hunting around the time Jack Jr. married Carly."

An interesting piece of info about Jack Jr.

"Are you going to stay, then?" Layla asked. "Oh, and is Conrad with you?"

"I'll hang for a day or so, and yes, Conrad is in the lobby. Don't worry, sis. I'm good. Any word from Rianne?"

Layla's voice tensed. "No. I've left her several messages. I think we lost her for good." Sadness made her words heavy. "I take it she hasn't contacted you?"

"No. Do me a favor? Dr. Vieira said you needed to rest. That means forget about Rianne while you're in Maine. How is it, by the way? The house? The ocean? You know we've always dreamed of living on the water."

Layla slumped her shoulders. "It's freaking beautiful here. I want a house like this one." She gave Jordyn detail after detail, giddy as she talked.

I knocked on the glass. I hated to burst her bubble, but I didn't want her to give away too much or linger on the phone.

She spun around and held up her finger. "Jordyn, I should go. I'm turning my phone off. Sam thinks Roman can track us."

"Layla, listen to Sam. Don't let your emotions overshadow logic. Roman can very well track you. Anyone with the means could. Besides, Rianne made her decision. When she's ready to show herself, she will."

Score one for Jordyn. I made a mental note to thank her. She was the most levelheaded of the sisters. Rianne was the hothead, and Layla was the stubborn one.

While Layla finished her call, I decided food was in order. My stomach growled the minute I pulled the roast out of the fridge.

A second later, Layla glided in, shrugging out of her coat and exposing her curvy body as she took in the floor plan. "I know I said it once, but this place is just *wow*."

Everyone had the same response after seeing it the first time. The inside was just as breathtaking as the outside. It was large with high ceilings and thick exposed beams traveling from one side of the house to the other, giving the place an expansive feel. A fireplace, a large leather couch, two oversized fabric chairs, and a couple of tables decorated one half, and the island spilled into the gourmet kitchen with windows overlooking the Atlantic.

I shoved the pot roast into the microwave then leaned my elbows on the island and watched her.

She was standing in front of the fireplace, rubbing her hands together.

"I have just the remedy to warm you up."

She spun around, rolling her eyes. "Did George leave?"

"It's just you and me." The microwave dinged, but I didn't move. "Are you hungry?"

Lust drifted in the air.

I grinned. "You're starving."

She lifted her sweater over her head. "Not for food."

I straightened. "I know. But we should talk first."

She unclasped her bra, and her tits bounced free.

Motherfucker. My erection was instant.

Then she kicked off her boots before she shimmied her hips out of her jeans. Once she was standing in nothing but her panties, her auburn hair flowing in waves around her, I groaned as my heart opened and my cock throbbed.

She gave me a flirty smile. "Well, vampire. You want me alone. Now what are you waiting for?" She tweaked one of her nipples.

I licked my lips, snapping mental picture after picture. Stupid me kept thinking we needed to talk. Hell, I couldn't articulate a word if my life depended on it. My fangs lowered as my gaze traveled down to her thigh.

She followed my line of sight and beamed. "You want me here." She touched that spot reserved for me as she opened her stance wider. "I'm all yours, Sam."

The aroma from the pot roast competed with the lust drenching the room. Fuck the roast. At the speed of light, I had her by the waist before setting her down on the leather couch.

She giggled. "I will never get used to your speed."

In one move, I ripped her panties off her.

She laughed again as she opened her legs as wide as she could.

Her pussy glistened, her scent driving me fucking mad. My eyes flashed silver, and before she could move, I sank my fangs into her sweet flesh. The first taste was always the best—smooth, sweet, and explosive.

She tangled her hands in my hair. "I know this may sound crazy, but this is the hottest thing ever. I could orgasm right now."

I retracted my fangs and licked the spot before kissing my way up to her pussy.

She pouted. "No, don't stop."

"A little at a time, baby doll. Now, legs over

my shoulders." I could lose my shit immediately at the thought of how she tasted.

She obeyed before I flattened my tongue against her swollen nub, gently at first.

The sound of her whimper sent the bolt of a thousand-watt electrical current to my balls. Then I feasted on her like a starved animal.

She clutched my head, trying to mash my face harder into her. "Suck, Sam. Please."

I finger-fucked her as I sucked and licked.

She rolled her hips as her ball-squeezing moans grew louder. "I'm close."

"You taste like heaven." As though I'd said the magic words, she screamed her release.

I sucked harder as she continued to orgasm, saying my name over and over.

Man, my name on her lips was right up there with the feeling of being inside her—orgasmic.

She untangled her legs from me. "That was amazing."

I pressed my hands into the couch and leaned in. "I would agree." I flicked my tongue over one nipple then the other.

She grabbed my cock through the fabric of my jeans. "I want you inside me."

I licked the light sheen of sweat off her chest

as my mouth travelled up to nip her chin. "Let's eat first." I wanted to take my time and space things out, since we had all day and into the night.

She sniffed. "It does smell good. But it can wait."

I sat beside her and draped my arms over the back of the couch. "Do as you please, then." Who was I to deny her my dick?

She straddled me. "Take off your shirt."

I wasn't a good listener, but I had no problems doing as she commanded.

She ran her hands up and down my chest and abs, her eyes hooded, her lust multiplying once again.

I moved her hair over her shoulder and exposed her long, smooth neck.

She traced her finger over my carotid artery, mesmerized as if thinking of biting me.

Whether she needed blood or not, I sank my fangs into my wrist then held out my arm. "Drink." Doc had said the baby would probably need my blood.

She looked at me with questions in her hungry gaze.

I didn't understand why the kid would need my blood. No woman pregnant with a natural-born vampire baby had ever needed blood as a food source. The only time the kid would need my blood was when he reached his teenage years and decided to lose his humanity. Until then, our kind was a normal human. But I wasn't about to question anything. That was Doc's department. All I cared about was making sure Layla and the baby were healthy and safe.

She licked the blood off me, but by the time she did, the puncture holes had closed.

I bit myself again. "Drink now." My tone was deep and commanding.

She sucked on me like she was a newborn vampire.

As she drank, I smoothed a hand over her hair in gentle strokes. "Don't ever be afraid to take what you need from me, Layla." She hadn't been up until now. I imagined the baby was messing with her mind. "In my world, logic isn't in play. So don't try and figure it out."

She lifted her head, and blood smeared on her lips.

The word *beautiful* came to mind. I pulled her to me and kissed her. "We are one," I said between our tongues tangling together.

She kissed me hard before she broke away and

sighed. "It's just weird how I crave blood. Hopefully, it's helping him."

"Him? Do you think it's a boy?" I couldn't believe I was asking that question or talking about a kid like I was all in. *Am I in?*

I zeroed in on her toned stomach. As if someone had dumped cold water on me, my dick softened. I grasped her hips, stood, and set her on two feet. I needed something super strong to calm the jitters in my stomach.

She followed me, her bare feet slapping on the wood floor. "What just happened?"

I rummaged around in the fridge until I snatched a beer. I wasn't ready for a kid. I wasn't ready to change diapers, and I certainly wasn't ready to worry nonstop about who in this world would hunt my child down for their own damn benefit or to gain power.

I flipped the top off the beer bottle with ease. "Nothing." *Liar. You're scared out of your mind.*

She wiggled her hips up to me, her tits bouncing, her pussy on display. "You don't lie very well."

Downing the beer in two gulps, I raked my gaze over every inch of her. Then my mind shut down, and my cock came alive again.

25

LAYLA

I stuck my hands on my hips as my cheeks flushed. Every sculpted inch of him bristled with strength, but underneath lay terror, which threw me off-kilter. I had yet to see Sam frightened of anything.

I wasn't exactly elated over my pregnancy. I wasn't sure I could wrap my mind around the concept. "Talk to me, Sam."

A shaky laugh escaped his full lips.

I pressed my naked body up against his, my tits mashing into his hot muscled flesh.

He set the empty bottle on the granite island, his green gaze never wavering from mine. "I can't think with you naked."

It was my turn to laugh as I unzipped his jeans. "You need relief and to relax, and I know how to take away your troubles. We can analyze us later." I inched back a step, plastering on a flirty smile as I tweaked my nipples.

He bit his bottom lip and kicked off his boots then his jeans, keeping his focus on me. "Play with yourself," he ordered as he removed his boxer briefs.

I squealed as warmth radiated throughout my body, doing as he commanded.

His fangs lowered, and on a blink, silver banished the green in his eyes.

I circled my finger around my clit as my gaze took a slow, sensual hike up and down his muscled body. *How did I get so lucky?* The draw to him was more than boy meets girl, more than a simple attraction. His pull was magnetic, an enticing craving feeding an addiction I never knew I had.

He pumped his massive cock, and on the upstroke, he stopped, closing his eyes briefly as if trying to ward off an orgasm. He let out a strangled sigh as he closed the distance between us. Then he whisked me to the living room, where the fire crackled and the music of the waves trickled in through a small opening in the glass doors.

There was no place I wanted to be other than right there with a man I was beginning to fall for—or maybe I already had.

He skirted the couch and set me down behind it. "Bend over." His dominant tone sent waves of ecstasy rippling through me.

I hesitated for a beat before I planted my hands onto the buttery leather sofa.

He shaped my hip with one hand and positioned his dick at my entrance with his other.

I widened my stance as I lifted my butt in the air.

Then he slid his dick inside me and stilled. "You okay?"

I whimpered, savoring the moment, the tightness, fullness, him, us, and the way we fit together. "Perfect."

He thrust into me slowly at first, saying, "So fucking wet." Then he stopped.

I glanced over my shoulder to find him staring at something ahead of us.

My heart dipped as fear suffocated me. I followed his line of sight, thinking someone was watching us or Roman had found us. But all I saw was a tranquil scene sprinkled in beauty. The early afternoon sun glistened off the Atlantic.

Then something occurred to me: he had better vision than I did.

"Do you see something?" I asked.

"Just enjoying the view and how fucking good you feel."

"Then fuck me, vampire. Like you mean it."

He threw his head back and laughed, and the glorious sound filled me to the brim with happiness.

He started thrusting. "I don't know what happens when we leave here or over the next nine months, but I will do everything in my power to make sure you're safe and no one ever hurts you again." His tone was low, as if he was chanting a mantra to himself.

Then he became a madman. He drove in and out. The sound of flesh slapping together echoed around us while the ocean raged in the distance. The waves were high as they crashed ashore, the soothing sound trickling in through the opened doors. I closed my eyes, enjoying the music, the scenery, the myriad of feelings running through me, and Sam. I couldn't believe how my life had changed on a dime. But at that moment, I didn't want to be anywhere else except in Sam's arms.

As he continued to fuck me, groans and moans

peppered the beautiful room. Our breathing was heavy. Then... on his last thrust, he pulled out, spun me around, lifted me so my butt was on the back edge of the couch, and shoved his cock inside once again. "Wrap those gorgeous legs around me." He clutched my ass, sank his fangs into my neck, and fucked me like a man possessed.

My heart raced. My mind shut down. I'd never thought I could feel anything greater than a mind-blowing orgasm, but I was wrong. With his blood running through my veins, I could actually feel his emotions—lust, love, and happiness. Or maybe I was feeling the same. Aside from a high school crush, I'd never fallen for any guy, but Sam wasn't any guy. The alpha vampire oozed power, passion, confidence, and so much more. I had no doubt he would protect me with his life, and that was both frightening and liberating. One part of me would die if he died, and the other part of me would fight to the death if anyone dared to come between us or hurt him in any way.

I had a strong desire to please him, to make him feel like he was my world, like I would give my soul for him.

He removed his fangs and kissed me, tenderly

but sloppily. The tanginess of my blood had acti-vated a wild hunger I didn't know was possible.

He broke the kiss, his hands traveling through my hair and down my back until he grabbed my butt cheeks. I wrapped my legs around his waist as he carried me over to the fireplace. The warmth of the dying flames commingled with the cold air seeping in through the doors, but I couldn't feel anything other than the heat from his body.

I flattened my hands on his bare chest then slid down his sweat-slicked skin.

He looked confused and angry until I dropped to my knees, my gaze glued to his. When I gripped his thick shaft, his eyes glowed a luminous silver.

We stared at each other for a long second, or maybe a minute, until he said, "Suck me off, baby doll. Take all of me. Take all you need." His husky tone spurred me into action.

I licked the head of his cock as he combed his long fingers through my hair and groaned. I squeezed around his erection and teased the tip with light licks and gentle kisses.

He rolled his hips, coaxing me to do more than tease. When I sucked him into my mouth, the head touched the back of my throat, and he bucked like a wild bronco.

I gave him a blow job that I was sure he would never forget. He growled, groaned, and fucked my mouth.

Just seeing the powerful, arrogant vampire come undone was almost enough for me to orgasm. He roared his release, and I swallowed every last drop of him, salty and sweet.

Now, we were ready for that tough discussion, and I was ready to face the world with Sam Mason at my side.

26

SAM

Dawn was about to break on the horizon as I jogged along the shore. The salt air and cold temperature were just what the doctor ordered. My bare feet dug into the sand as I pounded one foot after the other, replaying every moan, every position, every feeling from the night before. Bliss. Euphoria. Epic. Orgasmic. All described the feelings that had gripped me from head to toe, not to mention my cock.

The definition of sex wasn't the act of two people fucking or having intercourse. My new definition was passion beyond the world we lived in, passion so strong and addicting that Layla Aberdeen had another thing coming if she ever thought to walk away from me. I'd never known sex to be more than getting off. Now, I knew what it was to feel what she felt. To feel us orgasm together. I was beginning to enjoy my empath side. But it was her blood running through my veins that gave me an extra kick, a high that I wasn't sure I would come down from.

I grinned at the mental image of her naked body as she slept. So peaceful. So gorgeous. Her soft snores and low moans had me itching to devour her. But she needed rest, especially with a baby, my kid, growing inside her.

I came to an abrupt halt. No matter how many times I said "my kid," it still sounded foreign. Maybe reality would set in when she started to show. I bent over and caught my breath. A sand crab scurried by. To think that one day I could be teaching my kid about ocean life.

I shook my head then filed that whole child thing away for now. Nine months was a long time, and I had other things to prepare for first. Rianne came to mind. She'd been the reason I couldn't sleep.

As I was about to continue my run, one of the phones rang. I had Layla's with me too. No way was I leaving her cell on the nightstand, where she'd left it. But it was mine that rang again.

I walked into the surf just enough to allow the waves to slide over my feet. The cold Atlantic was a welcome relief to my sweat-soaked body.

"Morning," I said to Tripp as I answered.

"You're up early, but I'm not surprised," he returned.

It was barely six a.m. "Did Rianne show up?"

"Negative, dude. One of the reasons I was calling."

"What! Where is she? Do you know?" She couldn't be here. Jordyn only knew we were in Maine, and Layla hadn't been paying enough attention to give anyone directions. Unless she was more attentive than I thought and had noticed the address then somehow left a voice mail for Rianne after she'd talked to Jordyn.

"The plane landed last night. She might've stayed in a hotel. Maybe she'll show up this morning. No problems with you, I take it?"

"None. And Rianne hasn't contacted Layla. At least not yet. When Layla checked her messages before bed, she had none. And I have her phone now, though I can't get into it." Damn passcodes.

"Interesting," he mumbled. "Sawyer is checking airport cameras."

"You don't think Rianne has teamed up with Roman, do you?"

"Where the fuck did that come from?" he asked.

I scratched the back of my head. "Not sure. But she wants me out of the picture. Since she and her asshole cousin couldn't burn me alive, maybe she's been taking measures to find someone who can."

"If that's true, then Roman is in Boston. Maybe he never left."

"He wants us to believe he's not in Boston to throw us off his tail." That was Roman's MO. He'd thrown me off before, luring me to Layla's rental house so I wouldn't be on the military base when he stormed in.

Silence reigned over the line as seagulls squawked overhead.

"As soon as Layla is up, we'll get on the road."

"Did you two talk about plans and what's to come?" he asked.

Images of us tangled and naked jumped before me. "Negative, dude. But definitely this morning. I should go in case Roman is tracking me."

"Call George. Have Stan give you a burner cell," Tripp said. "Check in when you're on the road." Then he clicked off.

I took a minute to inhale the salt air. I hated to cut our getaway short. I wanted one more night of unbridled passion.

A seagull swooped in over the calm, serene Atlantic and plucked out what looked to be seaweed. The orange-and-blue hues of dusk grew brighter. In February, the sun didn't rise until seven-ish, which was about an hour away.

I powered down my phone, took one last slow breath, then took off down the beach and toward the house, listening, scanning, and sniffing to make damn sure no one was lurking nearby. There wasn't another house in sight, but someone could be watching us from high on the cliffs behind me.

When I reached the steps leading up to the deck, I scanned the area one last time. Satisfied, I ran up, punched in the password to unlock the accordion glass doors, and slipped into the house quietly.

Once inside, I downed water then blood. The latter tasted nasty since I had Layla's. The supply from blood banks sucked ass, although my favorites were anything other than O positive. It tasted like pure metal, and the only ingredients that made it bearable to drink were the different flavors our supplier added on our request.

I tossed the bottle in the trash then made my way up to the guest bedroom. I peeked in before I entered. The bed looked like a cyclone had blown through with the blankets scattered around. But no Layla. I held in the fear that was ready to surge forward as I crossed the plush carpeted room, opening my senses. Aside from the lingering scent of sex, I didn't detect her. I didn't even hear her heartbeat. The bathroom was empty. I rushed out, ducking into every room in the house like a crazy motherfucker.

Has Roman found me? I bolted out the front door, scanned the area, sniffed, and listened. Birds chirped, singing their morning tunes, but no Layla. I rushed down the driveway to the road and looked both ways.

"Where are you, Layla?" I said out loud. Shoving one hand through my hair, I pulled out my phone. She couldn't have gone far. My Jeep was in the driveway.

I jogged back into the house and was

about to power on my phone when I spotted Layla on the beach. *How the fuck did I miss her? Man, you better get your head out of your ass.*

Pocketing my phone, I scaled the steps three at a time.

She must've heard me because she spun around, her hair billowing in the wind. "There you are." She wore her coat zipped up to her neck. Her legs and feet were bare, and she was shivering.

"You're freezing." I wrapped her in my body's warmth.

She flattened her cold hands on my heated bare chest. "And your heart is racing."

"You scared the fuck out of me."

"You weren't there when I woke up. You freaked me out too."

I kissed her forehead. "Sorry. I went for a run. I didn't think you would be awake at this hour of the morning after our steamy night."

She giggled as she slid a hand down to my growing erection. "Seems you're ready to go round... ten, is it?"

I smirked. "Something like that."

"I love it here, Sam. I don't want to leave. It's

quiet. No distractions. No problems. No one trying to kill us or kidnap us."

Man, I wished with all I had that I could give her what she desired. Unfortunately, I had to burst her bubble. "I promise one day, you'll have all this and more."

"How do you know that?" she asked in a sleepy voice.

I kissed her nose. "Because I'm your personal genie who makes wishes come true."

She laughed. "No offense, vampire, but your magical abilities can't grant wishes."

"Well, if you rub my belly, the genie will in fact grant you a wish."

She snorted before dropping into a fit of giggles. "You mean your dick?" She rolled her eyes, which sparkled in the dawn's early light.

I lifted a shoulder. "That's the only genie you'll ever need."

She laughed so hard she cried, and it was fan-fucking-tastic to see her so happy, even if just for a brief moment. "Want a blow job right here on the beach?"

I smirked. "Fuck. Do you have to ask me?"

She circled her arms around my waist then rubbed my ass before she dragged her hands over the sides of my thighs. When she did, her gaze shot to mine as her hands felt along the pockets of my swim trunks. "Do you have my phone?" Her face twisted. "Because I can't find it, by the way."

Busted. "About that."

I swore steam came out of her nose. "Sam Mason, what are you doing with my phone?" She stuck her hands on her hips, pursing her lips and narrowing her eyes.

"You're beautiful even when you're angry."

"Shut up and answer me!" she shouted, clenching her fist.

I raised my hands, backing away. "Chill. You're getting really worked up for nothing. I can explain."

"My aunt and uncle stole my phone. I never expected you to do something like this. Have you ever heard of trust, vampire?"

To lie or not to lie.

"I'm waiting," she said. "And if you don't answer me in one second, I'm going to kick you in the balls and punch you in the nose."

Nose I could handle. Balls not so much. "When you calm down, I'll be more than happy to explain." I stormed up to the house, feeling more irritated with myself than with her.

She ran at my heels. "I am not going to calm down. I hate when people take things that don't belong to them."

I set her cell on the island then stuck my head in the fridge. I needed another round of blood. I almost snagged a beer instead. The quiet morning was turning into an explosive one, and not in the way I would have liked.

She checked her phone. She didn't have any messages. If she did, her screen would have shown it. Her nostrils flared. "Are you going to talk or overdose on blood?"

I growled, trying to control my rising anger at myself. I understood why she was furious. I understood that trust was the thread that held relationships together. And I wasn't one to trust easily.

She slapped a hand on the island. When she did, the lamp in the living room crashed to the floor.

She jumped a mile as she eyed the broken pieces of ceramic.

My eyebrows disappeared into my hairline.

She regarded me with equal parts fury and confusion. "Are you using your elemental powers?"

"Sunshine, if I was using them, this house would be a pile of rubble."

She stomped her foot. "'Sunshine'? Don't call me that."

I strode over to her and stuck my nose in her face. "Or what, sunshine?"

"Then how did that lamp fall?" she asked, taking her anger down a notch.

"No clue, but maybe you're experiencing some of my powers, given that you have a gallon of my blood in your system. And that's not the issue right now, is it?"

"No. You stealing my phone is." She gripped my balls. "Tell me why you took it." She bared her teeth.

I grinned like the ass that I was. "Or what? You can't hurt me."

"I can tear your nuts off."

I chuckled. "Then you would never experience last night again, now, would you?" She'd raved about the feelings from our orgasm together.

She poked a finger into my chest with her free hand. "Let's get something straight. If you want us to coexist, you can't be stealing my things or leaving me out of shit. You know something, and you're not telling me. And I would bet my right tit that whatever you're not saying relates to Rianne. You're trying to protect me. I get it. So talk." She let go of my balls.

I frowned.

She snorted, sticking her hands on her hips.

I sized her up. "Are you naked under that coat?"

She huffed. "Sam, this is your last chance before I bring down the house. I'm sure Webb and Jo won't like that."

I didn't exactly know how strong she could be with the amount of my blood in her system, and I didn't want to test her ability. Jo and Webb had renovated the home recently, and my sister would stake me if we ruined her perfect hideaway.

I tugged her over to the couch. "You'll need to sit down for this one."

She didn't argue. She crossed one leg over the other and began to move her foot back and forth.

I created some distance between us and sank into the chair across from her. "I'm sorry I took your phone. I should've come clean last night. But I wanted us to relax for one night at least."

Her foot stopped moving. "Thank you for the apology."

I leaned my elbows on my knees. "Before I fill

you in on what's going on, I need to know where your head is at with us."

"Are we about to talk feelings and I love yous?"

"Just answer the question." Irritation was scraping along my nerves. "Where's your head at, Layla? Baby, life, enemies, future... anything. We need to leave here today with a clear plan. Are we in this together or not?" Frankly, whether we were or not, I wouldn't let her out of my sight. But it would be easier if we sang from the same sheet of music.

Puffing out her cheeks, she stared at the tranquil Atlantic as the sun began to crest the horizon. On a long intake of breath, she pinned me with hard blue eyes. "I'm afraid to say anything right now. The minute I do, it's real, Sam, and I'm scared."

"What are you afraid of?"

"You. Me. Us," she said with surety. "How does a human fall for a vampire? I mean, I know how. But it's sad to think I will grow old and you won't and neither will our child."

She had a point. If I lost her and didn't die in battle, I would walk the planet as one depressed, hurt, and pissed-off vampire with so much rage I would probably wipe out humans with just one look.

"You're not frightened?" she asked. "We're having a baby, Sam. That doesn't scare you?"

"Fuck yeah. I'm flipping out. I don't know the first thing about being a dad. I'm not sure I believe it yet, either."

"Me too," she whispered.

I crossed the room and sat on the coffee table in front of her. "Look, the bigger issue right now is Roman and anyone who will want to profit off a Mason. Jo and I were used as lab rats. My kid isn't going through that. I'm a Mason, and I come with baggage you're not ready for. Hell, I'm not ready, either. It's bad enough I'm always looking over my shoulder. And then we have Abbey. Now our kid too. Don't even get me started on your family."

Her shoulders slumped.

I took her hands in mind. "Baby doll, I will give my last breath to protect you. I would do that even if there wasn't a baby in the picture. But now, we need to be more vigilant about our surroundings, who we talk to, who we tell about the pregnancy. Rianne wants me dead."

"She doesn't feel you're good for me," Layla

said. "She thinks falling in love with a vampire is suicide."

I reared back. "So you're in love with me?"

She pulled away and captured a fingernail in between her teeth. "I don't know. Are you?"

"I've never been in love. But if feeling like I can't breathe when you're not with me is love, then I guess I am."

Her mouth hung open as she held her heart. "Whoa!"

I was suddenly light-headed. The silence between us became deafening. *Did I just tell her I loved her?*

"Um..." she said.

I swallowed a lump in my throat that felt more like a big fat fur ball. "Baby doll."

She scooted to the edge of the cushion and mashed her fingers against my lips and said, "Shhh." Then she kissed me softly.

"What are you doing to me?" I whispered.

She giggled. "I could ask you the same thing."

I eased away. I'd been the one pushing her to talk, and suddenly, I didn't want to. I gulped in a boatload of air and pressed on. "Layla, the next nine months will be a test of our relationship. We need to settle some things, like where you want to live." *Please stay with me.* I would never force her, but she couldn't be out on her own without protection.

She shivered. "I was thinking. I could ask Harley if I could crash with her until I can figure things out."

I knitted my brows. "Harley? Fuck no. I was thinking you could stay with me."

"Like a married couple?" She bit her bottom lip. "I don't think we're ready for that."

I grinned. "Why? You don't want to fuck me every night?"

She snorted. "We wouldn't come up for air. Sam, I want to take us slow." Then the light snuffed out of her eyes, and she gave me a sad smile. "Everything is happening too fast." Her gaze drifted out the accordion glass doors. "I wish my mom and dad were here." Tears clouded her eyes. "I'm out here on an island. I feel like I can't trust anyone anymore."

I curled her hair around her ear as regret knotted my stomach. "Again, I'm so sorry about your phone. I am an ass. A big one."

27

LAYLA

I stared at Sam's lips, feeling the remorse coursing through him. Still, I couldn't have a relationship with him if he continued to do things behind my back.

"You're a gargantuan ass," I said. "You still haven't told me why you took my phone."

He pushed to his feet and went into the kitchen.

I followed like an angry eager beaver. He was not getting out of this. I didn't care if he'd just told me in a roundabout way that he loved me, which I would process later. For the time being, if we were in it together, it was the perfect time to clear out our demons—or at least some of them.

He removed a knife from the butcher block beside the six-burner stove.

I propped a hip against the farmhouse sink. "What are you doing with that?"

The blade glinted in the morning light spraying in from the windows.

"You look pale." He had a funky look on his face that I couldn't make out.

"I'll let you know when I need blood. Now talk."

"Fine." He set the knife down and crossed his arms over his chest. "Rianne was on a plane to Boston last night."

I swayed. "For real?" My throat closed up. After the major blowup between us, I was torn about how to knock some sense into her. Her words were sewn into my brain.

I'm doing this for you. Humans can't fall in love with vamps. I'm my own person, Layla. And we don't belong with vampires. I know what I'm doing. I'm ridding the world of one of the most powerful vampires. Then when I'm done, his sister is next.

I couldn't bring myself to tell Sam that last line. I was hoping I didn't have to. But if Rianne was in Boston, she was there either to finish the job or to go after Jo. Or maybe she'd come to her senses. "Is Noah with her? Where is she?" I pushed off the sink and checked my phone, which was on the island, knowing Rianne hadn't called.

Sam came over to me. "We don't know. And Noah isn't with her, as far as we can tell. Tripp thought she would show up at the gate on base. But she hasn't. She might've gotten in late and stayed at a hotel. We're thinking she might show up today."

His dread hit me upside my face. I sucked in air. He'd warned me that, in his world, logic wasn't in play and not to try and make sense of it. But to experience his emotions as though they were my own was unnatural. Sure, humans could sense others' emotions, and body language was always a good indicator. But to actually feel what he felt in the pit of my stomach was giving me a dizzying headache.

"To finish the job," I mumbled. *Please let her show up and grovel for forgiveness.* I laughed out loud. Rianne would never beg.

He peered down through his long lashes. "Or she's teamed up with Roman?"

Air whooshed out of me as I shook my head like a wet dog after a bath. "She wouldn't stoop that low." I was beginning to believe someone had given her a drug that turned off her humanity. "I don't understand. When we first arrived at my uncle's ranch, she was defiant about staying there." I dipped into my memory bank. I didn't remember seeing Rianne much while I was sick, but I'd slept most of the time. Still, I would've seen a change in her, especially that morning we chatted in the kitchen. "She hates Roman. Remember he strapped her with C-4. One of the reasons my uncles are hunting again is because of him. Ray is salivating for revenge."

He tipped up my chin. "Look at me. You make valid points, and I agree. But maybe she'd been compelled."

"No," I said sharply. "Not at all. She was well aware of what she was doing." That much, I was certain of. Granted, Noah might have had something to do with pushing her over the edge, but Rianne hadn't been compelled in Montana. "We can't forget your enemies want you alive for your blood and DNA. Roman even said you're worth millions, which means if Rianne has teamed up with him, it's to kidnap you. He'll use her to do his bidding. He still wants Abbey, right?"

A muscle ticked in his jaw. "I know you want

to talk some sense into Rianne. I would do the same in your shoes, but until we know her motives, you can't go near her. For all we know, she'll kidnap you to lure me in."

"Great," I said. "We have Roman to deal with and now my sister and cousin." I anchored my hand to the granite top as a wave of dizziness hit me.

Sam lifted me onto the island. For some reason, the act reminded me of my dad having me sit on the kitchen counter as a little girl to watch him make banana pancakes.

Sam grabbed the knife. "You need to have a small amount of blood. Seriously, your eyes are dull." He slit his wrist and offered it to me.

I licked my damn lips as though I was about to sink my teeth into the juiciest steak. "This is so weird. I don't think I'll ever get used to this."

"Drink before it closes."

I suctioned my lips to his wrist. The blood exploded on my tongue like Pop Rocks candy.

Sam smoothed a hand over my hair before kissing my head. "Take all you need, baby doll." Then his lips were on my ear. "I do love you, Layla."

I froze.

He petted me gently. "I am so in love with you," he whispered in my ear.

Flutters and fireworks went off inside my stomach as goose bumps blanketed me. I sucked one last time then sat up straighter.

He blew out a breath, and I had to hold my stomach. Those butterflies were having a dance party.

He wiggled his way between my legs, appearing as though the weight of the world had fallen off his shoulders. "You're so freaking beautiful." He swiped the pad of his thumb over my lips.

I grasped his wrist then sucked the remnants of blood off his thumb.

He trailed his fingers along my cheek, studying me as though snapping photos for an album.

I was suddenly dizzy for an entirely different reason, trying to find the words to respond or say anything at all. I wasn't ready to answer in kind. I *was* falling for him, but I needed more time to be sure. Once I said those three little words, my life would change once again, and things were already going at warp speed.

"We should get on the road," he said as though someone had thrown a bucket of ice on him.

"Hey, wait." I didn't know if he wanted me to say it back, but we needed closure on the topic for the time being.

As if he knew the war raging inside me, he said, "I know that when you're ready, you'll tell me your true feelings. No matter what they are, it won't change how I feel about you."

I gave him a huge smile that contrasted with the crease I felt in my forehead. "How do you go from caveman to sweet guy?"

He laughed. "Which do you like better?"

I tapped my finger on my lips. "Mm. I think... kind of both."

He laughed harder.

I gripped the waist of his swim trunks and leaned in. "Caveman doesn't mean you can order me around, though."

He lost his smile. "Then don't throw yourself in front of flamethrowers or try to protect me." He rested a hand on my stomach. "Protect him. Protect you."

"Him, huh?" I asked. "You think it's a boy?"

"No idea. But I want a boy," he said like a kid about to stomp his foot, trying to get his way.

I giggled. "It's not up to you. That magic sperm of yours has already decided."

He slid his hands up my thighs. "Seriously, Layla." His green eyes narrowed. "I know you're a fighter. That's what I love about you. But the stakes are now higher."

I pressed my forehead to his. "I promise, Sam. I will put myself and our baby first." *Our baby. Whoa! That came out too easily.*

As Sam's warm breath breezed over me, as my pulse quickened and my heart raced, something my uncle Jack said punched me in the gut. *"It's time to do something with your life."* Of course, he hadn't meant with vampires.

Still, Sam loved me. He had a soul, and he felt emotions just like humans. And we wanted the same thing—family and to rid the world of evil whether human or vampire. He hadn't come out and said that exactly, but he didn't have to.

He cupped the back of my neck and peppered kisses over my face. "Even over your sisters?" The skepticism in his tone wasn't a surprise.

"As much as you love your sister, I love both of mine. That will never change. But the baby's safety comes first."

He helped me off the counter. "That's all I

needed to hear." Then he tugged me to him, and my tits mashed into his chest.

"Ow." If I didn't believe I was pregnant before, it was beginning to become evident now.

He froze. "I'm sorry. Did I hurt you?"

"My breasts are a little sore."

He inched back and gently cupped them, grinning like a teenage boy touching a woman's breasts for the first time. "One thing I can promise you. I'll handle these babies with care."

I snorted. "You're definitely a tit man."

He massaged my breasts. "I'm a Layla man."

We both laughed, and wow—it felt freeing to laugh together.

"Sam, one last thing."

He gave me a wolfish grin and traded my tits for my hair. "You're about to rip my shorts off?"

"Sex would be great. But it's not that."

He pouted.

I rolled my eyes. "I'm going to need Dr. Vieira and Jo to guide me through this pregnancy. I can't do it alone. So I would like to stay in the women's barracks." As much as I wanted to curl up next to him every night, I needed a little more time by myself. I'd never had a chance to get to know who I was. My sisters or my parents had always been around, and given the new trajectory my life was on, it would be good to sort out my feelings, to understand myself. Because I didn't anymore.

28

SAM

Webb and Tripp were lounging in Webb's office when I sauntered in later that day. The car ride back from Maine had been fraught with tension—sexual and otherwise. I'd told a woman I loved her. The only two people I'd ever said that to were Jo and my old man. Declaring it to a woman I'd only met three weeks before had my stomach in knots.

I'd been ready to puke several times and had almost pulled off the highway to do just that. But it wasn't because I was in love with her. It was the fear of losing her. I was itching to find Rianne and Roman. I wanted to start building a life where I didn't have to look over my shoulder every minute, especially with a kid on the way.

Tripp and Webb stared at me as though I had five heads and four hands. I probably did look like I needed to spend time with a punching bag.

"What happened to you?" Webb asked from his spot on the couch, wearing a grin as if he could read my mind. Maybe he could since he occasionally drank Jo's blood.

"How was Maine?" Tripp, who was an empath like me, albeit a weaker one, also had a smile that said he knew my secret.

Secrets were hard to keep around vampires, particularly ones who had the ability to smell or read one's feelings.

I dropped into a chair beside Tripp and focused on the picture of an aircraft carrier hanging on the wall behind Webb. "Peachy. Did we find Rianne? Roman? Where's my father? How's Ben? Shifters?" Anything to take my mind off Layla. I wasn't upset that she hadn't expressed her true feelings, though I knew she was holding back. But that nagging voice in my head was telling me she was so scared she might run. She might not face her true feelings, and that would break me into a million body parts.

Webb chuckled. "You've only been gone a day, dude. Chill."

Tripp crossed one leg over the other. His sandy-blond hair was pulled into a low ponytail, his jaw clean-shaven, and his bronze eyes bright, looking as though he had good news. "Sawyer did some digging on Camden Industries. They specialize in developing weapons for the Department of Defense. That's on the surface. He's going deeper, though."

My mind scrambled. "Interesting. Rumor is that Jack has a new weapon. Lester Worthington had a case in the back seat of his SUV with 'Camden Industries' on it. Lester wasn't at the ranch to buy a horse."

"We'll see what else Sawyer finds," Tripp said. "As for Rianne... we don't have any leads on her or Roman. I'm sure Roman is covering his tracks."

Webb typed something on the iPad in his lap. "Roman could've kidnapped Rianne."

That was certainly possible. "Or Rianne teamed up with him."

"That's a stretch," Webb said. "The Aberdeens have a vendetta against him."

I shrugged. "So what? Rianne thought I was the cat's meow for saving her life but look how that turned out." I rested my right ankle on my left knee. "Or she could be lurking nearby and watching until she can get Layla alone." The latter seemed more plausible to me.

Webb clasped his hands together. "Rianne is a concern, but we can handle her. Roman, on the other hand, is our priority. In the meantime, we've beefed up patrol around and outside the perimeter of the base. We have extra guards on both gates leading into the base. Sam, I need you to escort Wyman up to the infirmary. I just got word that he's not feeling well. And I'm short a guard due to a family issue."

I hadn't thought of Wyman in a while. "Are we going to release him?" We could keep him locked up, but I didn't see the point. "We can always have a scout trail him."

"Alia's father, Victor, has agreed to hire him so we can watch him. Victor has a need for a computer geek, and Wyman accepted the offer."

The dude was smart in some ways but not so much in others. Still, he would fit in with us if he was serious about the job. Little did Wyman know that Victor Costner was one vampire not to piss off. The man could wield a sword like a Viking fighting off five opponents at once.

"You mean he jumped at the chance. Why?" I asked.

"He said something about watching over Layla," Tripp said.

I didn't know what to make of that, but I would take it if Wyman didn't have any notions of running to his former employer, the CIA.

Tripp studied me with a curious glint in his eyes. "Speaking of Layla, how did it go? I take it you brought her up to speed."

"Yep. At the moment, she's with Jo, but she wants to stay in the women's barracks. Will that be a problem?" I didn't think it would be, but I had to clear it with Webb.

Web scratched his chin. "We have a team of women recruits coming in for some training. What's wrong with your place?"

"She doesn't want to stay with me," I mumbled. "I'll ask Harley."

"Problems already?" Tripp said with a smirk.

I growled at him. "Nothing I can't handle."

Webb pushed to his feet. "Harley would be good for the short term. The chief of Viking II accepted orders to San Diego, and he and his family will be moving in two weeks. Layla can move into his house when it's ready."

I reared back. "For real?"

Webb crossed the room to his desk. "We're family, Sam, and I don't just mean because I'm married to Jo. You know we take care of our own." He picked up a sticky note and handed it to me. "Check in with base housing. They'll let you know the date it will be ready."

I stood and gave him a quick bro hug. "Thanks, man."

"Do I see a tear in your eye, dude?" Tripp asked.

I flipped him off despite the fact he was my superior officer.

Ignoring me, he continued, "You told her you loved her, didn't you?"

"Damn empath," I muttered.

Webb flinched as his usual blank mask fell, leaving pure astonishment in its place. "You did?"

I threw my hands in the air. "Okay, I did. Now, can I go?" They had good intentions, but my nerves were still frayed, and I wasn't in the mood to discuss my feelings.

"Did she say it back?" Tripp asked.

I sneered. "You sound like a nosy high school girl."

"Wait," Webb said. "She didn't, did she?"

I started for the door. "I'm out of here."

"She will," Tripp said, raising his voice. "She's just scared."

"Are you psychic now?" I teased.

Footsteps pounded outside the office before my father came in. He wore blue jeans, a Navy SEAL T-shirt, flak boots, and appeared to be well rested. "Good, all of you are here." He gave me a quick hug then blew past me to the chair I'd been in. "I need everyone's attention."

That edginess rattling my cage multiplied. From the sounds of his rushed tone, he didn't have good news.

Webb returned to the couch. I sat on its arm, facing my father.

"Son, where's Layla?" Dad set his phone on the coffee table.

"She's at Jo's house. Why? Does this have something to do with her?"

He held up his hand. "I want you to hear this." He tapped on his phone.

"Steven, Jack Aberdeen." His irritating gruff voice blared in the room.

Tripp and Webb snapped to attention.

"We should have that talk now." Jack's voice was cold as ice. "I suggest we meet halfway and on neutral ground. You pick the place. As far as when, call me. Oh, and make sure Layla is with you." Then the voice mail ended.

Webb typed on his iPad.

"She's not going anywhere near that asshole," I rushed out.

"Easy, son," my father said. "We're not jumping because he said so."

"The halfway point is in Wisconsin, not far from Chicago," Webb informed us.

I looked at the iPad. "Does anyone get the feeling that we're being pushed toward Chicago? Jordyn is there. Jack Jr. and his wife live there. Does anyone find that to be a coincidence?" My radar was pinging left and right. It would devastate Layla if Jordyn sided with Jack.

Tripp held his chin between his fingers. "Camden Industries headquarters is in Chicago."

"No shit? Something is up. With our luck, Roman will be there," I said.

Webb dug his elbows into his thighs. "If we meet Jack, it has to be in an unpopulated area. Chicago or any big city is off-limits."

My mind scrambled to sift through what Jack could possibly be up to. He wanted Layla there, which told me he would try and whisk her away from me. "Any idea why now? I'm guessing he wants to test out his new weapon."

My father relaxed. "Or it has something to do with your visit to the ranch."

My focus was still glued on Layla. Jack didn't want anything to do with her if she sided with vampires, so why include her?

"This is a bad idea," Tripp added. "Fucking bad idea."

My old man had a deep crease between his green eyes.

I traded the arm of the couch for a cushion beside Webb. "What's going on, Pops? You're thinking really hard."

He swiped a hand over his black hair. "There's something all of you should know." He groaned out a heavy sigh. "I'm still trying to understand it." He glanced anywhere but at us for a few seconds. "When I was under, I saw my father."

Tripp, Webb, and I exchanged a frightened look. Anytime my grandfather had graced Jo's dreams, it was never good. The air in the office thickened with a fear that we had buried five years ago.

Dad pressed his hands together in a prayerlike

position against his mouth. "A war is coming. One that could wipe out our existence."

"You mean erase vampires, humanity, and all supernaturals?" Webb asked.

Dad straightened. "I don't know. The last thing he told me before I woke up was that I couldn't die. I had to help my son."

I sucked in a breath. "Me? Are you saying I have something to do with a war breaking out?"

Dad lifted a shoulder. "I don't know, Sam. But it sounds to me like you'll be in the thick of it."

"Aren't we always?" I asked. "We're Navy SEALs. We fight. We protect. I don't see the big deal here." Unless I was the one to start a war. Maybe I would. With the exception of Jordyn and Layla, the Aberdeens were hanging on by a thread with me. It wasn't *if* I did something to stop them or end their hunting business—it was *when*. Same went for Roman. If we faced off, and we would, no one would kill him but me.

Tripp scratched his neck. "Sir, you said 'could wipe out'—'could' being the key word. It leads me to believe there's a way to stop whatever is coming."

Dad nodded. "I got that feeling from my father. I just wish I could fall into a deep enough sleep to see if I could talk to him. But I think I would have to come close to death again to have that happen."

"You have a point, Steven," Webb said. "Remember when Jo talked to your father in one of her dreams? She was close to death as well." Webb slid to the edge of the couch, clearly ready to stand. "Let's deal with Jack Aberdeen first. We need to keep the peace, as hard as that might be. And he may surprise us and want to help. After all, didn't Jordyn and Layla say the sole reason for Jack reviving the hunting business was because of Roman? That leads me to believe he doesn't want a war."

I eyed Webb. "His son, Noah, does."

"Jack will deal with his son," my father said with surety.

Instantly, I thought of my kid. "I'll do whatever it takes to broker peace. Layla's about to have my child, and I'll be damned if I'll have anything in the way of me seeing him grow up."

All heads swiveled my way with mouths ajar.

"What?" I asked them.

Tripp touched his chest with the tips of his fingers. "I'll speak for myself, but it sounds freaky to hear you say *my kid*. Just saying."

"Also," Webb said. "It's the conviction in your voice. You've always been a straight shooter and take no prisoners, Sam, but that's been your code because you were angry with the world. Now, you have a purpose. You're fighting for someone."

I could feel my forehead creasing. "I've always fought for someone. My sister. I also fight to protect humanity."

"Sure, son," Dad chimed in. "But now, you have a baby on the way, and I can tell you that's a different love altogether. Not to mention the love you have for Layla. I'm not discounting how you feel about Jo, but your own family brings on much deeper emotions. And if you're not careful about how you approach things, you could get yourself killed."

I gritted my teeth. "How did this go from Jack Aberdeen and war to me?"

"Sam, you have a kid on the way," Webb said.

"That doesn't mean I'll stop fighting. It means I'll be more vigilant in protecting those I love."

The room fell silent.

I wasn't about to tiptoe into battle. I would do what I did best—be the soldier and fighter I was trained to be.

29

LAYLA

Sam had dropped me off at Jo's house on base at her request, and I followed her to her office. Apparently, she wanted to chat. I imagined she wanted to pick my brain and see where I stood when it came to her brother or the pregnancy or both.

I didn't mind. I needed all the friends I could get. Plus, she was studying hematology and genealogy, so what better person to talk to? I hoped she could help me find a way to learn more about my mom and her ancestors.

Jo rushed in. "Excuse the mess. I've got finals coming up."

I giggled. "I think you need more books," I teased. "It's a mini library in here."

Three large bookcases were packed, an oblong table had several scattered on it, and her desk had a stack of medical textbooks about five books high. Beneath the chaos was a well-decorated room with soft-blue walls, sheer gray curtains covering one window, and a portrait of Webb, Abbey, and her hanging on the wall behind two tan fabric chairs.

"That's what Webb tells me all the time. But we have a great library on base and a more extensive one at vampire headquarters in Boston." She plucked a lap blanket off one chair. "You can sit here."

I would rather have curled up on the window seat, which seemed like a cozy place to drink a glass of wine and read a good book. Although I would rather have sipped bourbon.

Jo laughed. "You're a hard-core woman if you like bourbon."

I tore my gaze away from the motes dancing through the rays of sunlight spilling through the sheer curtains and angled my head at her.

"Sorry. I try hard to stay out of people's heads. But sometimes, it just happens."

I'd forgotten she could read minds. "No worries," I lied. I made a mental note to make sure I remembered her abilities. "Jordyn told me about the library in Boston." Since we were on the topic, it wouldn't hurt to ask for her help. "I don't know if Sam told you, but there are vampires on my mother's side. Do you think I could find anything in any of the libraries about her family? I understand you keep good records on most vampires." I sank into one of the chairs.

"It's possible. What's her last name? Not that I know every vampire. But I've been doing research on my own mom and her genealogy." She wiped her hands on her black leggings, which she wore with a peach top that hung to mid-thigh. Her feet were bare and her toenails painted pink just like her well-manicured nails.

"Drake. But she told us she didn't have any siblings and that her parents had died when she was young."

She snagged a lone book off the floor and placed it on the table.

I did a double take. "*The Science Behind Vampires*," I mumbled. "What? Someone actually wrote a book about your kind?"

She laughed. "You remind me of me when I

first found this book." She handed it to me. "I came across it in a funeral home, of all places."

I choked. "That's spooky."

She sat in the matching chair next to me then switched on the torch lamp between us. "It was quite freaky. I was human when I found it, but I had been experiencing some physical changes and had no clue what was happening to me. You have much to learn, Layla."

I opened the book. "No kidding. I have so many questions, it isn't even funny." I scanned the table of contents. My eyes widened on chapter nine, "Everything You Ever Wanted to Know About Vampire Sex but Were Afraid to Ask." I snorted.

"That's a good one." She giggled.

My cheeks flamed like I was standing over a fire. "Can I borrow this? It's not for the chapter on sex," I was quick to add. "The topics look interesting." I flipped open one of the pages she had bookmarked with a sticky note. "Wow! Genetically engineering a vampire. Have your adversaries gotten their hands on this book? I mean, isn't this the process that manufactures humans into vampires?"

"The chapter doesn't detail how. And it's

quite difficult to find the right... recipe, if you will. My uncle was a great geneticist, but he wasn't successful, although he came close before his death. As a result, his last batch of testing resulted in half-breeds like Ben."

"Fascinating," I muttered.

"And scary. This is the very reason Sam and I have been hunted and why Roman wants Abbey. It's also why your baby might be on the most-wanted list of power-hungry assholes who want to build armies and become rich in the process."

My pulse stuttered as fear needled across my arms. I'd heard Sam when he said something similar, but hearing Jo articulate it with more anger seemed to turn on my panic radar. Then again, ever since Sam told me he loved me, I hadn't been thinking of much else.

"I feel your anxiety," Jo said. "This is one of the reasons I wanted time alone with you. I like you, Layla. I think you'll be good for my brother. But I need you to hear me."

Closing the book, I gave her my full attention as my stomach sank like a ship in rough seas.

She crossed one leg over the other and impaled me with a stern look that shackled me to my chair. "You will be the number one target from here on out if anyone outside our circle finds out you're pregnant with a Mason baby. You cannot think for one second that you can handle things on your own or live by yourself. You must have a guard around you at all times. I don't know if Sam told you that or what you two decided on, but he's not the only one you're dealing with now. I will go to the ends of the Earth to make sure nothing happens to you and the baby. But I need you to tell me you understand. I need you to be 100 percent sure this is what you want."

Jo Mason was beautiful and well put together, inside and out. Manicured nails. Perfect makeup. Thick, shiny black hair with streaks of purple. Those casual clothes I was sure she'd bought at a high-end clothing store. Silver eyes that shone like diamonds—and when they transformed to vampire mode, the violet color reminded me of a rare amethyst. Inside, she was intelligent with a heart of gold, from what I'd seen so far in how she handled Abbey and Sam. But the curtness in her tone, her sharp glare, and her pursed lips told me she was more lethal than Sam could ever be.

Unease sliced across my skin as I raised my chin. "With all due respect, because I have a ton of it for you, I will not be held prisoner because

I'm pregnant with Sam's baby. I understand the danger. I understand that my child could be hunted. I will do everything I can to make sure he or she is safe. Is this what I want? Honestly, I'm not ready for a baby. But I've never run from anything. Well, maybe your brother." Nervous laughter rumbled free.

She smiled warmly. "You're not running from *him* but from your own *feelings* for him. He loves you."

A flush rushed to my cheeks. "He told me this morning."

She sucked in air. "Oh, my word." She held a hand to her heart. "I mean, *I* knew it, and not because I've been in his head. As twins, we have this connection, and it's stronger now that we're vampires. But to know he's said it to you, that it came out of his mouth, is epic. And how do you feel?"

"Frankly, things are moving at the speed of light. I haven't had time to process. But to be honest, he's everything I want in a man. He's caring. He knows what he wants and isn't afraid to go after it. He's hot. Powerful. Determined. Can be an ass, but so can I. And he's a hell of a protector when it comes to those he loves. The latter quality reminds me of my dad."

She lit up as though she'd won a prize. "Webb reminds me of my dad in some ways too."

I lowered my gaze to the book. "I need you, Jo. I need Dr. Vieira too. I'm swimming against the current here. I would like to think I know what I'm doing, but I don't. A natural-born vampire baby? I'm scared to death."

She moved quickly, and when I blinked, she was kneeling before me. Her silver eyes flashed to violet and brimmed with tears. "You're not alone. I'm in this with you. I will help you every step of the way." She clutched my knees. "You have the best doctor in the world at your disposal."

I grabbed her hands and let out a huge breath. "Thank you. It's great to know I can count on you. But Dr. Vieira hasn't dealt with a pregnancy where the fetus requires blood as a food source."

She pushed to her feet. "True, but he's working hard to find out why."

"You don't think I'll give birth to a baby vampire with fangs, do you?" The moment I said that, it sounded stupid. "Maybe that's the reason why the fetus needs blood."

She stared at me as though I was right.

"Oh my God. I'm right, aren't I?"

She tilted her head slightly. "We speculate but

aren't sure. No one during our existence has had a vampire baby."

The air jetted from my lungs "I think I'm about to be sick." I held my stomach, needing to escape, puke, run, hide—or all of the above.

Then something Dr. Vieira said hit me like a hard wind on a stormy day. *"In our world, Layla, you'll learn that some things don't have an explanation, especially when magic is involved. And you'll hear me say this many times: nothing is normal when it comes to Sam or Jo."*

I stood on shaky legs as nausea sloshed in my stomach. "I need to use the bathroom."

She pointed to her left, seemingly alarmed that she'd told me the things she had. "Down the hall. When you're done, meet me in the kitchen. I'll fix us some tea."

I rushed out as acid shot into my throat.

30

LAYLA

I barely made it into the spacious bathroom and over to the toilet before I puked. Holy hell. I was pregnant with a vampire—not just a natural-born vampire, but a true vampire, who would be born with fangs, who would have powers, and who would require blood in a bottle rather than formula or breast milk.

I hung my head in the toilet, waiting for another round of puke to burst free. I couldn't have the baby. A waterfall of tears poured out as a cluster of emotions flooded my senses, making it hard to breathe. I waited a beat before I sat on my haunches then pulled out my phone to call Jordyn.

She answered on the first ring. "Hey, sis. I was just about to call you."

I bawled my eyes out. "I can't do this, Jordyn. I can't have this baby. Things are happening way too fast. And Rianne is supposedly in Boston. Not sure why. The SEAL team is looking for her, but they're not having any luck. Sam told me he loved me. I couldn't say it back. Hell, I'm losing it."

"Layla." The pity in her voice was more heartbreaking than anything. "I need you to breathe. Breathe."

I shuddered and sniffled, crawling beside the toilet to rest my back against the peach-colored wall. "Sam loves me. I don't know what to do with that. I've killed his kind, yet he loves me, and now, my baby will be born with fangs." I cried harder. "I'm a fucking mess."

"Stop freaking out," she said softly. "Stop denying your feelings for him because you think it's wrong to love a vampire. I understand, though. We were taught to hate them. But it's time to follow your heart. And how do you know the baby will have fangs?"

"Jo told me. Dr. Vieira thinks that's the reason I'm drinking Sam's blood."

"Sounds to me like Dr. Vieira doesn't know

that for sure. I think your pregnancy hormones are kicking in and making you emotional. Look, I'm flying out tonight."

"I thought you were staying for another day," I said, sniffling.

"Conrad told me about Rianne, so I'm leaving early."

"Did you accept the job, by the way?"

"We'll talk in person." She sounded as though something had happened.

I flicked away a tear. "Jordyn, what's wrong?"

"Have you talked to Aunt Tab?" she asked.

My aunt was the farthest thing from my mind. "I have no reason to."

"She's worried about you. Call her."

"You didn't mention the pregnancy, did you?" My pity party vanished as a foreboding feeling clutched at my throat.

"Of course not," Jordyn said, "but Uncle Jack has reached out to Steven Mason. He finally wants to meet with him. I think he wants Steven's help."

I coughed then swallowed. "Why?" Jack was too proud to ask anyone for help.

"She couldn't talk. Call her, Layla. I'll see you tonight." Then she hung up.

Crap. We barely talked about Rianne.

A chill scraped down my spine as I flushed the toilet. Maybe Aunt Tab knew what Rianne was up to. I went over to the sink, which had a collection of soaps, lotions, and a basket of washcloths beside it. I turned on the faucet and let it run while I checked myself in the mirror.

My blue eyes were dull with faint black circles underneath them. My freckled nose was red. My lips were chapped, but not as badly as they had been the day before. My auburn hair didn't have the normal shine to it, and I had a pimple on my nose. Overall, I looked like death.

I splashed warm water on my face several times and checked myself again. I laughed through tears. No amount of water would change my ghostly appearance. Shuddering, I combed my fingers through my hair, attempting to fluff it up, but it was no use.

I gave myself a stern look in the mirror. "You're strong, girl." I rolled my shoulders back. "You can handle anything." I repeated those two lines as I turned and leaned against the sink.

A bathtub big enough for two was tucked in the far corner, a skylight above it. Suddenly, my mind took a trip back to the night when Sam had been the star of my dream. The memory quickly vanished when the doorbell rang.

I collected my phone, which I'd set on the counter, and tapped on Aunt Tab's number. The line rang three times before her panicked voice came through. "Layla, how are you? I've been going crazy not knowing if you were okay. Jack told me what Rianne and Noah did. I'm shocked beyond words."

I believed her since her tone pitched and rolled. "I'm okay. Confused as heck about Rianne. I don't think she and I will be working out our differences. Do you know why she flew to Boston?"

"She's in Boston? Oh, Jack and I have been looking for her and Noah. They seemed to have disappeared. Is Noah with her?"

"Not as far as I know," I replied. "What's going on? I hear Uncle Jack wants to meet with Steven Mason."

"It's true. He wants Steven's help to find Noah. After Jack yelled at Noah and Rianne for what they'd done to you, they disappeared. We've tried calling him and Rianne. It's like they dropped off the planet. But you said Rianne is in Boston, so that's good news."

I captured a nail between my teeth. "Maybe

Noah went to visit Jack Jr. in Chicago." Although if he did, Jordyn would've mentioned it, or at least Carly would've told Jordyn.

"He didn't. We checked with Jack Jr.," she said. "I'm afraid he might've been taken by that Roman vampire."

That didn't add up. Roman would go after those Sam and the SEAL team cared about, and Noah didn't fit into that circle. Rianne might, though. Unless my uncle Ray incited Roman recently.

My brain was about to explode with too many unanswered questions, but one in particular was nagging at me. "Was Jack involved in the plot to burn Sam?" I wanted to believe he wasn't.

"No," she replied emphatically. "I know you don't believe that, but I promise you, Jack didn't know what Rianne and Noah were up to. Layla, if you find Noah and Rianne, I need you to promise me that Sam won't kill my son."

"Aunt Tab, I wish I could, but I can't. But what I can tell you is that the vampires here don't go out of their way to take a human's life. That's what I've been trying to tell Jack, but he won't listen. The vampire military is not your enemy. But if Jack or Ray are out to hunt Sam or any others on his team, then all bets are off. If Noah tries to string up Sam again, he *will* defend himself."

A light tap on the door snapped my spine straight. "Layla," Jo said. "Are you okay?"

"I'll be right out."

"I've made some tea that should help the nausea," Jo said before her footsteps faded.

"Aunt Tab, I have to go. We'll talk soon." Then I clicked off before she begged me again. I had my own problems, and they were more important than worrying about Noah.

I walked into the kitchen, where sunlight pinged off the copper pots and pans hanging over the stovetop built into the white marble island. I blinked several times to adjust to the blinding light.

Jo was pouring hot water into three cups. "Layla, this is Alia Costner."

My gaze swung to a pretty blond woman with sky-blue eyes who was sitting on a barstool.

"It's nice to meet you, Layla. Come. Sit." Alia pulled out a stool next to her.

Jo slid a cup of tea to her. "Alia tutored Sam and me. Now, she tutors Abbey. I thought it would be good for you to meet her. She might be of more help with your quest to learn about your mom. She knows our history better than me, and she can get access to vampire records."

Jo gave me my cup. "It's ginger, which should help with your nausea."

I loved ginger, but at the moment, I wasn't sure if I could keep anything down. It had been a while since I'd had blood, and whether it was my taste buds or the baby, I wouldn't mind switching out tea for blood. But Sam wasn't there, and my parents had taught me to be polite when I was a guest in someone's home.

I slid onto a stool next to Alia. "Are you a vampire?"

Alia sipped her tea. "I carry the gene, but I chose not to turn because I wanted kids. Now, I have a wonderful son." She smiled, but it seemed forced.

I brought my cup to my mouth and blew before I took a sip. "Is he a vampire?"

"He is," she said despairingly. "So, Layla, tell me about you." It was clear she didn't want to talk about her son. "Growing up, my father told me stories about hunters. Your family is one of the legends in our history." She practically gushed with excitement, as though I was a celebrity.

"Legends, huh?" I imagined history books

teaching the children of vampires about the dangers of hunters. More than that, I would have to warn my own child about the Aberdeen clan. He could never step foot on the ranch, play with his cousins, or do anything with my family. A bolt of sadness stung my chest as I swayed to one side.

Alia caught me. "I think you need to lie down. You look pale all of a sudden."

Jo rushed over. "You can rest in the guest room. I'll call Sam too. I think you need blood."

Tears threatened as the women guided me down a hall that seemed never-ending. I couldn't have the baby. I just couldn't.

31

SAM

I stormed into Jo's place. "Where is she? Is she okay?" I padded across the carpeted living room, anxious to see Layla. "What happened?"

Jo blocked me from turning the corner toward the bedrooms. "Sit down, Sam." She stabbed a finger toward one of the chairs. "Layla's fine. She's resting."

"I thought you said she needed blood." The minute I'd gotten off the phone with Jo, I ran over to my sister's like a crazy motherfucker.

She pinned me with the sisterly look she always used to boss me around. "A minute more won't hurt."

Oh, how the tables had turned since she'd become a vampire. When we were human, I'd been the one in charge of our sibling relationship. And I wasn't one to back down, but it was evident she had something important to tell me.

I skirted past her and went into the kitchen. "What is it, then?" I opened the fridge, looking for something to drink.

"Layla is freaking out, and it's my fault. My intentions weren't to upset her, but I should've known to tread lightly. Anyway, our conversation led to why the baby required blood."

I bumped my head on the inside of the fridge as I tossed a look over my shoulder. "You know why?" My voice hitched.

She pressed her hands into the edge of the island. "We don't know for sure, but Dr. Vieira theorizes that the baby will be born a true vampire."

I shut the fridge door. "For real? Like you and me?" I scraped both hands through my hair. I could see why Layla was freaking out. I didn't know how I felt about that new information. I was still trying to wrap my brain around becoming a dad. "A baby with fangs and powers?"

"If I were Layla, I would be a little weirded out," she said. "Anyway, I also wanted to tell you that I overheard her talking to Jordyn and then her aunt while she was in the bathroom."

I massaged a knot in my right shoulder. The tension was mounting to huge proportions. "Yeah, I know about Jordyn. Conrad called Webb to let him know they were flying in tonight. Did you hear what she said when she talked to her aunt?" I settled my back against the sink.

"In a nutshell, the Aberdeens don't know where Noah and Rianne are. Her aunt is frightened."

"Then that's why Jack wants to meet with us," I said. "He wants our help." I wouldn't walk into a meeting with him banking on that, though. Her aunt could have been setting Layla up, and not by choice. Jack could have been forcing her.

Concern knotted Jo's eyebrows. "One more thing."

I cocked an eyebrow. "There's more, sis?" I could handle just about anything, but I swore if anyone added more to the already mountainous pile of shit I had on my plate, I might explode.

"I was in her head, and I'm only telling you this because we need to make her feel like she matters. She's special, Sam. But we're too focused on the baby and not her." Jo came up to me. "I know you love her. She told me. I couldn't be happier for you." Her smile was replaced with a frown. "But I also don't want you to be hurt by a woman. She's struggling hard with us... and now a baby. I'm afraid she's going to run."

My jaw tightened against my will. "Jo." My tone bordered on a growl. "Did you tell her if she hurts me, you will rip her heart out?" I could see my sister doing just that.

Her silver eyes flickered to violet as she poked a finger in my chest. "Not at all. But I would if she did."

We stared at one another for a long second.

"Sam, I'm sorry. I didn't mean for the conversation to take a downward turn. I know her hormones are probably all over the place, but she had to know about the baby sooner or later."

I kissed Jo on the forehead. "I'm not mad at you. And you're right. The last thing I want to do is hold anything back from Layla. We agreed that we're in this together."

"Then how do you feel about a pure-vampire baby?" Jo asked.

I slid around her. "I honestly don't know. I also don't have time to process it, either. My first priority is Layla."

I whipped my attention toward the hall as Layla's heartbeat tickled my eardrums before she came into view.

In three long strides I was gazing into her luscious blue eyes.

"Is that true, Sam? I'm your first priority?" Wariness etched her tone.

"I'll let you two talk. I need to meet Webb and Abbey, anyway." Jo hurried out.

Once the front door clicked shut, I lifted Layla and set her on the island. Then I wormed my way between her legs.

A calm quiet stretched between us, broken only by the *boom, boom, boom* of our hearts.

Her electric-blue eyes sucked me in, and for a split second, I forgot where I was until her cold hand touched my face. "Where did you go?"

I searched for words to articulate how I felt, but actions were far better, so I brushed my lips over hers, flattening my palms on her cheeks. "Kiss me?"

She studied me as though she didn't hear me. Maybe Jo was right. Maybe Layla had decided I wasn't the man for her.

My heart tripped. Suddenly, the space between us became charged like two opposing atoms ready to explode. I curled her hair behind her ear before lightly tracing a path around the shape of her ear.

She shivered. "I'm scared, Sam. Frightened out of my mind about this baby."

I kissed her nose. "I know. What can I do to put you at ease?"

She rubbed a finger over my lips. "I don't know."

"Don't ever think for a second you're not my priority." I smoothed a hand over her hair. "Layla, you own my heart."

She gave me a weak smile. "Even with a baby who will have fangs?" Tears clouded her pretty eyes.

I nibbled on her bottom lip. "Doc isn't sure about that. And even if he was, it doesn't matter. Fangs or not, our kid will be a vampire."

"What if it's a girl?" She blinked and a tear cascaded down her cheek. "Then she won't be able to have kids. At least if she's born human, she can make the decision to turn when she reaches the right age. Look at Alia Costner. She didn't turn so she could have kids. I want my child to be able to choose."

There was the crux of why she was freaking

out. But we couldn't control the outcome of the sex or whether the baby was human or not. "I do too. But my biggest concern right now is that you look extremely pale." I pulled a knife from the sheath strapped to my leg.

"I don't want blood."

My forehead creased. "Then you need to eat something." I helped her down and was about to forage through the fridge when she caught my hand.

"Sam, please tell me everything will be fine. That I can have our child."

My chest clenched painfully as I cocooned her in my arms, digging deeper for something to say. "I'm not going anywhere." I felt compelled to reassure her. "We can have this baby. You can have this baby. You're strong, Layla. And you have a whole team of people here, rooting for you."

Then I kissed her like she mattered, because she did, and I would continually show her that she had my soul.

32

SAM

Two days had passed since my old man shared Jack's voice mail with us. We'd been in planning mode, strategizing, running through scenarios, and listing the tactics associated with each. We were also searching for a meeting place, which we had yet to find. But we couldn't proceed if Jack didn't return my father's call.

According to Layla, Noah was missing, and the Aberdeens were concerned that Roman had taken him. If Jack wanted our help, he sure as hell wasn't making his son a priority—unless Jack had given in to Roman's demands. Though, Jack didn't strike me as the type to ask for help or give in to anyone. His pride drove his actions, and he was also a skilled hunter.

I skirted a table in the infirmary on my way to see Ben. I hadn't had a chance to talk to him. As I brought Wyman in, Jo had called about Layla, and I'd rushed out.

"Sam, don't take too long," Dr. Vieira called from his office behind me. "I want to start pulling your blood before Dane comes in."

I grumbled at the shifter's name. It had been over a week since the alpha of the Gray Pack had been there. Nevertheless, I came to an abrupt halt, spun on my heel, and strode to his office. "Did you find out why the drug is killing shifters?"

"The toxicology report isn't back yet. He's dropping off another supply of shifter blood. Ben's wound hasn't fully healed, but I think I know why. I just need to run some tests."

"You think the antidote we have on hand will help us when we meet with Jack?" I asked.

"I haven't tested it against that drug, but all of you will get the antidote just the same. I'll be out in about ten minutes." He yanked his cell from atop a stack of folders. "One more thing, Sam. Play nice if you're here when Dane comes in."

I nodded even though I couldn't promise Doc

anything, although I needed to thank Dane for his help.

Ben grinned the minute I strutted in. "Dude, finally. How are you? I heard you were almost burned alive. And shit, Layla is pregnant. Man, I missed so much. How are you holding up?" His jaw looked like it might come unhinged, as if he had just heard about the baby.

I ponied up to his bed and gave him a quick bro hug. "By a thread. Sorry I haven't had a chance to talk. You look better today." His reddish-brown eyes were clear. Color had returned to his face, although it was hard to see much beneath the thick beard that had grown in.

"I feel better, but for some reason, the wound isn't completely healed yet. I'm so ready to join the ranks of the living." He threw the blanket off him and exposed the injury on his hip. "Doc says my human side is fighting with my vampire side. He's waiting for more shifter blood."

"That looks a thousand times better, dude. Doc will come through," I assured him.

"I sure as fuck hope so. If not, I'm done with the SEALs." He replaced the bandage and pulled the blanket up to his waist. "I hear you're meeting with Jack Aberdeen. When? Maybe I can be part of that."

"Jack hasn't called to confirm. And before you ask, we don't have any leads on Roman or Rianne. I take it Doc or Tripp filled you in on that too."

He nodded. "Tripp is hoping I'm healed in time for whatever is coming." The one skill Ben brought to the table as a half-breed was his strength. He was stronger than the average vampire, which didn't make sense since he was half human.

"It's something big. I can feel it."

"You're usually never wrong about those gut feelings," he said.

"Do you remember anything when you were with Roman, by the way?" Tripp had questioned Ben the moment he became coherent, but he'd said Ben hadn't learned anything that would give us a clue as to what Roman had up his sleeve.

"As I told Tripp, I overheard part of a phone conversation. Roman had been talking to some guy named Fred, demanding more money."

Doc poked his head in. "Sam."

"I'll be right there," I volleyed over my shoulder. "Dude, I have to give blood. Apparently, my little guy needs it."

One of his thick eyebrows went up and the other down. "What? Why?"

"Million-dollar question. But I want to make sure Layla has a supply with her."

He smirked. "I'm still blown away that you're about to be a dad. And you said 'little guy.' Do you know if it's a boy already?"

"Too early to tell. Heal, man. I need you more than ever. I'll check in soon." I gave Ben a quick hug, spun on my heel, then left.

Doc was waiting for me on the other side of the infirmary next to his lab bench. He and Jo each had their own workspace.

I sat in a metal chair with wide wooden arms for ease of drawing blood. "Any luck finding out why Layla needs blood for the baby?"

Doc went to work hooking me up to the equipment. "I doubt I'll find an answer while she's pregnant, but Alia is helping me search records. Maybe this has happened to someone more than a century old. Regardless, I don't think it matters that much, as long as Layla and the baby stay healthy."

After having lain awake for the last two nights, thinking about my kid, I agreed. True vampire baby or not, the kid was mine, and that was all that mattered to me.

As soon as my blood started flowing into the bag, Doc's cell rang. He tore off his nitrile gloves and plucked it out of his lab coat. "I'll be right back." He sauntered toward his office with his phone to his ear.

I closed my eyes, thinking I could get a quick nap in. I had tuned out the hum of the lab equipment in the spacious room when the *whoosh* of the doors penetrated my eardrums.

"Sam, have you seen Layla?" Tripp's fury-filled voice boomed.

My eyes bulged open, and all I could think was that Layla had run, that she'd finally decided that dating a vampire and having a baby wasn't her gig. Then Rianne came to mind. I wondered if she'd called Layla and asked to meet her somewhere.

Tripp crossed the lab in a flash, his features pinched, his bronze eyes swirling to black. "She's not at Harley's, and neither is Jordyn."

"Motherfucker." My heart plummeted off a cliff. "I think she was meeting Alia at the library."

His mouth tightened at the corners. "She's not

there. I'm trying to get Lane on the radio, but he isn't answering."

I ripped the needle from my arm as Doc hurried over. "I just hung up with Alia. She overheard Layla and Jordyn talking about new clothes."

Tripp yanked the radio from his belt. "Lane, come in."

The radio crackled. "Go, lieutenant."

Tripp growled. "Why the fuck didn't you answer before now?"

"Sorry," Lane said. "I was using the head. I was about to call you."

"Where's Layla and Jordyn?" Tripp asked in a tone that brooked no argument.

"In the women's dressing room at the base exchange," he returned. "No need to worry. They're fine. I can hear them laughing."

My pulse slowed as I exhaled.

"Bring them to the war room. Now!"

"Copy that," Lane said.

"I'll go get them." It would help ease my nerves to see Layla.

Tripp caught my arm and tightened his grip. "No. I want you down in the control room. I have something to show you."

Doc and I exchanged a wide-eyed look. Tripp hardly ever blew a gasket. He was one of the most reserved SEALs on the team, even as our leader.

"What's going on?" I asked.

"Too fucking much to keep track of," Tripp said cryptically as he set his hard gaze on Doc. "Is he done?"

"Sam can come back later," Doc replied quickly. "Dane is coming in, anyway. It's best if you two aren't here."

"You're right about that," Tripp fired back. "Your father just spoke to Jack. I'll explain the rest when all of us are in one room." He marched out, slamming open the lab doors as he did.

I couldn't begin to think why he would be livid with the Aberdeen sisters.

As if Doc knew what I was thinking, he said, "I've only ever seen Tripp that furious maybe twice. Whatever is going on has to be monumental."

"They're Aberdeens," I mumbled.

"And you're tied to them for eternity, Sam." He sounded sad.

"Only Layla, man. Only Layla."

He gave me a who-are-you-kidding look. "I think you and she fit together nicely, and I'll support you no matter what. But Sam... you know as well as I do that it's not just Layla. Regardless of whether it's vampires or humans, a relationship always comes with the person's family. But—"

"If you're about to counsel me on what I'm in for with the Aberdeens, I know. Remember, two of them tried to burn me alive."

Pity colored his expression. "Then let me just reiterate something. It's ingrained in the Aberdeens to kill our kind. Has been for centuries, Sam. Now, with a kid on the way, your life will be filled with more strife than you've ever seen. And while I believe you can handle almost anything, everyone has a breaking point, even you."

"Do you have some new information I don't know about?"

"The Aberdeens will never let that kid be born, and it's not Jack that you have to worry about."

I angled my head. "Please tell me you're not about to say something like Layla's father is alive." Not that he would scare me, but it would throw a wrinkle into the mix.

Doc pulled on a pair of nitrile gloves. "Jack's mother. She's the one who runs the show," he said casually, as though I should have known.

Regardless, another Aberdeen hunting me or breathing down my neck didn't matter. Or maybe it did. "Layla has never mentioned her grandmother. My father hasn't, either."

Doc nailed me with a grim look. "You've only known Layla for a short time. You can't know everything about her."

"Why are you making a big deal out of her grandmother, Doc?" Jack had been the star of the show. "And why are you just now telling me this? Or why hasn't my father?"

"There wasn't a need to tell you. But now that she's pregnant..."

Then it dawned on me. My father had been trying to tell me something just before Abbey blew into his room at the medical facility in Boston. *"Sam, there are a few things you should know* —" But before that, he'd been adamant about her family not finding out about the baby.

My phone pinged. "I better go. Tripp might chop off my head."

"Sam, make sure you come back. I don't want Layla in a situation where she doesn't have any of your blood."

I didn't, either.

33

LAYLA

A chill tiptoed down my spine the minute I entered the theater-style room. The last time I'd been in there was with Rianne when Jordyn had been missing.

Jordyn glanced around in awe. "This is a war room? Looks like a great place to watch a movie."

We climbed down the stone steps with my bodyguard, Lane, leading the way.

"So what's this about?" I asked him for the hundredth time.

He tossed a look over his shoulder, his light-brown eyes full of frustration. "No idea. But Tripp is seething."

I'd been racking my brain over why Tripp

would be so enraged with Jordyn and me, or maybe it was just me. But neither of us had done anything wrong.

Since Jordyn's return from Chicago, which had only been the day before yesterday, we'd been lounging at Harley's house since the women's barracks were occupied. She'd given Sam the thumbs-up for Jordyn and me to crash at her place while she was out of town, visiting her mother.

Jordyn and I hadn't left her house until that morning. We'd met Alia briefly at the library, but then she'd gotten a message from her father and had to leave. So Jordyn and I decided to check out the base exchange to see what they had for clothes. The small amount Jordyn had packed before we left Montana wasn't enough.

Lane, who was about six-foot-four and broad, had a cute smile, thick dirty-blond hair on top that was shaved on the sides and back, and seemed like a sweetheart, waved for us to have a seat in the front row. "I need to duck out for a sec." Then he disappeared through a side door.

"What do you think is going on?" I asked Jordyn.

"No clue. Maybe they're monitoring our

phone conversations. I did talk to Intech this morning."

I gathered my hair and draped it over my shoulder. "You think Harley's place is bugged?"

She set her purse on the chair beside her. "What would that matter? We haven't said anything they don't already know."

"About Intech. Are you taking the job?" When we talked about her interview, she'd mentioned she was on the fence. Something felt off to her that she couldn't put her finger on.

The side door opened, and Tripp and Sam entered. I hadn't seen Sam since Jordyn arrived. Even if I'd wanted to, he'd been working, which was cool. I needed space to wrap my mind around a baby and the fact that he was in love with me.

My stomach dipped at the sight of him. He wore his black uniform—SEAL T-shirt stretched across his muscled chest, cargo pants, flak boots, and weapons strapped to his legs and waist.

Tripp was dressed the same, and both had their hair tied at the nape.

"What did we do to piss you off?" Jordyn asked Tripp before he could open his mouth.

Tripp balled his hands into fists as his nostrils flared like a bull about to attack a matador. He shot daggers at Jordyn with his eyes as he leaned on the table in front of the movie screen.

Sam stood with his feet shoulder width apart and his hands behind his back about five feet from Tripp. His attention was focused on his lieutenant, though he wore a vacant expression that reminded me of a robot programmed to do as Tripp commanded.

The hairs on my arms fired to attention.

Tripp snagged the remote device off the table and pressed on it. A slide appeared with eight bullet points beneath the name "Camden Industries."

I scanned over the words and zeroed in on bullet point five. Then I swung my gaze to Jordyn as my mind tried to unjumble the reason why Tripp's jaw was ticking furiously.

She shrugged with her lips tightened. "Camden owns Intech. So what? Is that why you hunted us down?"

She hadn't been around the SEALs as long as I had, which told me something big was coming next, especially if Sam's rigid posture or stone mask was any indication.

Tripp's wry grin dropped a heavy blanket of unsettling pressure over us. "Let me break it down. Camden Industries specializes in developing weapons for the Department of Defense. Not a big deal. Intech develops computer programs for the DOD. Camden owns Intech. Seems legit." Tripp pushed off the table and paced. "But here's where things start to make us scratch our heads. When Sam was in Montana, at that bar where Noah and Rianne kidnapped him, he spotted something in an SUV that made him suspicious."

Sam still hadn't shifted or batted an eye, and if not for his chest moving with his breath, I would've thought he was definitely a robot.

Tripp tucked a hand into his pants pocket. "At first glance, nothing gave us a red flag. Until we dug deeper." He came to a halt and pressed on the remote.

Another slide came into view. That time, it was a picture of a very familiar tall, brown-haired man dressed in a tailored black suit with a yellow satin tie.

It took a beat for my brain to click into place. "Is that Lester Worthington?"

Jordyn pointed to the screen. "That's the guy who came into the Deer and Elk. Sam said he was interested in buying a horse. I also saw him talking to Noah when Sam left to make a phone call."

Sam finally came out of his robotic state. "We're almost certain Lester wasn't at the ranch to buy a horse. We think Lester was there to sell Jack his new weapon."

Jordyn huffed. "I still don't see why you're upset with us. Our uncle is a hunter. You know that. So he's buying a weapon."

Tripp clicked the remote again.

I knitted my brows. Noah was talking to Lester outside of Intech as though they were old friends. "When was that taken?" My aunt thought Noah was missing or had been kidnapped by Roman.

Tripp settled his stance at the edge of the table. "This was the day Jordyn interviewed with Intech. Sawyer was able to hack into the cameras around the company."

"Any sign of Rianne?" I held my breath. Maybe she was in Boston but then joined Noah in Chicago.

Tripp shook his head hard. "None."

Sam's eyes flashed silver as he focused on Jordyn. "Are you plotting with Noah and Rianne to kill me or any of us here? Was your interview a hoax? Is your interest in working with us just a ploy to throw us off track? Are you their mole?" His voice grew deeper on each question.

I understood his anger. I could even jump on board with how suspicious it looked that Jordyn had trekked off to Chicago, given the pictures up on screen. But he had no right to unleash his browbeating fury on Jordyn. She was the one person who would never betray me.

I fisted my hands in my lap. "What gives you the right to bully her? And what happened to innocent until proven guilty? Not only that, but I trust her."

Sam's fangs descended as if in slow motion.

I rolled my eyes and popped up like a jack-in-the-box. "Puh-lease, vampire. Fangs don't scare me."

He marched closer to me. "Need I remind you that Rianne tried to hurt you? Almost killed you. And didn't you trust her too?"

I bared my teeth. "Jordyn isn't Rianne."

"Answer the questions, Jordyn," Tripp prompted in an even tone. At least he was keeping his composure together, although I didn't doubt he could snap at any moment.

Jordyn clasped her hands together as she fixated on the low pile carpet.

It felt like a bag of nails was poking my stomach. "Jordyn, say something."

She cleared her throat. "I promise, Layla. I don't know what's going on." Her voice was soft but shaky, and she still hadn't looked at me. "I'm not a mole."

My pulse pounded in my ears as I sat back down. I knew my sister. She was holding something back. Otherwise, she would be standing up for herself.

"Your elevated heartbeat says differently," Tripp said.

"I can feel your fear," Sam added.

She shuddered. "You do because I know what this looks like. I promise I'm not involved with Noah and Rianne. The reason my pulse is racing is because I'm trying to figure out what the fuck is going on. I declined the job this morning. Something felt off to me. After my interview, I spent some time with the man in charge of security, Fred Emery. He gave me the creeps, from the way he leered at me to how much he knew about me. I was about to tell you, sis, when they came in."

Sam flinched slightly. "Jordyn, you said Fred Emery?"

I jerked my attention to Sam. "Do you know him?"

"No," he said, then eyed Tripp. "But I think Roman does. Ben mentioned he'd heard Roman talking to a guy named Fred."

Whether it was Sam mentioning the word *talking* or not that triggered my memory, I suddenly recalled Lester chatting with his friend at the Deer and Elk. "You know, Lester mentioned your name when he was at the Deer and Elk, Sam."

Tripp and Sam jerked back.

"And I just told you that Lester was talking to Noah," Jordyn added then waved her hand at the screen. "You've got pictures of them together. Maybe Noah is driving the ship. Maybe he's working out a deal with Lester to profit off you, Sam."

"By killing me?" Sam asked. "That doesn't make sense. I'm usually wanted alive."

"Maybe Roman doesn't need you alive anymore. Maybe he has a contract on your head," I said.

Tripp scrubbed a hand along his jaw. "Possible. But we haven't found Roman mixed up with either of these companies."

"True," Sam said. "But after Roman escaped, his trail did lead to Chicago."

"Whatever Noah and Lester are up to," Tripp said, "we have work to do." He got on his phone and rattled off orders about Camden, Intech, and Fred Emery. "Dig deeper," he said in a tone that brooked no argument to the person on the other end of the line. "I want every detail of both companies from the CEO down to the mailroom guy. I want a dossier on Lester Worthington and Fred Emery to start." Then he hung up before he and Sam headed toward the exit.

Jordyn swiveled in her seat to face me. "You believe I'm telling the truth, right? I didn't know Noah was in Chicago, and if Carly did, she didn't say anything."

I studied her for a long second as a tiny voice whispered not to trust anyone. But Jordyn hadn't given me any reason not to believe her.

She sighed as she stuck out her chest. "You can always have Steven read my mind if it makes you feel better."

That didn't seal the deal yet. I'd been able to block Steven from diving into the deep recesses of my mind when I'd first met him. But Jordyn had always been truthful.

I captured her hand. "I do believe you."

She quivered. "Thank you. I would never betray you."

I hugged her. "I know."

"Jordyn," Tripp called. "We would like for you to take the team through your time at Intech. Come with me."

"I love you. I'll catch up with you later," she told me before getting to her feet and passing Sam as he strutted over.

"Can we find a secret island where no one will find us?" I asked.

He pulled me to my feet and kissed me on the cheek. "I'm for all that. But this is our life, baby doll. Your family and mine. My dad talked to Jack, by the way. We're meeting him outside of Chicago tomorrow night. He reiterated that if we don't bring you, he's walking."

Sam had told me about the voice mail Jack had left. I had no clue why Jack wanted me there. It would be nice to think he wanted to make sure I was okay, but that was a pipe dream.

"I would insist on going even if he didn't dangle me like a carrot."

Sam grinned, showing his heart-stopping dimples. "I know. But then I would have to tie you up." He waggled his thick eyebrows.

I flattened my hands on his chest and ignored his sexual innuendo for the time being. "Did your dad ask Jack why he wanted to meet?"

"He did, and Jack's response was 'We have many things to talk about and not over the phone.'"

"It's going to be a long nine months, isn't it?"

He studied me intently as if trying to find a way to tell me another piece of bad news.

"Just say it. I'm a big girl." Then again, with my hormones all over the place, I wasn't sure how much more I could handle.

That stone mask was back in place. "Stay with me tonight."

"Sam, you're scaring me. And that's hard to do."

He eased away and smiled, but it seemed forced.

"You found Rianne?" I held my breath. If they did, it wasn't good.

"No," he said. "I want you to prepare yourself. There are too many moving parts, given what we're learning about Noah, Camden, and Intech, not to mention your uncle. And then there's Roman and Rianne."

"You should just call Jack and tell him about Noah. After all, according to my aunt, that's why he set up the meeting. He wants your help finding his son."

Sam nodded. "We could, but as your uncle said, we have many things to talk about, which means there's more than Noah on the table. And we need to know what he's up to. Is he involved with Camden? Does he have a new weapon? What are his plans to hunt Roman?"

"He won't share his strategies," I said.

"He doesn't have to. We'll read his mind."

"Jo is going? I know your father can read minds, but he needs to touch Jack to do so, and my uncle won't let that happen."

"She is. Does Jack have a way to block anyone from getting in his head?" Sam asked.

"As far as I'm aware, no. But I haven't been around Jack for two years. You won't be able to compel him, though."

Sam smirked, showing that cocksure arrogance. "Remember, I don't compel like normal vampires."

"Careful," I warned. "Even the best can fail."

He hadn't lost his aura of superiority. "Not Jo and me. Together, she and I are unstoppable."

After witnessing his elemental powers, I had to agree, and combined with Jo's abilities, I wouldn't doubt him.

But the way things were going, the mighty could fall.

Two hours later, I stood in front of a wall of windows in Sam's apartment on the naval base, gazing out at the courtyard below. Piles of melting snow gave way to a mixture of brown and green blades of grass. A handful of round cement tables dotted the yard between the two buildings, and guards patrolled the roof of the one across from me.

If not for the open and spacious apartment behind me, I would have felt like I was in a high-security prison. I would have given anything to rewind the months and years to a time when I felt like I could breathe. Since my parents died, I hadn't had a day where I didn't worry about my sisters, our future, or the struggle to survive. If I'd never taken that job from Wyman, my sisters and I would still have been three peas in a pod.

Basking in the silence, I inhaled then released a breath. Sam had brought me to his place while the SEAL team peppered Jordyn with questions. I wanted to be there, but I was tired and nauseous. I would give anything to return to Maine, to hear the crash of the waves, to see the sun rise, to walk the beach with Sam, to do anything other than deal with the tons of crap hitting us all at once.

The landscape lighting turned on around the courtyard as dusk set in. A guard emerged from the prison building across the way. Sam had pointed out before he left that the jail cells resided in the basement of that building. I thought of Wyman. According to Sam, Wyman had been ill. Some type of stomach flu. But he had fully recovered and was working for Alia's father's security firm.

I made a mental note to see if I could talk to him. I wanted him to relay every detail of when he'd been with my father. I was growing more curious by the day about the woman my dad supposedly had been dating and if she'd been the one who ended his life.

The doorknob clicked before the door groaned open.

My pulse quickened as Sam swaggered in, appearing as though he could use a year of sleep. Right behind him was my sister.

Jordyn sashayed in wearing a huge smile. "So this is your hideaway?" She took in every corner of the room. "Nice penthouse."

"It's my father's half the time," he said. "I'll let you two talk." Sam strutted down the hall.

I skirted a chaise lounge before perching on the edge of it. "How did it go?"

Jordyn sat on the couch across from me. "Um. Steven read my mind. And before you say anything, I asked him to. I got the feeling the SEAL team wouldn't trust me, and I want them to. I want them to know I'm on their side."

"I hear a *but* coming." Dread crawled through my chest.

Her brown eyes lit up. "Chill, sis. It's all good. I finally had a chance to talk to Steven. He's offered me a job. He learned yesterday that one of his staff members, who was in that explosion, didn't make it. So he has an opening. And he said he would do anything for me since we're family now."

My mouth hung open. "Family, huh?" It was weird to even think of vampires as family. I guessed I'd better get used to that. "Anyway, you look excited, but your voice says otherwise."

"I'm headed to Boston in an hour. Steven is

putting me up in his apartment at their headquarters. I start work tomorrow. He wants to get me situated before he leaves for his meeting with Jack, so I won't be here for you."

I joined her on the couch. "Don't worry about me. Besides, you're only two hours away at most. I'm stoked for you."

"I know, but I'm also worried about you meeting with Jack. To be honest, the other reason I didn't take the job at Intech was Carly. I don't want to be around our family. I'm irritated with myself that I even interviewed for it. My heart has always been with the vamps here."

"Don't beat yourself up. I pushed you to go to the interview. I'm glad you did, though. Now, you know for sure that vampires are your thing." I laughed.

She giggled. "We're vampire lovers, sis. Mom and Dad would freak."

"I don't know about Mom." I sighed, pushing out some frustration over our dead mother. Considering she had vampires somewhere in her lineage, Mom could very well have loved the bloodsuckers.

She rose. "We'll find out more about Mom.

With me working for Steven, I'll have access to records and their library in Boston."

A spark of excitement tickled my stomach as I stood and hugged her. "You will."

Maybe things were falling into place for us.

34

LAYLA

Fire rose on both sides of the long stretch of road. I was running for my life, screaming for them to stop. "Please!"

A pinging noise made its way into the deep recesses of my brain, jarring me into sitting up position. Disoriented, I blinked several times, trying to figure out where I was. The room was dark with a ray of light spraying in from the window. The clock on the nightstand read 3:00 a.m.

I kicked off the covers as sweat coated my naked body. That pinging noise started again. I flicked on the bedside lamp, and my phone's screen brightened with a text from Sam: *I'm on my way up.*

383

He'd left hours before to finalize tactics and strategies for the meeting with my uncle. I thought he would've been back already.

I propped the pillow against the fabric headboard and shook off the remnants of my dream. Then I noticed another text from Jordyn: *Hey, I tried to call but you must be asleep or with Sam. I made it to Boston. The apartment is fab. Call me before you take off in the morning.*

I hadn't been able to shake the macabre chills since Tripp showed us those slides of Noah talking to Lester. Maybe that was the reason for my dream—or what I could remember of it, anyway. Fire and...

The steel door opened, and Sam strutted in with an air of danger as menace poured off him. "Well, this is a nice surprise. I thought you'd be asleep." He locked us in as his gaze devoured every inch of my naked body.

"I had a bad dream."

He started peeling off his clothes. "Want to talk about it?"

"Nothing to talk about. It was darkness and fire. Then I woke up."

"Sounds like you're having PTSD about that night."

I shrugged. "Maybe. It was a nightmare to see you hanging over the fire. But enough about that. I need a distraction or to do something to keep my mind from wandering." We were scheduled to fly out at around eleven the next morning, which meant we had plenty of time to tumble between the sheets.

He fixated on my tits. "I want to suck those babies until the sun comes up. Is that a good enough distraction?"

I gently rubbed my breasts. "You can't have these. They're sore."

He grinned as his green eyes flickered to a glowing silver. "I'll be gentle." He tore the leather strap from his hair and shucked off his boxer briefs.

Sheer power and dominance rippled across the room. Waves of heat and lust wrapped around me, and I moaned as if he was licking my pussy.

With slow, casual steps, he came toward me, stroking his erection.

I lost my breath and my mind. Nothing mattered anymore except having him inside me.

He crawled onto the bed like an expert cat burglar about to snag the most expensive jewel in the world.

A squeal escaped as my breath caught in my throat. The anticipation of his tongue on my clit had my stomach in knots as though it was the first time we'd seen each other naked.

He peppered light kisses over my left breast. "I heard that pregnant women are quite horny."

I snorted. "How do you know this?"

"I've been reading."

Shock rendered me speechless. There was so much I didn't know about the alpha vampire.

"Your lust is strong tonight, baby doll."

"Is that so?" I was still processing his admission that he'd been learning about pregnancy.

But my astonishment vanished as he straddled me before adjusting my body so I was lying flat. "Tell me what you want." His voice was husky as he positioned his hands on either side of my head and lowered his lips to ghost over mine. "Fast, slow, or somewhere in between."

I giggled. "I don't think we're slow types, vampire."

His grin was all imp. "You're right, but I'm in the mood for long and slow."

"Shut up and fuck me, please."

He threw his head back and laughed. Then he slid down my body, the heated glide of his full lips everywhere at once and tormenting me into a squirming frenzy. When he reached the apex of my legs, he groaned as the tips of his hair caressed the sensitive flesh on my inner thighs.

I nearly shot off the bed as he chuckled then struck without warning. He sank his fangs into my thigh. The beelike sting sent a wave of pleasure straight to my clit. *Odd that a sting elicits such a euphoric sensation.* It wasn't the time to analyze why but to give in to the vampire who was stealing my soul, minute by minute and day by day.

I lifted my hips, ready to touch myself, when he withdrew his fangs and snarled. "Impatient."

I snarled back. "Fast, not slow."

"You're glistening." A rippling growl escaped him as he lowered his head. When the tip of his tongue touched my clit, I bucked up from the bed.

He grasped my hips, feasting on me like an animal who hadn't eaten in days. He dove into a rhythm that made me wriggle, sweat, and moan his name over and over again. I fisted my hands in the sheets and clutched for control. I wanted the swirling feeling to last, but I was on the precipice of having the best orgasm ever.

I took in steady breaths. Then boom—Sam bit, sinking his fangs in once again, this time into my other thigh as he worked my clit to a heated frenzy with the stroke of his finger.

Like quicksilver, my release blindsided me, and I screamed his name so loudly that if the room hadn't been soundproof, the whole building would've heard me. I wasn't done coming down off that mountainous high when he jammed his cock inside my dripping wet channel and roared like the animal he was.

My heart sputtered. My belly swirled, and in that moment, I knew I was in the right place with the right man. Predator or not, Sam was mine, and I dared my family to fuck with us again.

I tangled my fingers in his silky strands, guiding him to one breast then the other. His fangs grazed along the peaks of my nipples, never hurting me, treating my tits as if they were his precious gems. He didn't linger long, making his way up my chest to nip at my chin. I closed my eyes, relishing in his tender touch as he rocked and I rolled, meeting him thrust for thrust. Our breathing was in sync. Our hearts beat as one, and just when I thought he would kiss me, he pressed his lips on my nose, my cheeks, everywhere but my mouth.

My body hummed, and my clit sang, my limbs languid.

I could sense he was on the verge of exploding.

I opened my eyes, looked up, and lost my breath. His eyes were a luminous silver with dots of green bleeding through. He was a beautiful specimen, hand carved out of stone by the gods themselves. I was mesmerized as I watched him watch me.

"I'm yours, Sam."

As if those were the magic words, he fucked me hard and fast. Sweat slicked our bodies, our breathing labored. Then a flash of pain pinched his features before a guttural sound tore from his lips along with my name.

Tugging his hair, I squeezed my pussy around his cock. "Kiss me, vampire."

He didn't bat an eye and obeyed as if he'd been programmed to do so. Our tongues fought for dominance as he rode out his orgasm, his dick pulsing inside me. A galaxy of emotions overwhelmed me, and I was close to shedding a tear for some fucked-up reason.

I shook off whatever was going on inside my

heart and flattened my hands on his scruffy jaw. "Sam?"

He rolled off me and pulled me to him—nose to nose. "What is it?" His tone was lazy and low.

"I need—"

His phone blared, jarring me out of my lustful stupor and severing that intimate connection that strung us together.

"Fuck." He climbed out of bed to cross the room.

So much for telling him how I feel.

"Yeah." His tone was caustic as he answered the phone. "Now? Are you kidding? Copy that." He flung the phone onto the bed, scowling.

"You're leaving?"

He shoved his hands through his hair. "You are too. A snowstorm is brewing, and if we don't leave within the next three hours, we probably won't make the meeting with your uncle."

"So? Postpone it." I didn't care if we met Jack or not.

"Not a chance. We have a short window with your uncle. He wanted to meet. If we back out because of the weather, we feel we won't get another opportunity."

He had a point. Jack wasn't one to give anyone

a second chance, and he wouldn't buy a snow-storm as an excuse. After all, he and Ray had flown through a blizzard to come to my rescue. Besides, one of the main goals was to read Jack's mind. I wanted to know everything going through his thick skull.

"Once this is over with Jack, I don't ever want to see him again," I said.

"We're in agreement on that." He held out his hand. "Come on. I'll wash your hair."

Jack fell to the back burner as my eyes bugged out. I couldn't picture Sam washing anyone's hair. Regardless, I hoped I would have more of those moments with him.

35

SAM

I held Layla's hand as though she would be able to save me if the plane crashed. Flying wasn't my gig. I wasn't afraid of much but sitting in a metal tube that could burn my ass at forty thousand feet was one of my biggest fucking fears.

"Sam, can you let up a little?" Layla asked in a pained tone.

My eyes flew open as I eased up and peppered her hand with kisses. "Sorry, baby doll."

She giggled. "You know the safest form of travel is on an airplane."

Suddenly, the plane dropped, and my stomach went with it. The air pockets and turbulence had me ready to hyperventilate.

A burst of air escaped from Layla. "I take that back. Flying sucks."

"You know what would help?" I opened a telepathic connection. I wasn't sure it would work, but she had been drinking my blood left and right.

She raised an eyebrow.

Me sucking on your pussy.

She flinched. "I'd forgotten you could do that."

Do what? Lick you until you scream my name?

She swatted at me. "Telepathy. It's freaky."

Since we can't fuck, talk dirty to me.

You'll be hard in a flat second. Then what?

I clenched my teeth. *Good point.*

She laughed.

The pilot came on. "We're five minutes out. Everyone, take your seats. And please make sure you have your seat belts on. It's going to be a bumpy landing."

"Fuck me," I muttered.

Jo peeked over the seat in front of me. "Breathe, Sam."

"I will when we land," I fired back.

Tell me something about yourself that I don't know. Layla's siren voice was in my head. *I mean, there's a lot I don't know about you. And we're having a baby, so it's time I learn more about his father.*

His? On several occasions since we found out she was pregnant, she and I had been referring to our kid as a boy.

She shrugged. *I have no idea. But I would like to know. I don't want to wait until I give birth. Do you want to know?*

I don't like surprises. So yeah.

Sam, do you think we'll make good parents? Anxiety flowed off her in waves.

Of course. I have no doubt you'll make a great mom. As for me, I will love our kid hard. I don't ever want him to go through what Jo and I have been through. I will make sure he's protected, loved, and cared for. No foster homes. No wondering where his next meal will come from or what bed he'll sleep in.

Her mouth parted. "You and Jo were in foster care? I don't think you told me that," she said out loud.

Jo muttered something that I couldn't make out. I was too busy clenching my teeth and holding my breath as the plane rocked and rolled.

I let out the air I'd been keeping in. "The short version of the story is that it sucked, and no kid of mine will ever experience that." I didn't know if my old man, who was seated in front of Jo and Webb, heard me or not. It wasn't a dig against him, although he and I had had a tense relationship from the outset because of it.

"I can see why you're so protective of your sister," Layla said.

The closer the plane got to the runway, the more it shook. I swore we were in for a crash landing if the pilot couldn't straighten out. Then the tires touched down and screeched before the plane bounced and lifted into the air once again.

I squeezed Layla's hand.

She giggled. "The pilot's got this."

"Now, you know what scares me," I said.

I inhaled and exhaled as the wheels touched the tarmac, and that time, the pilot was successful. When the plane finally coasted down the runway, a long, relieved sigh came barreling out of me. I pushed my hands through my hair as my nerves began to settle. "We are not leaving until the weather is clear and the fucking sun is shining."

Webb chuckled.

I kissed Layla on the cheek. "Thanks for keeping me calm."

She snorted. "Calm? You were far from it."

Jo peeked through the opening in between the seats. "He's actually getting better."

"He should," Webb said. "Because there will come a time when he's parachuting out of a plane at twenty thousand feet."

"It's not the jump that bothers me, dude." During my SEAL training, I had no problem jumping out of a plane, and I wasn't afraid of heights. Again, the idea that a plane could blow midair was the issue.

The plane came to a stop in front of a boarded-up building that had several bay doors separating each hangar.

"Your fear makes you human, Sam," Layla added for support.

I stood from the aisle seat, ready to breathe some fresh air. "But I'm not human," I volleyed back.

Layla slid over to my spot. "Exactly. A vampire with heart. Most of the ones I've come across are animals and dead inside. It's all about them, or they feed off human terror. That's what I've tried to tell Jack. You guys are not like the vampires we've killed."

I always fed off fear, human or not. It was one

emotion that kept my mind sharp, especially in battle or tough situations... although fear could make me do things that didn't serve me or the team well.

Jo popped up then knelt on her seat as she faced us. "Our mission from the day we turned has always been to use our abilities to protect humanity and to find a way for our people to flourish and coexist among humans."

Webb unbuckled his seat belt. "We would like Jack to understand that. We would like him to join us to help us police our kind and bridge the gap between humans and vampires. Eventually, more and more humans will come to learn of us, and fear will take over. Then chaos will erupt."

Tripp and Dad pushed to their feet, both stretching in the process. Dad checked his watch. "We're an hour early. Before we sweep the area around the airport, I want to go through the plan one more time."

We'd failed to leave at the crack of dawn due to a problem with one of the plane's engines, another reason I'd been in freak-out mode.

Tripp tied his sandy-blond hair with a leather strap before he tossed two bulletproof vests at me.

Webb climbed to his feet and collected two vests for him and Jo.

There were only six of us. We decided to keep our best soldiers on base and left our backup SEAL team, Viking II, in charge. Roman could storm the base again, but he wouldn't find Abbey. She was in a secure location with Alia Costner. We thought it was best to keep the team to a minimum. We didn't want to spook Jack or incite him.

My father's phone trilled, the sound bouncing off the metal tube and echoing. He snagged it off his seat. "Damon, is anything wrong? Sure." My dad put Doc on speaker.

"I received the toxicology report from the drug Layla used on the vampires and the shifter at the club a few weeks ago. The drug in the darts contains ketamine, known as Special K on the streets. Loads of side effects on this, but mainly used as an anesthetic. Easily attainable if you know the right dealer. In addition, we found traces of cobalt oxide and a plant known as gelsemium or heartbreak glass. With the right dosage, this plant has the ability to cause loss of muscular power."

"Holy shit," I mumbled. "That's a hell of a cocktail."

"Exactly," Dr. Vieira said. "What I'm concerned about is the cobalt oxide. In extremely high amounts, it will cause us to burn from the inside out."

"I can tell you, it felt that way to me," I added.

"Do you think the cobalt oxide is Jack's new weapon?" Layla asked.

"Maybe," Doc said. "After all, your family has had a supply of it. We need to find out where they got it. Jo, when you're in Jack's head, look for the answer."

"Tell me more about the cobalt oxide," my dad said to Doc.

"Not much to tell, Steven," Doc replied. "Cobalt oxide can be purchased in powder form, and one of its uses is in the ceramic industry. Scary part is... all this can be made in a garage."

"Dr. Vieira," Jo piped in, questions dancing in her silver eyes. "What about the dead shifter?"

The sound of papers rustling together came through the line. "Her toxicology report showed low levels of wolfsbane in her system. I suspect the wolfsbane mixed with ketamine and gelsemium is what did it. Wolfsbane alone is deadly to shifters in the right amount."

"So someone was poisoning her?" Layla said.

"Roman," I threw out.

Layla's pretty eyebrows came together. "But he was dating her."

Webb leaned his elbows on the seat in front of him. "The shifter is none of our concern at the moment. Doc, the antidote we took before we left —will that help some?"

"I can't say for sure. It might prevent you from passing out, but it won't help the cobalt or the paralysis," Doc replied.

"That's why Roman didn't pass out at the club," Layla said. "He must've taken an antidote too."

"Highly possible," Doc said. "I'll inform Dane what we found. Let me know how things go and stay safe." He hung up.

Everyone was silent for a beat.

Tripp cleared his throat. "We have less than an hour. We need to scope out the landscape and make sure we're alone."

"As we discussed, the three of you will stay out of sight." My dad pointed to Webb, Tripp, and me. "Jo, Layla, and I will wait inside. If anything goes awry, you know where to meet."

We didn't expect any hiccups, but we were dealing with an Aberdeen, and if things went south, our plan was to meet at a highway rest stop about five miles from the airport.

Let the games begin.

36

LAYLA

S now fluttered to the ground, and I was quickly reminded of that crazy night when Roman cut off my uncle Ray's thumb and had Jordyn wrapped in C-4. It had been snowing then too.

I glanced skyward at the gray clouds. At least it was midafternoon, so we could see our surroundings and enemies coming at us. With the open fields on all sides, it would be hard for anyone to hide unless they were lying flat on their stomach, hidden by the tall grass and dense brush.

As I inhaled the fresh air, I descended the plane's short staircase behind Jo. She seemed ready for war, and not because she was dressed in skintight leggings or had daggers strapped to her legs, or even because of the gun on her hip. She had an aura about her that dared anyone to fuck with her.

Webb held out his hand to her at the bottom of the stairs. It was at that moment that I realized how in love they were, from the way he flashed his striking blue eyes at her to the smile that wasn't meant for anyone else on the planet.

My heart skipped a beat. I wanted that. I wanted to feel the rush of my heart and the wild flutters of butterflies when a man looked at me that way.

Sam loves you, that voice in my head supplied.

He said he did, but I had yet to notice him looking at me as though I was the only woman for him. Or maybe he did look at me like that, and I hadn't noticed. After all, I'd been too busy worrying about my sisters, the baby, and my uncle... and feeling sorry for myself. I needed to take off the self-pitying glasses, straighten my ass out, hold my head high, and tell everyone to fuck off.

When I reached the bottom, strong hands landed on my shoulders from behind, severing me from the stern talk I was giving myself.

Sam grabbed my hand. "You're nervous. I can smell your fear."

I wrinkled my nose, sizing up the imposing vampire. His ebony hair was tied at the nape. His green eyes glistened even on such a cloudy day. He was dressed to fight like a badass motherfucker, and not an ounce of trepidation showed on his handsome mug. It was as though he lived for the battles, the fights, the war. Then again, I would, too, if I knew I couldn't die easily.

"What does fear smell like?" My curious mind wanted to know, even though he was right. The last time I was among family, it didn't go well.

He smirked, showing his dimples. "Each person is different. But you have a salty scent that mixes with your deodorant when you perspire."

I snorted, not quite sure how to take that.

A gust of wind whipped around us and ruffled my hair to the point where I couldn't see for a moment.

Sam brushed my strands out of my face before he produced a leather strap from one of his pockets. Then he tied my hair back. "My dad always scolds us if our hair isn't secure before going into battle."

I giggled. "First, you wash my hair, and now, you're my stylist? Who are you, Sam Mason?"

He peered down at me with a serious expression. "I'm a man who is hopelessly in love with you. A man who wants you around for eternity."

A swarm of butterflies had taken flight inside me until he said that last part. I wouldn't be around forever, and those flutters died a quick death in my stomach. "Sam—"

He placed a finger on my lips. "Shh. Whatever you're about to say, you can say it when we're back on the plane. Right now, I need you to be alert. Fear is good. It keeps you on your toes, but only if you have one thing on your mind, and that's staying alive." He flattened his strong hands on my cold cheeks. "Can you do that for me?"

I didn't want to believe my uncles would harm me. But I'd never thought my sister would, either, or even my cousin, for that matter.

"Jack is a wild card," Sam said. "Your aunt might believe he wants our help to find Noah, but we need to operate like he doesn't until Jo reads his mind."

I agreed. Jack Aberdeen could be a loose cannon. He could also be working with Lester Worthington and using the meeting as a ploy to get the SEALs in one place.

"What if—" I swallowed a big boulder. "What if Jack shoots everyone with that drug? What if Dr. Vieira is right, and it burns all of you from the inside out?" I blew out a breath. "Maybe that's why I'm here. So he can take me back after all of you are dead." The nausea swished around, and suddenly, I wanted to hop on that plane and fly it out of there myself.

"That won't happen," he assured me. "He can't take all of us down at once, even if he has backup."

He might be right, but my stomach didn't agree. Still, I wasn't one to cower. So I gave him the best confident smile I could, knowing he could feel my true feelings since he was an empath. "I can handle my uncle." I had to. Besides, like Jo, I was dressed to fight, and I wouldn't hesitate to use my daggers or gun if I had to, despite family ties.

Sam studied me as his lips curled at the ends. "There's the feisty vampire huntress I love."

Warmth spread through my chest.

"Sam," Webb called. "Time to go."

He brushed his lips over mine.

"If you find Rianne lurking around here, bring

her to me." We still hadn't heard from or found Rianne. If I knew my sister, she had her eyes on our every move. "I'll handle her." I was ready to go two more rounds with her. *Fuck talking.*

He checked that my bulletproof vest was secure. "We'll find anyone who's around here. And if Noah is out there," he growled, "he'll leave in a body bag." He gave me a chaste kiss. "Be safe." He started to walk backward. "Remember, you and the baby come first." He blew me a kiss, spun on his heel, and jogged over to Tripp and Webb, who were huddled together.

I pushed out a breath, ready to get the show over with. I was ready to return to Jo's house in Maine, tell Sam how I felt, and figure out what to do next. Of course, I didn't think things would go back to normal after our meeting with Jack. Hell, I knew the battle was just beginning. But a girl could hope.

"Layla." Jo's sweet voice penetrated through my haze as I watched Sam disappear around the hangar building. "We need to go inside."

Blinking, I shuddered as a sinking feeling gripped my stomach.

Steven broke the lock on one of six bay doors. "We'll wait in here."

The snow began to fall more heavily, and the wind whipped around.

The moment Steven rolled up the door, a foul odor rushed out.

"Did someone die in there?" I pressed the back of my hand to my nose and swallowed the bile that was ready to burst free. A large wooden box sat ominously in the middle of the somewhat empty hangar. "Do you think there's a body in there?" There had to have been, judging by the stench.

Steven tore the top off the box with his bare hands, and the disgusting smell increased tenfold.

Vomit was about to hurtle out of my mouth, but I shuffled in anyway, holding my breath. I wouldn't put it past Jack to drop something off before he arrived. Maybe that was the reason he wanted me there, to send me a present—as in a vampire or.... Kendra came to mind.

Jo gave me a nod as though she couldn't smell a thing, which was odd, given her acute senses.

The blood drained from me.

Steven examined the body like he was the official coroner. "Whoever it was has been dead for quite some time."

I sidled up to Jo who was also inspecting the

corpse. "You don't think my uncle dropped this off here?"

Steven's head shot up as his green eyes bled to silver. "Why would you think that?"

"He's been looking for a vampire my father dated. He told me the PI he hired found a lead on her recently. Maybe he wanted me here to show me. I know that's a long shot." But that idea vanished when I laid eyes on a decomposed body that looked male, not female.

"Jack wouldn't know what hangar we were in, anyway," Jo offered before she walked around the space. In addition to the coffin, several crates were scattered about.

The sound of a vehicle's engine whirred in the distance.

Steven closed the box just as the dark-blue car drove past then backed up.

Jack wheeled up to the open bay door then cut the engine. He and Uncle Ray looked at each other. Then Uncle Ray's mouth moved as he said something to Jack from the passenger's seat.

A violent storm surged in my stomach. My uncles were up to something. "I don't like this," I mumbled.

Jo and I flanked Steven as we stood behind the

wooden box as if it would keep Jack and Ray from attacking us. The stench didn't smell as strong. Maybe because it had burned the hairs in my nostrils.

My uncles got out, and Ray opened the back door while Jack strutted in.

"What's this?" Jack waved a hand at the coffin. "Please tell me my son isn't in there." His face turned dark red.

I was about to respond when Ray dragged a woman out of the car and yanked her along with him. "Move." If there was anyone among my clan I despised, it was Ray. He was more irritating than Jack, to the point that I hated even to look at the man who resembled my father with his red hair and blue eyes.

Jo and I exchanged a surprised look. Even Steven had questions written on his pinched features.

"Do you know her?" Jo asked me. "Is that your aunt?"

I wanted to be snarky and say Jack would never allow Ray to drag his wife around like she was the scum of the Earth, and my aunt wouldn't put up with Ray's shit. She never had in the past. In fact, Ray had only talked down to Aunt Tab once, and after she grasped his balls like she was twisting them off, Ray learned his lesson.

"My aunt isn't blond," I replied.

The shackled, handcuffed woman almost fell when Ray pushed her.

Her fangs shot out. "Shove me again," the woman said with a sneer, "and I'll chop off your other fingers."

Ray narrowed his blue eyes to slits. "You can try."

"When are you ever going to learn your lesson, Uncle Ray?" Sarcasm dripped from my voice.

He pushed out his rangy chest. Where Jack was bulky and beefy, Ray was a beanpole. "When are you going to stop hanging out with blood-suckers?"

Steven growled, stopping any further argument between Ray and me. "Who's this?"

Jack's nostrils flared. "You first, Mason. Who the fuck is in the box?"

The woman gawked at me. "The resemblance to your father is uncanny." The blonde had hair down to her shoulders. Her eyelashes were covered with a thick coat of black mascara, bringing out her green eyes even more. Her makeup was painted on to perfection, and she had a beauty mark near the corner of her right eye.

"And you must be Kendra," I replied.

Her light-brown eyebrows rose. "You know who I am?"

"Enough," Jack snapped. "Who is in this box?" His tone was colder than the day outside.

Steven crossed his arms over his chest. "It's not your son. This was here when we came in. Now tell us why this young lady is here."

"He brought Kendra for me," I said. "That's why I'm here, isn't it, Jack?"

"You wanted to talk to her," Jack said. "I'm giving you that opportunity."

"Yeah, before we burn her to a crisp," Ray added quickly.

I was itching to lunge for him, which would have been easy since he stood across from me.

He jerked his head at Jo as he clutched his throat.

It took me a second to realize what Jo was doing.

She had her hand raised, palm facing up, fingers slightly curled and aimed at Ray. "We're not here to throw threats around. I suggest you keep your mouth shut, or I'll make sure you leave here in this box."

As he choked, Ray's face deepened to red.

"Ease up, Jo," Steven said.

She lowered her arms. "Next time a derogatory comment comes out of his mouth, he won't like my next move."

The lethal tone she used gave me chills, and if Ray didn't heed the warning, he was an idiot.

Jack glared daggers at Ray, who hadn't stopped rubbing his throat. "Take the restraints off her."

Reluctantly, Ray obeyed as he coughed.

"Kendra, can you wait outside? Or rather in the plane, which will be better for you," Steven said in a polite, gentlemanly tone.

She massaged her wrists, giving Steven a warm smile. "Thank you." Then she left at the speed of light. Whether she would wait or not, it didn't matter. My intuition told me she would find me when she thought it was safe for her.

"You wanted to meet. You said we had many things to discuss," Steven said to Jack. "So talk."

"Where's your son?" Ray tossed a look over his shoulder. "I'm sure he's around here somewhere."

Jo shook her head. "He's here to kill Sam. Un-believable."

"What? Is that what you read in his mind?" I gaped at Jack. "Is that the real reason you're here? To start a war?"

A muscle ticked in Jack's jaw. "I'm here to ask for help and to discuss other matters. And Layla, you should know I never ask for help."

"Stupidest thing ever," Ray mumbled.

"Jack is telling the truth," Jo said, not taking her eyes off Ray.

Ray was about to suffer a worse fate than a severed limb if he didn't shut his brain down.

Jack regarded Steven with concern. "I'm worried Roman took Noah and Rianne. Let's face it. Ray and I can hunt all day long, but we don't have the tools you do to find Roman. Which is another topic for discussion. I want to help you find Roman regardless of whether he has my son and niece or not."

Jo placed her hand on one of the daggers on her leg. "Ray knows where Noah is. Don't you?"

Lines dented Ray's forehead. "I do not."

I rolled my eyes. "Are you that stupid? She is reading your mind."

"What's going on?" Jack asked, completely

oblivious to whatever Ray was scheming. At least the shock on Jack's face told me so.

Jo stayed quiet, as did Steven. I was ready to pull my gun out and shoot Ray's foot just so he would stop acting like we were the morons.

"Start talking, Ray," Jack ordered with venom in his voice.

"What else is going through that pea-size brain of his?" I asked Jo.

Ray belted out a laugh that needled my nerves. I was ready to hurt my uncle in the same ways we maimed vampires.

I clenched my hands into fists before the ground beneath me shook. I could feel my eyebrows drawing down. I didn't know whether it was Jo, Steven, or me causing the vibration. I recalled a lamp crashing to the floor when Sam and I argued at Jo's house in Maine. He'd seemed to think I'd been responsible since I'd been drinking his blood.

"Talk!" Jack shouted at Ray. "Do you know where Noah is?"

Jo leaned in and whispered something to her father.

Ray studied his brother with a calculating glare. "These bloodsuckers will never help you.

You're as bad as our dead brother. Our family has hunted them for centuries, and now, you want their help. Sorry, bro. But I'm not jumping on board with that."

"What have you done?" Jack asked through gritted teeth. "Where's Noah? Rianne?"

"What's he thinking, Jo?" I asked.

"He's blocking me now," Jo replied.

"This meeting is over," Steven said. "Jack, before you ask me for help, check with your brother first."

Ray slowly backed toward the open bay door. "You're right. We're done here."

Steven's growl was deathly. "Do you want to die today?"

Ray saluted Steven. "Not my day to die. But it is for your son." Then he ran out like the building was on fire.

Oh hell no. "Sam!" I sprinted out of the hangar and banked left behind Ray when the chuff, chuff, chuff of a helicopter echoed in the distance.

I pumped my legs hard, keeping my eye on Ray, who was running like the wind. Murder came to mind.

"Layla!" Webb shouted my name from somewhere nearby.

But I kept going, breathing heavily, my legs burning, and my heart on a collision course with hell.

Ray's beanstalk body was fading fast as he ran farther and farther away from me.

Jo rushed up beside me and grabbed my arm. "Stop, Layla. He's not worth it."

I labored for breath as I snarled at the pretty vampire. "He is. He's up to something that involves Sam."

Webb finally came into view.

"Where's my brother?" Jo asked him.

Webb shook his snow-covered hair. "He's patrolling the north end of the airport, last I saw him."

The helicopter's engine grew louder.

I didn't know which way was north. "We have to find him. Ray is going to kill him."

Webb's face twisted as he pressed a finger to his ear. "Sam, come in."

I wasn't waiting. I took off in Ray's direction once again just as the helicopter approached.

"Layla, come back!" Jo yelled at the top of her lungs. "We'll get Ray."

I couldn't give a shit about my uncle. I needed to find Sam. I pumped my legs as hard as I could as that rainy night when I was running to save Sam flashed before me.

We would never be able to live freely, not with my family around.

I kept up my pace, searching the open landscape in all directions. Not a person in sight. Not even Ray. He'd probably darted around the hangar building.

That damn helicopter was annoying as hell as it lowered a basket as though they were about to rescue someone.

I stopped cold. *Or capture someone.*

My heart rammed against my ribs. *Holy fuck!* Maybe Sam wasn't the target. I was.

I started to turn around and retreat when a voice that awakened those butterflies shouted my name over the whirr of the helicopter blades.

My gaze darted ahead and slightly to the right.

Sam jogged toward me as the helicopter seemed to chase him.

Then that pounding in my ears blasted as though I was standing next to a bomb. I rushed up to Sam just as the basket swung behind him. It was like the jaws of life were about to capture him.

"Run, Sam!" I screamed at the top of my lungs.

But he didn't. He stopped, turned, and raised his arms high above his head. Then he lowered one arm and closed his hand into a fist.

He was about to unleash his elemental powers. That was the same move he'd done to Roman that night on the naval base. But when Sam opened his fist, nothing happened. He quickly tried again. No fire. No wild weather. Nothing.

He looked at his hand a little too long.

I was about to bolt over to him when someone grabbed me from behind.

Ray laughed in my ear. "You'll never see your vampire lover again."

I screamed like a banshee, and when I did, Ray collapsed. I was ready to kick him in the throat when I noticed blood coming out of his ears. He wasn't moving, but I couldn't worry about him.

I sprinted toward Sam, only it was too late. A guy dressed in full SWAT gear was shooting at Sam from the helicopter while another propelled down and shot Sam several more times.

"Noooooooooo!" I was about to run into the fray until another set of hands came around me.

"It's too dangerous," Steven said in my ear.

Jo came to a halt beside me and raised her arms, ready to use her elemental powers, but when she whipped her arms around, nothing happened. "My powers aren't working." She tried again but failed. "They must have something stopping us," Jo said.

Steven tried to use his powers, but he failed too.

Sam stumbled to his feet and roared. The men just kept shooting and shooting and shooting until he became a rag doll. Then one of the men in the helicopter aimed his gun at us while his partner loaded Sam in the basket.

I shrugged out of Steven's hold. *Screw this.* I pulled out my gun and started shooting at the man on the ground. It took me three shots until he fell.

I rushed over to Sam, whose limp body was sprawled inside the basket. I reached in to drag him out when the helicopter lifted. If they were taking him, then they were taking me too.

I was about to hop in with Sam's lifeless body, but fate had other plans. The basket's door snagged the sleeve of my sweater, and I tried frantically to get free as the helicopter took off. But my fucking sweater wouldn't come loose. I scrambled to climb in, but the wind was too strong, and the helicopter was moving faster now. I grabbed onto the grated door, hanging on for dear life.

But the higher the copter climbed, the more the wind thrashed me around. My fingers began slipping as pain careened up my arms. It felt as though my shoulders had popped out of their sockets.

Oh God. The baby. We're going to die. I promised Sam I would protect our child and me.

My heart beat wildly as my sweater ripped, and I lost my grip. "I love you, Sam. I'm hopelessly in love with you too."

Then I was free falling, and as gravity took the wheel, I prayed and prayed and prayed that fate was on my side.

To be continued...

ABOUT THE AUTHOR

Bestselling author **S.B. Alexander** is an independent author with over 25 titles to date. She writes paranormal, new adult, and sweet romances that feature hot heroes stealing hearts.

S.B. or Susan as she likes to be called is a navy veteran, former high school teacher, and former corporate sales executive. She's a lover of sports, especially baseball, although nowadays you can find her glued to the TV during football season.

When she's not writing, she's a full-time caregiver to her soul mate of twenty-three years who got a bad deal in life when he was diagnosed with ALS. Her motto: "Life is too short to waste. So live every moment like it's your last."

You can connect with S.B. Alexander in the following ways:

Reader Group: https://sbalexander.com/beastsandbitches
Author Website: https://sbalexander.com
Newsletter: https://sbalexander.com/newsletter
Email: susan@sbalexander.com

NEVER MISS A NEW RELEASE:

Sign up for her Author App
iTunes: https://bit.ly/sbalexanderitunes
Android: https://bit.ly/sbalexanderandroid

facebook.com/sbalexander.authorpage

twitter.com/sbalex_author

instagram.com/sbalexanderauthor

amazon.com/author/sbalexander

bookbub.com/authors/s-b-alexander

tiktok.com/@susanbalexander

ALSO BY S.B. ALEXANDER

MAXWELL SERIES

Upper Young Adult/New Adult Contemporary Romance

Dare to Kiss

Dare to Dream

Dare to Love

Dare to Dance

Dare to Live

Dare to Breathe

Dare to Embrace

THE MAXWELL FAMILY SAGA SERIES

Young Adult Sweet Romance

My Heart to Touch

My Heart to Hold

My Heart to Give

My Heart to Keep

THE VAMPIRE NAVY SEAL SERIES

Paranormal Romance

On the Edge of Humanity

On the Edge of Eternity

On the Edge of Destiny

On the Edge of Misery

On the Edge of Infinity

VAMPIRE NAVY SEAL: SAM & LAYLA SERIES

Paranormal Romance

The Hunted

The Predator

*The Union**

*The Dawning**

STAND-ALONES

New Adult Contemporary Romance

Crazy For You

Unforgettable

Holding Onto Forever

Breaking Rules

Rescuing Riley

THE HART SERIES

New Adult Contemporary Romance

Hart of Darkness

Hart of Vengeance

*Visit https://sbalexander.com/all-books/ to learn more about S.B. Alexander books and future releases. Please note release dates are subject to change based on reader demand and the author's schedule. Subscribing to the author's newsletter or following her on Facebook is the best way to stay updated with planned new releases.

GLOSSARY OF TERMS

Natural-born vampire: A human born with the vampire gene that, when activated, will turn them into a vampire.

Activation process: Those who carry the vampire gene can only turn by drinking the blood of their vampire father at the age of sixteen years or older.

Council of Elders – A group of five vampires who set the laws.

Genetic engineering: Turning humans into

vampires through a process of restructuring their DNA.

Cobalt – A vampire's kryptonite. The metal will kill a vampire if staked through the heart. It will also burn a vampire's skin if they come in contact with it.

Reproduction: A natural-born vampire is born by a male vampire and a human female with a rare blood type of Vel negative.

Council of Eternal Affairs: The legal department of the vampire government.

Vampire characteristics: Sunlight doesn't burn them. Their hearts beat at <5 bpm. Skin temperature is ten degrees cooler than a human. Eye color changes to black except for a few chosen ones.